Trail of the Blue Agave

Trail of the Blue Agave

Trail
of the
Blue Agave

George Bixley

Published by Dagmar Miura
Los Angeles
www.dagmarmiura.com

Trail of the Blue Agave

First published 2023

ISBN: 978-1-956744-67-5

ONE

SITTING IN THE PASSENGER seat, Slater looked over the interior of Claudine's old truck, the wooden dashboard and the spindly gearshift. It was a true pickup, without a second row of seats, and it was older than either one of them, but the engine sounded solid. They'd been at community college together, in horticulture, and even though Slater worked as an insurance investigator these days, Claudine was still in the landscaping game. She'd called him in to consult on a gardening case.

Confident with the manual transmission, Claudine downshifted on the ramp when they exited the freeway, slowing the engine without the brakes. Like Slater, she had dark Latin coloring, but she was less assimilated than he was—she actually spoke Spanish.

"So your client had some plants stolen," he said.

"Her name is Hester." Claudine threw up a hand. "I have some ideas about what's going on, but I want fresh eyes on it. I'm not going to tell you anything more because I don't want to bias you with my own thoughts."

"That works."

Slater looked out at the neighborhood rolling by, somewhere in the southeast part of Los Angeles County. Eventually Claudine turned off the boulevard, onto a street lined with big houses spaced well apart.

"Where are we, exactly?" he said.

"Downey."

"I had no idea Downey had such a bougie neighborhood."

"It's not very extensive," she said. "Just a few blocks. Technically it might be unincorporated, but in my mind it's Downey. I did four different yards for Hester, all right around here. Her own place and three houses she owns that she rents out."

"The streets here are in a grid pattern."

"Is that significant?"

"It makes it easy to get away on wheels," Slater said. "That's way more attractive to a burglar than a neighborhood with cul-de-sacs and loops and dead-ends."

"See, I knew you were the guy. You're already earning your pay."

"We need to talk about that at some point. Is she paying me, or are you?"

"I'll pay you for the consult."

Claudine slowed the pickup and pointed out the windshield. "This is one of Hester's rental properties."

It was a low ranch house set back from the street by an unfenced yard, dramatically planted with succulents and some dryland grasses. Claudine parked at the curb, and they both got out.

"This is really tight," Slater said, surveying it from the sidewalk. "The layout is inspired. Why isn't the yard fenced?"

"Hester figured a fence would hide the plantings, and nobody was going to trample them anyway, since they're not as inviting as turf is."

They climbed back into the pickup, and Claudine drove a few blocks, and turned a corner, and stopped in front of another yard. The plantings here were the same combination of succulents and grasses, and the yard was similarly unfenced, but it was bigger, and the house behind it was a hulking two-story monolith. Painted white, with Greek columns fronting the entrance, the upper floor had big evenly spaced windows with black shutters.

"This is Hester's place," Claudine said as she popped open her door.

Slater got out and looked it over. "That house belongs on a plantation. You should have put in cotton instead of the dryland stuff."

She chuckled. "I'm glad I'm not the only one who thinks it's a little much."

The driveway curved up to the house and back to the street again, encircling the plantings in a wide arc. As they walked up toward it, Slater saw a gaping hole in the landscaping. Something big had been pulled out by the roots.

From between the white columns a woman appeared, stepping out the front door of the obnoxious house. Wearing jeans and a green plaid jacket, she was trim, and walked toward them.

"Hester," Claudine called to her as she approached,

and then introduced Slater. From a distance Hester's expensive blond coiffure had implied youth, but at close range he could see that she had to be in her sixties. If she'd been surgeried, it was subtle. A neck lift, maybe, or a restrained face lift.

"Claudine is the only landscaper I've needed," Hester said, and waved at the yard. "You can see that she's a genius, but she says I need you."

"Tell me what's going on," he said.

"I'm ready to pull my hair out. This is the second time they've stolen from me."

"They came back? How long was it between hits?"

"Maybe a week. The first time it wasn't here. They robbed another yard that Claudine did for me." Her brow furrowed. "What do you do, exactly?"

"Mostly I investigate fraud." Slater dug in the hip pocket of his jeans, and fished out a dog-eared business card, and handed it over.

"Insurance," Hester said, briefly glancing at it before she tucked it away. She met his gaze. "I hope your skill set extends beyond that industry."

"Do you have photos of what the yard looked like before the theft?"

"Let me get my tablet." Hester turned and walked back to the house. Once she'd disappeared between the columns, Slater eyed Claudine.

"She called you a genius to your face. I hope you've got her on the hook big time."

"Hester pays me well." Claudine gestured vaguely. "Really well. I'm on retainer."

"Of course you are, because succulents require near daily maintenance."

She chuckled. "I send a guy to do the weeding

every few weeks. The downside is that I feel like I have to be on call for stuff like this." She spoke in a higher tone: "'Oh, the bentgrass turned a weird color, can you come and diagnose it?'"

Hester appeared in the driveway again, walking out from the house, a tablet in hand. She handed it to Slater. On the screen was a photo of the yard.

"That's last fall," she said.

Zooming in on the section where the hole was, he saw what had been there before.

"That's a blue agave." He looked up at the yard. There was one other blue agave still in the layout. The thieves had taken the one closest to the street.

"Claudine didn't tell you that?" Hester said.

"I didn't want to bias his process," she said, and waved an arm.

Slater tapped the screen. "When did this specific plant go in?"

"We landscaped all the yards at the same time," Hester said. "About five years ago, wasn't it?"

"That's about right." Claudine nodded. "I put in two-year-old agaves. They liked the soil and grew in nicely."

"That makes them the ideal age for tequila production."

Hester's eyebrows shot up. "Is that why they steal them?"

"Only one species is used to make tequila," Claudine said. "The blue agave."

Slater gestured to the one that remained in the yard. "This cultivar grows more slowly than the ones they farm for the booze industry, but it looks showier, and I bet it would make a better tequila product." He eyed Claudine. "I'm sure you keep the stalks tightly trimmed."

"The *quiotes*. Of course."

"Why does trimming them matter?" Hester said.

"If you let the stalk grow and flower," Claudine said, "the plant dies."

"For tequila production, you want the same thing," Slater said. "No stalk or seeds, so all the plant's energy goes into the body."

Hester waved a hand. "So someone is stealing them to make liquor?"

"It's the most logical explanation," he said. "You have other plants here that are worth more, but they're only used for landscaping. They didn't steal those."

Claudine took a deep breath. "I'm glad you came to the same conclusion."

"So why am I paying for two of you," Hester said, "if you have the same information?"

"I'm a horticulturalist," she said, "but Slater can do something about the thievery."

"Like what?"

"They're going to come back." Slater nodded to the agave. "For that one and the ones at your other properties. I'd like to put a tracking beacon on each of them. That way I'll know where they wind up."

"Fine by me. What'll it cost?"

"Two grand to get started," he said. "We'll reassess the work in a few days."

"Ouch." Hester frowned. "But I guess I have no choice. Can I wire it to you?"

"Cash is always better."

"I don't keep that kind of money lying around."

"Fine," he said flatly. "Send it to the phone number

on my card. I'll set up the trackers on this one and at your other properties."

"I'll text you the addresses," Claudine said.

"How many blue agaves are there?"

Hester looked to Claudine and raised her eyebrows.

"I planted five total across all the yards. There's three left."

"I'll plant the trackers at the other properties first," he said. "It's more likely they'll hit those than come back right after robbing this yard."

"When can you start on this?" Hester said.

"I'll be back this afternoon. If you see me out here doing stuff, don't shoot at me."

She frowned. "We're not Okies." Eyeing Claudine, she added, "Can you find something to fill the hole?"

"Do you want another blue agave?"

"You're the landscaper." Hester shrugged. "I know whatever you do will look great."

As she walked back to the house, Slater stepped in among the plantings, and went over to the surviving blue agave. Squatting, he looked it over, gently prodding the sharp terminal spine on one of the leaves. Claudine followed him, standing nearby.

"Wasn't Downey settled by Okies back in the day?" Slater said.

"Undoubtedly."

He lifted a couple of leaves to look at the heart, a pineapple-size solid mass in the center. "Do you think gun ownership is actually higher among Okies than people like her?"

"It's just a slur, Slater. She doesn't even know what it means."

"I don't think it's even a slur anymore." He stood up. "There's a whole Okie festival in Bakersfield. Music and food and everything. Up there being an Okie is a badge of honor."

Claudine waved a hand. "You'll put the tracker in the piña?"

"Is that what you call the heart?"

She nodded.

"This one has a big healthy piña," he said. "I'm afraid it'll damage its growth."

"They're going to steal it anyway. Just do what you need to do."

"So Hester's not an Okie, but I wonder what she calls us brown folks when we're not within earshot?" Slater said.

"She can call me anything she wants, as long as she keeps paying me." She frowned. "That reminds me. Give me a minute."

Claudine stepped over to the driveway and walked toward the house. It really was a lush layout, Slater thought, looking it over, and it was meticulously groomed. Claudine was earning whatever Hester was paying her.

Farther from the street was a *Dudleya,* and he stepped over to it, maneuvering among the plants. It was healthy, and thick, and well maintained. He dropped to his knees to look under it, and touched the underside of a leaf, then felt the waxy chalk between his fingers.

A big pickup had pulled into the driveway and stopped halfway up. Slater glanced briefly at the man who climbed out of it. White and Anglo, his short graying hair was in a stupid side part. He wore a loose white shirt open to the middle of his chest, and tan jodhpurs, and English riding boots. That look and that truck smacked of pretense. It made him want to punch the guy in the face. But he wasn't unpleasant to look at. He might be fuckable in a pinch.

The guy waved an arm and called to him. "Can I help you?"

"I doubt it," Slater said.

"Come out of there."

"Don't tell me what to do."

"You're trampling the plants. *No entrada, cholo.*"

Moving toward him, Slater stepped carefully around the plantings and onto the driveway. The guy didn't flinch, even when he was right up on him. That was typical of a moneyed person—he never saw it coming because no one ever stood up to him. Slater slapped him hard, left and then right, a rapid kovac.

"I am not a *cholo,*" Slater said through his teeth.

He stumbled back, and put a hand to his cheek, his eyes wide.

"I'm calling the police."

"Go for it," Slater said. "I know they'll send a prowl car on the double for a fancy guy like you. When they get here I'll tell them you groped my ass, and I slapped you in self-defense."

"I never touched you," he said, and scowled.

"You can't just grope people, even if they're the help. How would Hester feel about reading that kind of accusation in a police report?"

"Stop saying that," he said, his tone rising. "It's perverted."

"You're perverted. You can touch my ass if you ask nicely, but you have to ask first."

"I don't want to touch your ass," he shouted.

Slater put his hands on his hips. "Are you sure about that? You seem a little uptight. It might be cathartic." He raised his eyebrows. "Help you release some of that tension, if you know what I mean."

Claudine appeared from the direction of the house, walking down the driveway.

"Hey, Big Mike," she called to him as she approached, and flashed a smile. "How's the horses?"

He gestured to Slater. "Are you responsible for this?"

"That's one of my assistants."

"What kind of people do you hire? He's a brute."

"He's new," she said. "I'll get him out of your hair."

Placing a firm hand on Slater's shoulder, she guided him down the driveway toward her pickup.

"Hester's husband, I'm thinking," Slater said, once they'd climbed in.

Claudine revved the engine and pulled away from the curb, raising a hand to wave to Big Mike, still standing in the driveway by his truck, a scowl on his face, watching them.

"He was as red as a stoplight," she said. "What happened?"

"He called me a *cholo,* so I gave him a kovac."

"You don't look anything like a *cholo.* Technically that word means bald-headed. And what the hell is a kovac?"

"You know—the old two-for-one." Slater mimed the action. "*Ksh-ksh.* A double slap. In Japan they call it *oufuku-binta,* a round-trip slap. Irish people call it the paintbrush, and a cop I know calls it the Joan Crawford. She used it in her movies."

"What a lovely trip around the world." She frowned as she glanced over at him. "Why would you do that?"

"You know I'm not a right guy."

"You make a habit of slapping your clients? Or worse, my clients?"

"Only the ones who ask for it. Why do they call him Big Mike? He's actually on the scrawny side."

"He probably chose it himself. It makes him sound like a big shot."

"I wonder if he'll try to get Hester to can me?"

"Hester doesn't like him very much. She says if it eats grass and farts, Big Mike loves it more than her."

"He's a horseman."

"Plus he sleeps around," she said, "and he thinks Hester doesn't know."

His phone buzzed in the pocket of his jeans, and he pulled it out to check.

"Hester just paid me," he said, studying the screen. "Two large. She won't be getting that back no matter what Big Mike says."

Claudine navigated onto the 5, headed for downtown LA, the truck's engine purring contentedly as it accelerated up the ramp. Slater thumb-typed a text to his tech supplier, Svetlana:

Can you see me today?

"So how's that man you were macking on?" Claudine said.

"You mean Pike?"

"I don't remember his name. The last time we met you were on the fight."

"That happens sometimes. Even so, our narrative

complex burns with the intensity of all the stars in the sky."

She chuckled. "A narrative complex means a romance?"

"What we're doing is a lot more complicated than a romantic story. It's multidimensional, so it needs a bigger word."

"I'm happy for you."

"He transferred his job here, and he kind of moved in. I'm still totally obsessed. I can't keep my hands off the guy."

"So it's true love."

"I can confirm that the *l* word has been used," Slater said.

"Nice."

"I used to just work and work till I was half dead, but now I've got something to look forward to."

"It puts things in perspective."

"For me it kind of obliterated any hope of having perspective. Like I'm in his thrall." He waved a hand. "What about your romantic life? What's the skinny?"

"In a nutshell, men are animals." Claudine checked her side mirror to change lanes.

"Preach," Slater said, and listened as she talked about it for a while, her relationships with different guys, and how they hadn't worked out.

Soon they were off the freeway and in the Fashion District. As she pulled up to the curb in front of Slater's office building, his phone buzzed with Svetlana's response:

I am always here for you.

As he stepped onto the sidewalk, before he closed

the passenger door, he leaned in. "Thanks for the work."

"What do I owe you for the consult?"

"Zero. Hester already hired me."

Claudine nodded. "I might hold off on replacing that agave until you do your thing."

"I'll let you know."

"Even if you don't, I'm sure I'll get a full report from Hester."

TWO

▨▨▨▨▨▨▨▨▨▨

NOT BOTHERING TO GO upstairs to his office, Slater hustled across the street in a break in the traffic to the surface lot, where his classic Thunderbird, sleek and black, waited patiently for him. It wasn't really a practical ride, and far from stealthy, but he loved it, loved the throaty engine, the cherry interior. He climbed in and twisted his key in the ignition.

Svetlana's workshop was in a seedy part of Glendale, and he headed that way. She and her brother, Igor, sold Slater all his illicit tech, bugs and cameras and trackers, along with a web interface to keep track of it all. Cruising the streets of downtown, he got on the freeway headed north, and soon merged onto the 5.

Moments after he'd made the transition, there was a loud visceral *clunk* from the front end, and the car slowed. The engine was still running, but its response to the accelerator was sluggish, indifferent.

He could smell exhaust fumes.

"Damn it," he snapped, and rolled down the window.

Nosing onto the exit ramp, he followed it off the freeway into a residential neighborhood. He turned onto a quiet street, and pulled to the curb, and killed the engine. On his phone he found Duarte in his contact list, and dialed, and listened to it ring.

"*Cabrón,*" Duarte said when he picked up. "How's it rolling?"

"Not great today. I broke down."

"Just now? Is it drivable?"

"I don't think so."

"Where are you?"

"Right off the 5. In Frogtown."

"That's not far," Duarte said. "Text me your location. I'll be there soon."

Slater spent a minute sending him a map link, then climbed out, and leaned back on the front fender, and folded his arms. With his eyes closed, and his face turned to the warm sun, he could still hear the sound of the traffic on the nearby freeway, and the subtle *tick-tick-tick* of the engine cooling off.

It was frustrating, as he had stuff to do, but he knew he couldn't get too upset about it. This kind of incident was the price he paid for driving a fifty-year-old vehicle. At least he had Duarte. The guy knew all about classic cars, and appreciated their value, and knew how to take care of the Thunderbird.

A few minutes later Duarte rolled up in his tow truck and pulled in ahead of the Thunderbird. Painted red and white with the amber light bar on the cab, it looked smaller than a regular tow truck, and had a lower profile. He'd gotten here fast. He must have dropped whatever he was doing. That gave him some insight—it meant Slater was a valuable customer.

Duarte stepped out of the cab. Skinny, with his long black hair bundled behind his head, he was wearing board shorts, and a powder-blue bowling shirt, and incongruous yellow work boots.

He called a greeting, and as he walked over, Slater could see the concern in his eyes. He briefly grasped Slater's arm and met his gaze.

"Are you OK?"

"I'm not injured," Slater said.

"What happened?"

"I heard a bang, and lost power, and then I started breathing fumes. I wondered if it might be the exhaust manifold."

Duarte nodded. "It sounds like it. On that 351 Windsor engine the manifolds are made of cast iron. That's nineteenth-century technology. They tend to fail eventually."

"Can you get the parts?"

"Of course. I'll tow it to the shop and let you know how it looks." He gestured in the direction of the freeway ramp. "Vera will be here any minute. She's bringing the '63 Polara for you to use until we can fix it."

"I hadn't even thought that far ahead," Slater said. "You're right, though, I'll need wheels."

"We got you, man. I'm not going to make you rent a Prius."

Duarte stepped over to the tow truck and pulled a lever to lower the arms that would grab the Thunderbird's wheels. Before he'd even finished, a warm-red vintage car pulled up behind his, its chrome polished to a high shine, with that beautiful toothy grill, and the sweet original hubcaps—the Polara.

Vera stepped out from behind the wheel. Curvy, wearing tight jeans and a stretchy black blouse, she had a lot of dark hair, and heavy black eye makeup. Duarte's wife. He'd met her a couple of times at their garage. Vera's brow furrowed in concern as she approached him.

"Sounds like you're having a rough day, Slater. Are you OK?"

"It wasn't a collision. I'm fine."

"I mean emotionally." She squeezed his arm the way Duarte had. "A classic car is like a member of the family."

"Slater," Duarte called to him. "Keys."

Digging in his pocket, he tossed them over to him, and watched as he pulled open the driver's door.

"I know your man can fix anything," Slater said, eyeing Vera.

She nodded. "We'll take excellent care of him, or her—does your vehicle have a specific gender, or a name?"

Slater had to grin. "I haven't assigned any. So maybe just 'it.'"

"Well, the Polara is no substitute for your baby, but it'll get you around." Vera handed him the keys. "I know this is traumatic. Something that helped me a lot in similar situations was the idea that rather than avoiding the pain, and turning away from it, you should lean into it. Just sit with it for a minute, and let it hurt, and get familiar with that."

"You sound like a shrink."

She chuckled. "Duarte does most of the wrenching, but I'm better with the emotional support. Just remember that you're not alone. You can call us anytime, day or night, if you need to talk. Even if it's just to check in."

"I might do that." He studied her face. "You're very compassionate. Lots of gearheads are a little rough around the edges."

"It's part of the job." She raised her eyebrows. "I can be a hard-ass when I need to be. A customer in crisis doesn't need that."

Duarte stepped over. "I got it on the rack. You should probably bug out before I lift it."

"It can be a little upsetting to watch your baby being towed away like an invalid," Vera said.

Slater flashed the keys. "Thanks for the Polara."

"Garage door openers," Vera said, "parking passes, phone chargers, other personal items?"

"Good thinking."

He stepped over to the Thunderbird and pulled open the driver's door. Besides the pass for the lot at his office, he grabbed his garage door opener and his phone charger, and from the backseat the box of latex gloves he kept there, and his stakeout binoculars. There was some gardening stuff in the trunk, but he wouldn't need it.

Closing the door again, he stepped back. "You two are truly amazing."

Duarte laughed. "We're getting paid."

Climbing into the Polara, Slater put the binoculars and the box of gloves in the backseat, then clipped his garage door opener to the visor, and adjusted the mirrors. When he started the engine, it felt as smooth as the day it had rolled off the assembly line.

As he pulled into the street and rolled past the Thunderbird, Duarte and Vera were standing by the tow truck. They were waiting for him to be out of view before they hoisted it, he realized. They were being so careful with him, like a couple of gravediggers trying to show respect before they started to fill in the hole. Maybe they were right—he did feel a little queasy thinking about the Thunderbird being towed away.

Making a couple of turns, he navigated back to the freeway ramp. This vehicle was much older than his own ride, but the accelerator was a lot more responsive, and it felt like it had pep. As he picked up speed he rolled down the window. The steering was really sensitive too as he changed lanes. It wouldn't be so bad to drive this baby for a day or two.

Svetlana's workshop was a long low building, and the ivy was starting to disguise the seedy facade, he saw, pulling up in front of it. Claudine had planted that, after he'd recommended her when Svetlana had asked him for landscaping help.

There was an ancient disused doorway facing the street, but the real entrance was around back, and he walked to the alley, and down to the heavy steel door. He pressed the bell and lifted a hand to the camera overhead, looking up into it so that he'd be easy to identify.

The door lock clicked open, and he stepped into the anteroom, and waited for Svetlana's electronics to scan him for weapons and explosives. He must have passed muster, as a moment later the inner door lock snapped open, and he stepped inside.

Lining the windowless room were workbenches, strewn with tools, and wire, and bits of metal, and circuit boards. The air was redolent of machine oil and hot plastic. Standing in front of a computer screen perched on the workbench, Svetlana was wearing a flower-print red dress over her bulky frame. She turned toward him as he stepped in.

"You're driving a new car," she said, her Slavic accent flattening the vowels.

It was no surprise that they had cameras on that side of the building, but it was interesting that she'd monitored him pulling up.

"That vehicle is older than both of us," he said. "I borrowed it from my mechanic. Mine is in the shop."

"I like the color. Like a ripe tomato." She waved a hand. "What can I do for you today?"

"I need a tracker that can go inside something woody."

"Like a tree?"

"Like a succulent. About this big." Slater held his hands a foot or so apart. "Ideally it could be completely concealed."

"A succulent is what?"

"It means dryland plants with thick leaves. Agave and yucca. You have some planted along your front wall."

"It must broadcast for a few days, I'm thinking?"

"As long as possible."

"I have something that will work."

Svetlana stepped toward the far end of the room, gesturing for him to follow. Plucking a little black object from a shelf above the workbench, she handed it to him. Tube-shaped, it was about the size of a D battery but longer. At one end a few inches of black insulated wire stuck out.

"This is the antenna," she said, fingering the wire. "The device can be buried deeply in the plant, but as much of the wire as possible should be exposed. Here's the power switch." She pointed out a tiny recessed slider. "It will function for about a week. Positioning data comes from sensing Wi-Fi signals, so it won't work well out in the country. It reports its location through the cell network."

Slater turned it over in his hands. It was heavy, and with that kind of life span, it had to be mostly battery.

"This will work great. What's it going to cost me? I need three of them."

"Special price for a loyal customer, six dollars for the set. I'll get the others."

When she tapped her wrist to the reader beside the door into the next room, the lock snapped open, and she stepped through, then closed the door behind her.

It was quiet here today, with nobody else in the workshop. He looked around the space. How many clients did Svetlana have, he wondered, and how many of them were as shady as Slater was, buying blatantly illegal surveillance gear? She'd once told him that she did on-the-books business with some big company, manufacturing some kind of sensor. Most likely she used that to launder her income from the illicit stuff.

Svetlana stepped back through the door with a brown paper supermarket bag in hand.

"Leave that one on the counter," she said. "I have three new ones for you."

Back at her computer, she spent a minute scanning the bar code label on each unit, then peeled it off and put the device in the shopping bag.

"All of the tracking devices are connected to your account," she said finally. "Once you switch them on, you'll see them in the interface."

"Excellent." Slater pulled his wad of cash out of his jeans, and riffled off six C-notes, and handed them over. Once she'd counted them, Svetlana unselfconsciously tucked the cash into her bra.

"Always a pleasure," she said.

"Back at you," he said, taking the bag from her. "Have you had any word from your brother? Is he ever coming back to LA?"

Svetlana scowled. "He's very selfish. Igor has no means to support himself, but he won't come back to work."

"He's still in Russia?"

"That's where I send his allowance. The far east. Siberia. Here the flowers are already blooming, but in Siberia the snow is just starting to melt. Who would choose to be there instead of here?"

"I get it," Slater said. "Family is complicated. *Spasiba bolshoye.*"

She cackled at that. "You sound like a native speaker. Keep learning."

Once he was outside, and walked around to the street, for a split second he thought the Thunderbird had been jacked. But he knew where it was: in Duarte's capable hands. Today he was driving the Polara.

It was such a decent ride. Accelerating effortlessly up the ramp and into the traffic, it felt light, like the tires were floating just above the asphalt. He exited the freeway into his own neighborhood, the hilly streets north of downtown LA. On his block the magnolia was still flowering, the big blossoms losing some of their dramatic starkness as the tree started to leaf out.

His house was a monolithic modern box built by gentrifiers, out of sync with the historic neighborhood. It had a garage and an ADU on the ground floor, and two bedrooms above that. The top floor was the kitchen and the living room and a deck.

Pike's SUV was nowhere in sight. He'd gone up to the Central Valley yesterday for work, and Slater didn't know when he'd be back. If he was around, he parked on the street out front, and his ride was hard to miss, with its dents and scratches and the New Mexico tags. He'd driven it out when he'd moved from Albuquerque.

Pulling up to his garage door, he waited for it to roll up. He still wasn't used to having somebody around all the time, sharing the space, but he was crazy about the guy, and couldn't get enough of him.

Nosing the Polara inside, he killed the engine and rolled the door down. He didn't need to go upstairs, and instead went to the wall rack farther back that held all his tools and gardening stuff.

He'd need the drill, and he grabbed that, then compared the drill bits to Svetlana's trackers, choosing a couple of options. When he carried it all to the back end of the Polara, and opened the trunk, he saw that the rug inside was immaculate. It felt wrong to put his dirty gear on it, so he piled it on the concrete floor, and grabbed a moving blanket, and lined the trunk with it before he loaded the tools in.

Next he grabbed a shovel, and his pickax, and some moldable silicone putty. That was for plugging leaks in irrigation lines, but it would work for what he needed to do today. Thinking about it for a minute, he found an awl and some screwdrivers, just in case.

Once he'd slammed the trunk of the Polara, he backed into the street and waited for the garage door to roll down. The addresses Claudine had sent him were all within a few blocks of each other. He put one into the navigation app on his phone and headed back onto the 5, south toward Downey.

Traffic wasn't heavy yet, and the drive went fast. When he pulled up in front of the landscaping, it was a smaller yard than the other one Claudine had shown him, with fewer plantings. Back near the house was a prominent blue agave. Like the others, this yard had no fence around it.

He climbed out and opened the trunk, sliding one of Svetlana's trackers into his hip pocket, then grabbed a trowel and the drill and the awl. Stepping into the landscaping, he made his way over to the blue agave. Before he got there a woman stepped out of the house, wearing a pink track suit, her dark hair tied back.

"Excuse me," she called to him. "What are you doing in my yard?"

"Technically it's Hester's yard. I'm a gardener, and I'm working for her. So you can spare me the static."

"The guy usually comes early in the morning, not at this time of day."

"That sounds like a you problem."

Slater knelt beside the agave and started to scrape the sandy earth away from the heart with the trowel.

"What exactly are you doing?" she called to him.

Ignoring her, he picked up the drill and attached the hole saw bit. The heart was solid and fibrous but softer than wood, and the bit cut into it easily. He felt guilty about damaging such a beautiful plant. If it didn't get stolen, doing this would stunt its growth and shorten its life.

Glancing toward the house, he saw that the nosy tenant was gone. He used the awl to pry around the disk of woody material in the surface he'd cut into, and it popped off in one piece. Next he put a wood spade bit on the drill, and spent a minute deepening the hole into the heart. Pulling the tracker from his back pocket, he switched it on, and pressed the black cylinder into the cavity he'd made. The width was right, but he needed to drill it in a bit deeper. He pulled the tracker out again, and once he'd made the hole deep enough, he pressed it back in, leaving its attached wire extended.

He pressed in a thin layer of the putty on top of the device, then put the fibrous cap back on. With a little pressure, the putty held it in place. The wire he folded over the base of a leaf, leaving it invisible unless someone looked closely. With the trowel he covered the base again, smoothing out the soil to look like it hadn't been disturbed.

It was totally obvious something unnatural was there, he saw, studying his work. But whoever was going to steal it would be doing it late at night, and it likely wouldn't get inspected until later—and by then he'd know where it had been taken.

THREE

RISING, HE PULLED OUT his phone, and checked Svetlana's tracking app. A new device appeared in the list, labeled "труб-2." He had no idea what the Cyrillic letters meant, but when he zoomed in on the map, the dot was in the right place, right here, on a residential street in Downey. Svetlana spoke English well enough that her interface didn't need to have all the Cyrillic, but he suspected she outsourced the coding to people back in the motherland, and it ended up a mishmash of the languages.

Gathering up all his gear, he carried it back to the Polara and loaded it into the trunk, then drove to Hester's other rental property. This was the place Claudine had shown him this morning. The lone blue agave here was farther from the street, closer to the house. Once he'd grabbed his tools, he stepped into the landscape and knelt beside it.

No car was in the driveway, and nobody appeared

from the house to challenge him. As he was drilling out the hole in the plant's heart, it felt like this one had more moisture in the fiber. Maybe it was younger, or it was getting more water.

As he clicked on the tracker's little recessed power switch, he noticed that the cylinder had a dent on the bottom rim, like it had been dropped. Svetlana said they were new. He studied the dent, and probed it with a fingernail. The metal of the cylinder might have separated a hair from the base.

Digging out his phone, he found that the app showed a new device online now, "труб-3." Its dot on the map was his current location. Even with the dent, the thing was working. He wedged it into the heart of the agave, then sealed it up and hid the protruding wire.

Once he'd rearranged the dirt, he carried his tools back to the trunk of the Polara, then drove to Hester's. There was one more blue agave, amid her sprawling landscaping, and he spent time with it on his knees. It was so lush and healthy, it seemed like a crime to drill a hole in it, but he did it anyway.

When he'd finished with it, he rose, and eyed the stupid pretentious plantation house, and carried his tools to the Polara. The tracking app on his phone showed three devices now, all labeled "труб" and numbered 1 to 3. The markers were in the right spots on the map, all in this neighborhood.

As he was looking at the map, standing next to the open trunk, the phone rang in his hand. The caller ID said it was Duarte. He picked up.

"We were right," Duarte said. "It was the exhaust manifold. It has a big crack in it."

"Is it a lot of work to fix it?"

"It's an easy fix, but it's not so easy to get the parts. Vera is on her way to Sun Valley now."

Slater knew exactly where that was, a neighborhood with lots of auto wreckers. Anyone who maintained a classic car knew the way to Sun Valley.

"How long will it take?"

"I'm thinking a couple days," Duarte said. "I want to replace both of them as a preventive measure."

"That sounds wise."

"It might cost a little more than a typical repair."

"I get it, man. You're scouring the junkyards. I'm not worried about the cost. You and Vera are full-service professionals."

He laughed. "How is the Polara running?"

"Like a dream. It's my second favorite car now."

Once he'd ended the call, he slammed the trunk and walked up the driveway toward the house. He wanted to wash his hands, and tell Hester he'd placed the trackers. Walking between the pompous columns, he stood at the front door and rang the bell.

A minute later Big Mike pulled the door open. Instead of the jodhpurs he was clad in chinos and a black T-shirt now. He scowled in recognition.

"You again. The slappy gardener."

"The name is Slater, and you earned that slap. I need to talk to Hester."

"She's not here."

"I also need to wash up."

Big Mike scoffed but pulled the door open wider. "It's over there. On the left."

Slater stepped into the foyer, a big double-story space with black and white floor tiles and a curving staircase leading up. He found the little half bath under the stairs. When he stepped out again, Big Mike was still in the foyer.

"I wanted to talk about that," he said. "When you slapped me."

Slater raised a palm. "If you need to complain about it, big guy, I'm not interested. If you're going to try to make trouble for me, bring it. Otherwise you can spare me the chin music."

"Calm down." He frowned. "I don't want to make trouble. I was thinking maybe I would like to touch your ass."

"Seriously?" His eyebrows shot up. "That changes things. Is Hester out for a while?"

"Hours and hours."

Slater waved a hand. "I can fuck you, Big Mike, if that's what you want. It can't get sticky though."

"What does that mean?"

"I've got a smoking hot man at home, and we're embroiled in a sprawling romantic narrative complex. The rules are that I can have sexual experiences with other people but not romantic ones. What do you want to do?"

"What you just said." Big Mike held his gaze. "I want you to fuck me."

"You'll need a condom and lube."

Big Mike turned and started up the staircase, and Slater followed him, into a bedroom with windows over the front yard and the street. As Big Mike stooped to dig in the bedside table, he sat on the bed and leaned down to untie his boots.

Eyeing him, Big Mike waved an arm. "Not here. This is where Hester sleeps."

"So we're cheating on your wife, just not in her bed."

Big Mike scowled. "We have an understanding."

That's not what Claudine had said, but Slater didn't need to point that out.

"There's a sofa in my study," Big Mike said, and walked out.

Slater followed him down the hall, into a big room, brightly lit by big windows, with dark wood furniture. The sofa looked comfortable, but in front of the desk was a heavy armless chair. Putting his hands on it, he assessed its sturdiness.

"This will work." Slater pulled it out and turned it to face the room, then dropped into it, spreading his knees. "Come here."

Big Mike hesitated, shifting his weight from one foot to the other. "This is crazy."

"I'm going to demolish you," Slater said, raising his voice. "Get your ass over here."

With a sharp inhale, Big Mike stepped over, and Slater reached for his arm, and pulled him into his lap. Big Mike sat sideways, and put his arms around Slater's neck, and leaned in to his mouth. It was warm and taught, and Slater spent a minute with it, then mouthed his neck and his ear.

"I can feel you getting hard," Big Mike said.

"Let me get my pants down."

Big Mike rose, and Slater unbuckled his belt, and popped his fly. Big Mike pushed down his chinos and stepped out of them, revealing his tighty-whities.

"What happened to the riding boots?"

"I don't wear them around the house. They're downstairs." His brow furrowed. "You want me to wear them?"

"You have to. It's not optional." Slater pulled his cock out of his jeans and held his gaze. "Toss me the condom, son, and look sharp."

"You know I'm older than you, right?" He handed it to him and then stepped out.

Slater pulled his shirt off, but decided not to bother with his boots. He shoved his jeans down, then sat in the chair again, and rolled the condom on.

A moment later Big Mike stepped in, wearing the black riding boots and nothing else, already chubby.

"Nice," Slater said, and waved him over.

He straddled him, bracing his hands on Slater's shoulders, and Slater guided him down, slowly pressing into him. Big Mike closed his eyes and tilted his head back, moaning with the intensity of it. Once he was all the way down, Slater grasped his waist, breathing hard, and bounced him a little.

"You feel that?" he said in Big Mike's ear. "You're in the saddle. You're in charge. You're the only one that can make this happen."

"You're so hot," he said, his face red, and leaned in to kiss him.

Soon he was bouncing intently, with Slater guiding him with one hand and stroking his cock with the other.

"Keep doing that," Big Mike said, panting. "I'm close."

"Come on, man. Ride the pony."

Slater slapped his butt, and with that Big Mike climaxed, straining into his hand. That was enough to push Slater over the edge, and he pressed into him, grasping his waist, pulling him closer.

Big Mike slumped forward, leaning on him, and

Slater wrapped his arms around him, supporting him while they caught their breath. He could feel his heartbeat gradually slowing.

Eventually Big Mike rose, flaccid now. "You like the boots, huh."

"You want to get on this horse, you need the right gear."

He took a breath. "You're a lot of man, Slater."

"So I'm told." He rose, and pulled off the condom, and handed it to him.

Big Mike frowned but took it. "I should ask for your discretion."

"I know how to keep my mouth shut, big guy." He pulled his jeans up, and met his eye as he buttoned his fly. "At least until I need some quick cash."

His eyebrows shot up. "Blackmail?"

"In my world it's called the squeeze play. A way to generate a consistent revenue stream."

"You sound like a syndicate banker."

Slater chuckled as he pulled on his shirt. "I'm just messing with you."

"It might be kind of hot to be blackmailed by a guy like you. As long as there was more sex in the equation. You'd ravish me, and I'd pay you, and I'd hate it but I'd love it."

"Have you heard of the blackmailer's ultimate reward?"

"What's that?"

"A shallow grave up in the Angeles National Forest."

Big Mike frowned. "I'm not that guy."

"Neither am I."

Slater walked out, and trotted down the stairs to

the foyer, and out to the driveway. His phone had buzzed a minute ago, and he checked it. The notification said there was a text from Reddy Kilowatt. That was his nickname for Pike:

Headed home this evening.

Slater wasn't supposed to hook up with other people when Pike was in town, and he'd said he might be up there for a few days. If he wasn't actually in town yet, he hadn't violated his sex rules. Either way, it was great that Pike would be back tonight.

Walking to the Polara, he thought about that word he'd used, *home*. "Headed home." If it were anyone else, he'd have to school them on whose house it was. But this was Pike. *Home.* It implied more than just where he lived, where they lived. It meant their relationship, their narrative complex, whatever it was that they were building.

Once he'd climbed behind the wheel, he took a minute to text Hester. Numb-nuts Big Mike would likely neglect to mention that Slater had been there:

I planted trackers in all three blue agaves. Let me know if any of them go missing.

The late-day traffic was sluggish through downtown, and when he turned onto his street, in the rearview he saw Pike's familiar SUV turn in behind him from the other direction. Once he'd pulled into the garage, he stepped into the street to watch Pike climb out of his rig and sling his day pack over his shoulder.

With luxy dark hair, wearing a white shirt and dark trousers, Pike was thick, with a perfect little paunch over his belt. When he caught sight of Slater he cracked a smile, that look that made his heart soar.

"That was fast," Slater said.

"I was already on the road when I texted. What are you driving?" He gestured to the Polara in the garage. "I thought I got stuck behind somebody's grandmother."

"That particular grandmother could smoke your rig any day of the week."

Pike chuckled, and embraced him, and met his mouth, getting lost in it. Slater relished the electric warmth of his arms. This moment, the intense connection—it always felt like time just stopped, like he lost track of everything else.

Pike pulled back. "I feel like we're giving the neighbors free porn."

"Nobody's watching us."

He pointed to the house across the street. "That place has a doorbell camera, and that one has a camera over the side gate. It probably catches part of the street."

"You're so observant. It's actually useful to know that."

They went inside, and Slater hit the garage door button, and they climbed the stairs to the next floor, where the bedrooms were. They slept in the one that faced the street, and the other one, at the back, had a bed in it plus a desk under the window so that Pike could have some privacy when he worked remotely.

Slater pulled his boots off and stretched out on the bed to watch him undress.

"So what happened to your hooptie?" Pike said, unbuttoning his shirt.

He explained the breakdown, and about Duarte and Vera. "I never had to ask them to come out before.

I always drove over to their garage. The pair of them were treating me like grief counselors."

Pike pulled on a T-shirt. "They know how you feel about the T-bird. It's kind of amazing they provide that level of service."

"You have no idea how much I pay them."

Pike lay down beside him, and Slater lifted his head so he could slide his arm under his neck.

"You seem chill," Slater said.

"It was a pretty easy day. Just pounding the pavement, interviewing knuckleheads, visiting hock shops."

"Nobody was shooting at you today."

Pike chuckled. "I'm feeling rested too. I haven't for a long time."

"All the flying back and forth to Albuquerque. I'm sure it was exhausting."

"That was part of it, but it was mostly about you."

Slater eyed him sidelong and frowned. "Do I snore or something?"

"It's been hard work cozying up to the forty-niner. I couldn't sleep. I just thought about you, day and night. Now that we have a groove, I can finally get some rest."

"I'm glad that happened to you too. To me it felt like I was walking around high on drugs. Euphoric but also kind of out of it."

He beamed and squeezed Slater's neck in the crook of his elbow. "You got crushed out on me."

"You know damn well I did. You're a dangerous man. I couldn't see straight. I wasn't even sure which way was up for a long time. There's still some residual effects of that."

"Rosa came yesterday morning after you left," Pike said.

"I thought things looked tidier."

"I tried to explain that she needs to clean the stovetop. She acted all offended, and said she cleans it every time. I let it go, but if she thinks that's clean, she's either crazy or she's playing you."

Slater scoffed. "I hope you didn't tell her that."

"I gave her a raise, by the way. You weren't paying her enough."

He laughed and shifted onto his side. "You crack me up."

"Because I want her to actually do the work?"

"Because she's not doing what you want, but she needs to get paid more for it."

Pike raised his eyebrows. "Those things aren't necessarily connected."

"I love the way your mind works." He caressed his face. "Adore it. I adore you."

———◦———

LATER THEY ORDERED SOME Thai food, and ate on the patio table out on the deck as the daylight faded, chatting about nothing and agreeing on everything. After dark it was too cold to lounge outside, and they sat on the sofa that faced the French doors onto the deck, and read the book they were currently immersed in—the *Iliad*.

No way could Slater's brain handle the actual poetry of the *Iliad* at the end of the workday. This version was an analysis of each section, written in modern language. It covered all the details but didn't feel too dense, and the symbolism was all clearly explained, alleviating the need for him to decipher it. Neither one of them were especially passionate about the classics, but when they'd met, Pike had been reading a primer on Greek mythology, and they'd read it to each other, and now that had become their thing.

It was Slater's turn to read, and he leaned back on Pike, relishing the warmth of his big arms encircling him, and found the page.

"When Aphrodite saw the attack on Aeneas, she swooped in and covered him with her robes so that he'd suffer no further injury …"

FOUR

BRIGHT SUNLIGHT STREAMED THROUGH the sheers when Slater woke. His head was clear, so he must have stuck to his ration of bourbon last night. It was definitely easier to adhere to his booze rules with this guy around. Pike distracted him from the routine, but he also inspired him to behave himself.

He watched the regular rhythm of Pike's chest gently rising and falling, and studied his face, so soft and guileless, his mouth agape. A while later Pike woke, and looked at him, and cracked a smile.

"What's going on?"

"You're so beautiful," Slater said. "I can't stand it. It's like you're intentionally trying to drive me crazy."

"Even in my sleep?"

"Like you said yesterday, it's getting more familiar. When you first started staying here, my heart would get all messed up. Like physically. It was beating too fast. That seems to have eased up."

Pike shifted next to him and wrapped an arm

around his chest. "It's because you love me."

"I plead no contest to that one." He caressed his cheek. "Let me smoke you."

Not waiting for a response, Slater threw back the covers, and shifted down the bed, squeezing Pike's morning woody, then took him into his mouth. Gasping at the intensity of it, Pike shifted position, and grabbed Slater's cock, and went down on him too.

Pike climaxed first, straining into him, and a moment later Slater came, then rolled onto his back.

"I feel like a damn teenager," Pike said. "It happens so fast."

"That's why you get a woody in the morning. You're supposed to do something about it."

Pike chuckled and got up, and a moment later Slater heard the shower go on. He pulled the pillow under his head and yanked the covers over himself. Just for a little while, to enjoy the warm glow of satiety a moment longer.

Eventually he forced himself out of bed, into the cold air, and pulled on a pair of skivvies and a T-shirt. Trudging up the stairs, he started the coffeemaker.

When Pike came up a while later, he was dressed for work.

"You're going to the office?" Slater said, and poured him a coffee.

"I have a meeting. I'll be there for a few hours."

Pike pulled some fruit out of the Frigidaire and sliced a couple of bagels in half, setting it all on the dining table. When he finished eating, Slater sat back.

"Is my street understanding of explosives correct, that an M-80 is the same as an eighth of a stick of dynamite?"

Pike gestured with the rind of the orange slice he'd just eaten. "It's apples and oranges. The explosive in dynamite is a different chemical than the flash powder in fireworks. Dynamite has percussive force, so you can dig holes and dislodge rocks. Fireworks are mostly flash and bang."

"So what's in dynamite?"

"Nitroglycerin is the explosive. It's combined with inert stabilizers."

"I know that stuff," Slater said. "In my business we call it safecracker soup."

Pike frowned. "I wouldn't be hanging out with people who'd use that to open a safe. You'll get yourself blown up. As a liquid it's unstable, and dangerous. That's how the Nobel prize guy made his money. He figured out how to stabilize nitroglycerin as dynamite."

"Flash powder still has some kick to it, though, doesn't it?"

"You can definitely blow your hands off with flash powder too." Pike picked up his coffee mug. "Why are you asking?"

"I've been working a case with these stolen succulents. I was thinking I could hollow one out and fill it with flash powder from some M-80s. When the thieves started to chop them up, *kaboom*."

"That's a really stupid idea," Pike said, his brow furrowing. "Flash powder won't explode from percussion, like chopping into it. It needs an ignition source. A flame."

"But safecracker soup will ignite from percussion."

"More likely it'll blow up while you're trying to get it into the plant." He scoffed. "Besides that, booby traps are illegal. If someone got hurt you'd be on the hook for battery, manslaughter, maybe even murder."

"All right. I get it." Slater threw up a hand. "A boy can dream, can't he?"

"I have to go." Pike rose and put his mug in the dishwasher. "No explosives," he said intently, jabbing a finger at him.

"Sure thing, pop."

"Are you going to do it anyway?"

"I have other options."

"Like what?"

"That's need-to-know type information," Slater said.

"Why can't you just tell me the truth?" Pike raised his voice and waved an arm. "It's about that Russian, isn't it. I know there's more going on there than you've said."

He frowned. "There's no need to get steamed about it."

Shaking his head, Pike scoffed and headed down the stairs.

Slater slammed the last of his coffee and sat there thinking about it. What was Pike so pissed about? Just the mention of safecracker soup had set him off. He hated this part—not knowing why, trying to read someone's mind, trying to figure out what the hell was really going on.

It was too much work to rig the agaves anyway, plus he'd already planted the trackers. He grabbed his phone and checked Svetlana's app. His heart started to pound when he saw that one of the trackers had moved. This was already happening.

On the map the marker for the tracker showed

that it wasn't far from where it had been planted in Downey. When he zoomed in, he found it was a residential neighborhood, a street lined with apartments. The green circle for the estimated location was in the front yard of one of the buildings. It might be off by a few feet. Svetlana's Wi-Fi sniffing tech wasn't always super accurate. The blue agave was more likely inside that building, not out on the lawn.

The marker was labeled тру6-2. That was the first one he'd planted, in the yard at one of the rentals, not at Hester's house. Scrolling through the movement history, it had started its journey at 3:47 a.m., and took sixteen minutes to get to where it was now. Someone had dug it up and taken it home.

Rising, Slater went down to his bedroom to get dressed. Yesterday's jeans smelled a little funky when he gave them the sniff test, so he pulled on a clean pair, along with a black buttoned shirt. In the garage, when he flicked on the light, the rich red of the Polara was startling. He'd almost forgotten that this was his ride today. He backed it into the street, and waited for the garage door to descend, then cruised down to Sunset.

Glancing at his phone, he saw that the tracker hadn't moved again. The neighborhood it was in was over near Rio Hondo, in Pico Rivera. The navigation app took him on the 5, and when he turned onto the street where the tracker was, he slowed down and cruised past, looking over the scene. Cramped tight together, run-down apartments lined both sides of the block, with little patches of lawn along the sidewalk.

At the next corner Slater pulled a U-turn and

then parked across the street, a ways up from the building where the marker was. From here he had a view of it and the street out front. He killed the engine and zoomed in on the map. The green ring that showed the location was sizeable—it encircled part of the front yard and a stretch of the sidewalk fronting it, but it didn't touch the apartment building. There was definitely no blue agave sitting on that patch of scrubby crabgrass and bare dirt. The estimate could be off, and the blue agave could be a few yards outside the circle, inside that building. But the circle hadn't glitched or hopped at all, both signs that the software was struggling for accuracy.

The circle also covered the cars parked tight together along the curb, he realized, staring at the screen. Looking up, the vehicles closest to the center of the estimated location were a dark SUV with flashy rims, and a mid-'90s powder-blue Town Car. If the agave was in one of those, the thief must be taking it somewhere else—this was just where they slept.

It made sense that it wouldn't be delivered to its final destination at four in the morning. That was just the optimal time to jack it. The tracker also hadn't stopped anywhere else, so it was likely still in the possession of the thief, not the moving man who'd fence it or the ultimate tequila maker.

Slater shifted to get comfortable. The Polara's seats weren't as plush as the Thunderbird's, plus stakeouts were usually lengthy, and always boring. He looked at stuff on his phone, emails and bills and other bullshit, keeping one eye on the vehicles at the curb.

There were lots of people strolling the sidewalk, including a group of teenagers who walked past, even though school had to be in session by now. Idly watching them, he wondered if he really needed to be here. He could follow the tracker to the next destination from anywhere. But if it was in one of those vehicles, he'd be able to see who had custody of it from right here.

A while later a woman walked out of the apartment building, her long hair bundled back, wearing jeans and a blue nylon jacket. She climbed into the SUV with the rims and started the engine. Slater grabbed his binoculars from the backseat and zeroed in on her face. She studied herself for a moment in her rearview mirror, wiping at her lips.

This was it—she could be the thief. Slater sat up, ready to twist the key in the ignition, and watched the tracking map. When the SUV pulled out and rolled past him, the location circle didn't budge. He stared at it for a minute, and refreshed the screen, but nothing changed. The agave was in the Town Car.

Or was something else going on? Another possibility flashed in his mind—maybe the thief had spotted the tracker, and extracted it, and dumped it in the gutter here. Popping the door handle, he climbed out and walked across the street, and strolled up the sidewalk. He scanned the scruffy turf, and the verge, and the gutter. There was empty junk food packaging, a half-eaten chicken leg, and lots of wrappers for those little cigars, but he couldn't see anything that resembled the tracker.

It had to be in the Town Car. As he passed it, he looked in, but the side windows had a heavy tint on them. It was likely in the trunk anyway. Crossing the street, he walked back to the Polara. Keeping the blue agave in the darkness of the trunk would damage it, and stunt its growth. But it didn't matter. If someone was going to use it to make tequila, it wasn't going to be replanted. It was already destined for destruction.

Sometime later a guy walked out of the apartment building, wearing jeans and a blue plaid shirt. He was Latin, and a little chubby, with his black hair slicked back. With the binoculars Slater got a look at his face, and his heart started to pound when the guy unlocked the driver's door of the Town Car and got in behind the wheel. He started the engine and revved it, then pulled into the street and rolled past. Slater instinctively shrank back into his seat, but the guy didn't even glance at him. On his phone the location marker was on the move now—this was the guy. Hester's blue agave was definitely in the trunk of that Town Car.

Slater waited a minute, then started the engine and popped it into gear, and made a three-point turn in a driveway. The Town Car wasn't in sight ahead, but he could see it on the map on his phone, the green location circle hopping down the street and resizing itself as the tracker sniffed out new Wi-Fi stations and cross-referenced their locations in the public databases. A few blocks ahead the marker headed right on the boulevard, and a minute later Slater made the turn. The circle was stationary again, he saw, and it shrank as it got more confident about its location. When he came up on the Town Car, it was parked at the curb in front of a taqueria.

Farther up the block, Slater made a quick U-turn in a break in the traffic. That was totally illegal, but the Polara was peppy enough to pull it off so fast that no one would see more than a vague red blur.

Before he got to the taqueria, he pulled to the curb and killed the engine, then grabbed his binoculars. He couldn't find the driver of the Town Car, in that blue plaid shirt, but he could see the entrance to the place, and he watched people coming and going. A few minutes later the driver stepped out. There was nothing in his hands—he must have eaten in there. Through the binoculars he got a better look at the guy's face—a broad nose, hooded eyes. He had that familiar look of so many Angelenos whose roots were on the ranchos in Zacatecas and Durango.

He stepped into the street and climbed into the Town Car, then pulled into the traffic. Slater watched the marker for a minute before he started the engine. It had moved just a few blocks and stopped again, and Slater kept an eye on it as he nosed into the boulevard traffic and headed that way.

The vehicle was parked in the angle spaces in front of a block of low-rise commercial buildings, sagging and in need of paint but still hosting retail storefronts—a laundromat, a seedy-looking insurance agency, and García and Co., whatever that was. The laundromat was open, but the other businesses looked dark. Except the one with the faded sign above the door that said MONDO ALEGRE, he realized, watching a guy step out, the door swinging closed behind him. The silhouette of a martini glass was painted next to the name. Mondo Alegre was a bar. It seemed a little early in the day for boozing for anyone but a professional alcoholic, but it felt more likely that his target would have gone in there than into the laundromat.

Slater turned onto the next side street and found a parking space half a block up, in front of a row of crowded-together little bungalows. He walked back to the boulevard and the retail strip, and pulled open the door to Mondo Alegre, and stepped into the dim interior.

FIVE

RANCHERA MUSIC WAS PLAYING low on a tinny speaker. A few booths lined the walls, and at the back was a long bar. Nobody was in the booths but four people sat on the stools at the bar, none of them together, drinking even though it was lunchtime on a weekday.

The linoleum was grubby and ancient, and the ratty barstools had been repaired with duct tape. This was a dive bar, but not the kind where hep white kids came to groove. These were working-class Latin folks.

Looking over the patrons as he stepped toward the bar, Slater saw that they were all men. Was that a red flag? He recognized his target even though the guy was facing away from him—he remembered that shirt. He was sitting a few stools up from the corner of the bar, and Slater walked to the end. No one was sitting on this side, and he took the middle stool, where he could watch his target and the other patrons. The guy already had a glass of beer in front of him, and sat gazing into the blue glow of his phone screen.

As Slater sat down, the bartender stepped over. She had her hair pulled back, and wore a stretchy purple top that showed the outline of her bra straps, and way too much eye makeup.

"*¿Cheve?*" she said, raising her eyebrows.

Slater didn't know the word. "A small of whatever lager you have on tap."

As she walked away, he dug out a sawbuck and set it on the bar top. He pulled out his phone and gazed at the screen, not seeing it but using it as cover to surreptitiously watch his target. The guy was thumb-scrolling, and had the sullen empty expression of someone killing time.

When his beer arrived, the bartender whisked away the sawbuck, and he took a sip of the watery ale. His target looked up and said something to her as she made change at the register. He spoke in Spanish, way too fast and clipped for Slater to parse any of it.

The woman raised her voice when she replied, jutting her chin, like she was telling him off. The word she punctuated it with was "Mauricio." That was either this guy's name or the name of someone she was invoking to intimidate him.

In the guy's hand his phone rang, a shrill electronic sound, and he answered it in unaccented English.

"This is Mauricio … I got it last night … I was waiting for you, gringo … Keep your pants on. I'll be there soon."

Slater sipped his beer. The guy was talking to his client, or maybe to the fence, but this was definitely the person who'd gone into the landscaping and uprooted the blue agave. Mauricio was the thief.

Then he felt eyes on him. One of the other men at the bar, sitting a couple of stools past his target, was studying him intently, he realized, his brow furrowed. Slater avoided his gaze and looked back to his phone.

Someone walked in from the street, and Slater glanced toward the doorway. A guy dressed in denim and a red golf shirt. He walked up to the bar and clapped his target on the shoulder.

"Mauricio," he said, followed by a string of staccato Spanish.

After a brief exchange the guy wandered farther down the bar to talk to someone else. Eventually Mauricio drained his glass and rose. There was no rush for Slater to leave—he knew this guy's face, and knew his ride, and could easily find him with the tracker.

Taking another sip of his beer, Slater arched his back and rolled his neck. The man on the stool beyond Mauricio was still eyeing him, and when their eyes met, the guy jutted his chin and called to him in Spanish.

"*No comprendo,*" Slater said. "I've only got the one language."

"I said, have you got a looking problem?"

He frowned. "What are you talking about?"

"You're looking at my boy here, and you're looking at me. What are you looking at?"

"How should I know?" Slater said. "I never studied zoology."

"What the fuck does that mean?" he demanded.

"I'm not looking at you, or your friend. I'm trying to have a drink in peace."

"You're definitely looking around, *paisa*. Who sent you here?"

That word, he'd heard before. It meant somebody from the sticks, a hick, a hillbilly. Slater scoffed, and sat up straighter to tuck his phone into his jeans. "Spread out," he said.

Mauricio had paused, after tucking away his change, and stood behind his barstool now, also watching Slater, his brow furrowed.

"You didn't just walk in here," the other guy said. "Nobody does that. Who are you working for? I've never seen you before. Have you seen this one before, *primo*?"

"Never," Mauricio said. "Who are you, *vato*? I'm confused."

"Don't feel too bad. I know you can't help it," Slater said, and shrugged. "Lots of people are stupid."

The other guy jumped off his stool. He wasn't very tall, but he was built thick, and he came at him. Slater managed to get up off his stool, but the guy was fast, and almost instantly on him. He punched Slater in the shoulder and then in the gut. The double shot. It was an effective street-brawling technique as it was hard to block.

Slater managed to land a blow on his chin before he had to crumple around the pain in his gut, and then swung wildly from below, striking the guy in the neck. The guy stepped back for a second, then lunged at him. Slater saw his trajectory, and ducked lower, and head-butted the guy's crotch, grabbing his thighs. It was a wrestling move to flip him over his back, and it wasn't difficult when you knew how to do it—you just had to lift from below your opponent's center of gravity. At that point there was no way for him to keep his feet on the ground, and the guy had already generated all the momentum required for the throw by rushing him.

Slater threw him over, and the guy landed flat on his back, looking stunned for a second. Standing erect and taking a step back, Slater growled at him.

"Stay down."

The bartender shouted something in Spanish, and at that moment he saw a fist coming at him in the periphery. He had no time to react, and it struck his eye socket, spinning his head. Stunned, he stumbled a step away and crouched lower. His assailant was fast approaching, and he punched hard at his dick.

The first guy was on his feet now, and the bartender was shouting louder. That dick punch had landed—the second guy stepped backward, cupping his crotch with both hands, his expression pained.

Slater stood erect, but neither of them came at him again, instead just glaring at him, murder in their eyes. Mauricio hadn't been one of his assailants. He was over by the bar, standing there watching the brawl, his expression sanguine. Why were they not pounding on him anymore? Maybe it was something the bartender had said. Then the pair of them approached him in unison, one on either side. Slater wound up to throw a punch, but each of them grabbed one of his arms, and hauled him out the door, and threw him down on the grubby concrete.

He managed to roll as he landed. That was another move from middle school wrestling, a technique to distribute the impact so that nothing got broken, hopefully not even bruised.

One of them shouted at him in Spanish, waving an arm. Slater got to his feet, and swatted the dust off his butt, and walked away. As he neared the corner, he glanced over his shoulder, but no one was following him. They'd gone back into the bar.

What the hell was going on? They thought he was up to something. That was actually true, but he wasn't doing what they thought he was doing: working for someone to case the bar. Obviously he hadn't been as stealthy as he thought he was in surveilling Mauricio. His heart was still pounding, burning through the adrenaline, as he came up on the Polara. At least nobody had shot at him.

Incidents like this were the reason he parked out of view of the entrance. He looked back up the empty street once more, just in case, but there was no one around, and he climbed into the Polara.

He took a deep breath to calm his racing pulse and pulled the rearview mirror down to take a look at himself. He massaged the tender spot around his eye. It was probably going to bruise. Digging out his phone, he found a supermarket nearby, and fired up the engine, and drove over.

In the freezer aisle he found a packet of frozen peas, and once he'd bought them, sat in his car in the parking lot with the cold plastic pressed to his eye. With any luck this would avert the swelling and the worst of a bruise.

Why had he strutted in there, like a damn tyro, swinging his dick? He should have sensed that it wasn't just a bar. It was somebody's clubhouse.

With his free eye, he checked Svetlana's app. труб-2 had moved—Mauricio had left the bar, and stopped somewhere a little closer to downtown. East of the river and north of the tracks. That was an industrial zone. When he zoomed out, the map label said the neighborhood was called Soto Junction. He'd never heard of it. When he zoomed in, the tracker looked to be inside a structure.

Dropping the peas on the floor of the passenger side, he started the engine and drove toward the marker. In a few minutes he was on the wide boulevard that ran through the neighborhood, plied mostly by box trucks and semis. Long stretches of chain-link fence topped by razor wire protected the factories and warehouses. He cruised under a heavy railroad bridge dense with graffiti, then under the steel pylons of a high-voltage electric line.

Eventually he turned onto a quieter side street. The marker was a few blocks up, and he drove slowly past the site. It was a corner lot surrounded by a fence made of narrowly spaced steel pickets painted black. Next to the gate a sign mounted on the fence said EASTSIDE LIGHTNING, along with the building number. The gate was rolled open, and he could see the structure, a long single story set well back from the fence. On this side, facing the gate, was an office door and windows. Farther down, along the side of the building, there were no windows, but there was a truck loading dock with a big roll-up steel shutter. Vehicles sat in the stalls in front of the office, but none of them was the blue Town Car.

Slater made a right at the next corner and parked along a tall hedge fronting the blank wall of another lengthy building. There was barely room for the greenery to thrive in the narrow verge, but he knew why it was there—to block access to the broad empty graffiti-ready canvas of the side of the structure. Any would-be artist would move on to easier pickings rather than fight through the hedge.

On his phone, Slater zoomed in on the marker. It was definitely back there in that building, on the map shown as a vague rectangle. If the marker was accurate, the blue agave was near that loading dock door.

Next he searched for Eastside Lightning, and found the company's website. It was the brand name for an artisanal tequila, "brewed at our distillery in Soto Junction." This neighborhood was Soto Junction, so this was the distillery—and Mauricio had brought them the blue agave, the primary input for brewing tequila.

The website had an airy and stylish vibe, with a few vague paragraphs describing the company, "an exciting new venture in premium tequila."

It also explained that "Eastside Lightning is the vision of Zane and Kim," along with a posed photo of the pair of them beaming at the camera. Zane looked to be in his early thirties, with mousy brown hair and a beard around his chin but no mustache, like a nineteenth-century New England mariner or a 1950s Venice beatnik. Kim was older than Zane, in her forties maybe, with her hair in the short pixie style so many Asian women wore when they hit middle age.

As he went through the website, it seemed the company's only product was the tequila. The description for it said it was "based on centuries of tradition but with a unique artisanal twist you haven't experienced yet. Eastside Lightning is the new go-to tequila for people in the know."

He'd seen this kind of marketing before—take something ordinary and call it "artisanal" or "one of a kind" and you could charge a whole lot more for it.

Briefly glancing at Svetlana's app again, he saw that the other trackers were both still in Downey, where he'd planted them, in front of Hester's plantation house and at her other rental property. He tucked his phone away and thought about it for a minute, gazing absently at the empty street.

This was a tequila distillery, and even though there was no sign of Mauricio or the Town Car, he knew the stolen blue agave was in there because the tracker was in there. He had no doubt about why they'd acquired it. He needed to confront them about it.

A quiet street like this was a prime break-in spot, and when he climbed out, he left the Polara's door unlocked so that they wouldn't break the glass. There was nothing to steal apart from his binoculars, except maybe the whole car.

Slater strode to the corner and around to the open gate. Up close he saw that the Eastside Lightning sign was printed on a long sheet of clear plastic, attached to the fence with bolts. The asphalt on the lot ended just past the loading dock, but there looked to be plenty more space beyond it, at the back of the building. A gravel lot like that would be for freight trucks to turn around and for storage, but there was nothing parked back there now, except a stack of a dozen shipping pallets along the wall just past the dock.

The office door faced the street, and parked in front of it was a black Bimmer sedan. Next to it was a little round-topped SUV with a Benz logo on the lift gate. He didn't know they made anything that small and odd-looking. It must be new. Beside the Benz was an empty stall, and then a beat-up maroon-red pickup with a utility rack and locking tool boxes in back.

Striding past the vehicles, he walked up to the office door. No security cameras covered this entrance, he saw. Maybe they thought the fence and a locking gate were all the security they needed. A hand-lettered sign was taped inside the glass: BUSCA AYUDA. He'd seen that often enough over the years to know what it meant: help wanted.

When he pulled on it, the door was unlocked, and he stepped inside. The lone desk in the front office had nothing on it, apart from a phone and an empty paper tray, like it wasn't in use. Maybe like him and Max, this outfit was too small to need full-time clerical help. There were no obvious cameras here either, and no signs of life, but a wide hallway led farther back.

Slater stood in front of the desk and called, "Hello."

A moment later a guy stepped out of one of the doorways in the hall. This was Zane, shorter than he'd expected, and still with the gnarly half beard. At least it was tightly trimmed and not all shaggy. He was wearing a tweed sport jacket with a silky yellow ascot. It was a pompous look, but he had to admit it actually worked with the beard. Zane was thick, and wore his chinos tight, revealing his not unimpressive junk. The guy was basically fuckable.

At the sight of him Zane's face clouded. With mangled Anglo pronunciation, he said, *"Buenos días."*

Even monolingual Slater knew it was too late in

the day for that phrase. People only said that in the morning.

"I actually speak English," Slater said, and scowled at him.

"Good for you. I guess you should come in." He beckoned him to follow, and as he turned, called sharply, "Kim."

Stepping around the front desk, Slater walked back to his office. It was carpeted in dark gray and contained a basic glass-topped desk, a little conference table with four chairs, and a credenza with a TV set and several fifths of their tequila lined up on it. It was flashy but not overblown.

Kim stepped in behind him, with the same short haircut as in her portrait. In real life she looked a little older, maybe mid-fifties, and her photo hadn't shown that her rack was way out of proportion with her slight build. That degree of augmentation wasn't unusual in this town, although nothing else about her was glam, as she wore light makeup and basic black trousers. Her blouse was unbuttoned to show some cleavage. That made sense—when you spent that much on them, you'd want to show them off.

Standing behind his desk, Zane raised his eyebrows. "Have a seat, Mr. ....?"

"Slade," Slater said. "John Slade."

As Slater sat across the desk from him, Kim took the other guest chair, shifting it half a turn so she was facing him.

"I assumed you'd be from Mexico," Zane said. "This is Kim, and I'm Zane."

"I know who you are."

"Right."

Zane's gaze was so intense, his eyes a little too wide. A vein was pulsing on his forehead. Was this guy on something? Either that or he had a thyroid condition.

"Mr. Slade," Kim said. "What can we do for you?"

"Where do you obtain your blue agave plants?"

Her brow furrowed, and she held his gaze. "We have an outside contractor. They deal with the farmers. We only use agaves grown in Southern California. Nothing imported." She waved a hand. "We're not interfering with any production channels in Mexico."

"We're a small operation, Mr. Slade," Zane said. "We don't actually use a lot of agave."

They'd both said his name, and both used that intense eye contact. It seemed odd coming from both of them. Like it was a technique they'd learned in some business training session.

"Big picture," Kim said, "we're not a threat to the Mexican tequila industry. By comparison our sales are minuscule. Mostly limited to the Southwest."

"We're also no threat to the protected appellation," Zane said, raising his eyebrows. "Our product only uses the word *tequila* tangentially, and it doesn't appear on the bottle."

Slater looked from him back to Kim. It felt like they'd rehearsed this. "What's the protected appellation?"

Kim's eyes narrowed. "Isn't that your people? We were told you were going to drop in."

"Who told you that?"

"I thought you were from the Mexican agricultural appellation body."

"That's not me," Slater said.

"So who do you work for?" Zane demanded.

That flash of anger, the sudden shift in demeanor—he'd seen it before, and it was characteristic of tweakers. This guy was on meth.

"It feels like you're afraid of these appellation people," Slater said. "Are they like a drug cartel?"

"Why are you here?" Kim said, raising her voice.

Slater sat up and met her gaze. "I saw your help-wanted sign in the door."

"Fuck," Zane roared. "You're just a day laborer?"

Slater raised his eyebrows. "Has the position been filled?"

Kim rose. "That's about the factory, not about us."

"Isn't this your factory?"

"You need to talk to Rogelio," she said, and headed toward the door. "He's the production manager."

"Go on, then," Zane said, gesturing toward the door. "Stop wasting my time."

Slater's instinct was to step around the desk and punch him in the face, but that wouldn't fit with the play he was making. He rose and stepped into the hallway. Kim's office was on the opposite side, and as he walked by he saw that hers had a pair of long file cabinets. Zane's office didn't have any of those. That meant Kim was the one who did the paperwork.

At the end of the hall was a wide fire door with a little glass window in it shot through with reinforcing wire mesh. When he tried the handle, it was unlocked, and he stepped into the factory.

SIX

A COUPLE OF TOWERING STAINLESS-STEEL vats dominated the far side of the big space, along with other machinery connected by a network of black plastic pipes. That was about processing liquids—this must be the still. At the side, near the wall with the loading dock in it, were two long worktables and a big red tool cabinet. On top of one of the tables was a beautiful blue agave, dramatic and out of place in this dull industrial place. The roots were still mostly intact. That was one of the plants he'd put trackers in yesterday, the one that had been in Mauricio's car.

On the other side, opposite the loading dock, a pony wall split the space. It was about eight feet tall, with another eight feet of air above it. Through the wide gap in the wall he could see a yellow forklift with a roll cab parked in the space beyond.

"Hello?" he called.

A guy walked out of the back and stepped toward

him. He was dark, Latin or black or maybe both, with a tight little mustache, wearing a work shirt and jeans. Pushing fifty, he looked sinewy but moved with the confidence of someone who worked with their body. Fuckable, he decided.

"Are you Rogelio?" Slater said.

"What do you need?"

"Kim said I should talk to you about the help-wanted sign in the door. The name is Slade."

Rogelio nodded. "I do the production. I need some help moving stuff around. I don't have enough time to do it all myself."

"You're the only one working here?"

"Usually. The job is pretty basic. Maybe you can do some production work later on, but you have to learn it. For now, can you drive a forklift?"

"Sure."

"You got certified?"

"I'm not going to lie to you, Rogelio," Slater said. "I did not."

"It doesn't matter. Forklift school is mostly about learning not to lift too much stuff and then crash. Driving one is like driving anything else. As long as you only lift pallets, and don't lift pallets that are too heavy, you'll be fine."

"I'm sure I can handle that."

"They pay minimum wage."

"I can handle that too."

"It's too late today," Rogelio said, "but can you start tomorrow?"

"No background check, no references?"

"Nobody wants to work anymore, *morro*. If you can lift twenty-pound boxes, you're hired."

"Can you show me around?"

Rogelio sighed but stepped over to the worktable, and picked up a bottle, and handed it to him. "We make tequila."

It was a fifth, with the Eastside Lightning label and the cap on it, but it was empty. Rogelio turned and walked toward the vats. Slater set the bottle down and followed him over.

"The tequila is aged in the tanks," he said. "This machine does the bottling."

Slater looked over the equipment. Next to the tanks were several pallets with blue plastic barrels on them, each marked with a big fire-diamond label. He didn't know the whole meaning off the top of his head, but he knew the bigger numbers meant whatever was inside was more dangerous. One of the squares contained a 3—that meant it was either very caustic or very flammable.

"Is the distilling also done in those tanks?" Slater said.

"We don't make the alcohol. We mix our flavorings with pure alcohol. The bottling isn't complicated, but you have to watch it closely. You're not going to be doing that for a while." Rogelio walked back to the worktable by the loading dock. "Tequila is made with blue agave plants, like this one. We process it to add flavoring."

There was still dirt on the roots, Slater saw, and a machete sat beside it on the table, ready to chop off the leaves. Outside the loading dock a horn honked, and Rogelio turned and hustled over to it, and pressed the switch to roll up the steel shutter. As it rose a box truck came into view outside, slowly backing up to the dock.

Rogelio wasn't paying him any attention, so he pulled out his phone and held it down by his belt to snap a couple of photos of the blue agave. He knew it had just arrived here, a few minutes ago in the trunk of that old Town Car—it was unlikely that Rogelio had seen the tracker yet. Mauricio definitely hadn't noticed it or he would have extracted it.

Rogelio was squatting at the end of the box truck, talking to the driver outside through the gap. It was just a few steps over to the tool cabinet, and Slater grabbed a flat-blade screwdriver, and turned the agave over, and popped off the plug of woody fiber. He dug out the putty and balled it up, then extracted the tracker by pulling on its antenna wire. Stuffing the tracker in his hip pocket, he replaced the plug in the piña. Looking around for a trash can, he saw a barrel lined with a black leaf bag near the tool cabinet, and stepped over to drop in the ball of putty.

Rogelio was hard at work, loading white cardboard boxes from a pallet onto the box truck. Emblazoned with the Eastside Lightning logo, the boxes looked heavy. They had to be cases of the product— all the bottles he'd seen were fifths, and each of those boxes would hold a dozen of those. Finally the driver came in to inspect the load, and signed a clipboard Rogelio handed him, then pulled down the gate on the truck. Once the driver had gone outside, Rogelio rolled the shutter down on the loading dock. As he walked over to the worktable, he eyed Slater.

"That's what you'll be doing—moving the cartons around, and loading the trucks."

"Got it," Slater said. "I'll see you tomorrow."

He walked out through the offices, and saw that

Zane's door was open but Kim's was closed. Out the front door, he strode through the gate to the street, briefly glancing over his shoulder. Of course no one was following him. Around the corner on the next block he spotted the Polara, glad that it was still here and unmolested. As he sat down the tracker jabbed him in the butt.

"Damn it," he muttered, and arched his back, and pulled it out. It felt damp, as if the piña had some moisture in it. Peering at it to find the little power switch, he snapped it off, then tossed the device on the floor of the passenger side.

Digging out his phone, he dialed Claudine, glad that she answered.

"Your prediction came true," Claudine said when she picked up. "Hester told me another blue agave was taken last night."

"I knew they'd come for them. Sitting out in the open and just the right age for booze production. It's way too tempting."

"Is your tracker working? Do you know who took them?"

"I'm working on that," Slater said. "Listen—do you know someone at the college who could tell me about protected appellations for stuff like tequila?"

"I'm sure any prof could fill you in, but I have a contact in the state agriculture department who specializes in that. Do you want to talk to her?"

"Can you text me her details?"

"I'll call her first," Claudine said. "That way she'll definitely take a meeting."

Once he'd ended the call, Slater started the engine, its throaty rumble edifying under his feet. The freeways must have been jammed with late-day traffic, as his navigation app sent him on surface streets through the Arts District and on Temple. When he passed the four-level, he could see the 101 was a parking lot, bright headlights in one direction and a sea of taillights in the other.

Once he was in his garage, he grabbed the tracker from the floor, and the packet of peas, soft now at room temperature. He set the tracker on his workbench and then hustled up the two flights to the kitchen, where he tossed the peas into the icebox. There were already several in there—it was the cheapest ice pack ever.

Pike called to him from the main room, and Slater walked through to find the coffee table had been moved over by the French doors, and Pike was on the floor, kneeling on lush green grass. A few square yards of it filled the space between the sofa and the easy chairs.

Slater had to laugh. "What's this?"

Pike sat back. "I suppose I should have checked with you first."

"This can't be real." He crouched to feel it. The blades were realistic, but it was definitely made of plastic.

"They sell it at the hardware store," Pike said, and stood up. "I figured this space needed a carpet."

"What made you think of artificial turf?"

"I just saw it, and thought it would work. Are you digging it?"

"It looks good." Slater stepped back to survey the space. "We can never let a dog visit, though. They'll piss on it."

Pike frowned. "I hadn't even thought of that. Help me put the coffee table back."

They each grabbed an end, and lifted it onto the grass, and stood back to look at the room.

"It's extremely groovy," Slater said.

"You have to try it with bare feet."

Dropping into an easy chair, he pulled off his boots and socks and walked on the faux turf.

"It's not as cool as real grass, but it's close."

Slater's phone buzzed in his pants, and he pulled it out to check. It was a text from Claudine:

> You have a meeting at 8:30 tomorrow. Her name is Alejandra MacDougall.

A second text had a street address and an office number. He didn't have to look it up—he recognized that address. Her office was in Fort Ronnie, the hulking state office building downtown.

He sent a brief reply:

> I'll be there.

Pike sat on the sofa, and Slater stretched out next to him, and rested his head in his lap. Just the feeling of Pike's hand caressing his chest made him feel calmer, like it was the end of the day, like he could start to unwind.

"I thought you might have moved back to Albuquerque," Slater said. "You were so pissed at me this morning."

"I wasn't pissed at you. But it is frustrating that you don't trust me enough to tell me about your work."

"I tell you plenty. I can't have you meddling in my cases."

"Why would I do that? Unless you blow something up or murder somebody, I'm not going to get involved."

"Tracking devices."

Pike frowned. "What?"

"That's what I put in the blue agave plants. Tracking devices. I got them from the Russians."

"There you go. Thank you."

"I can't afford to lose my connection with Svetlana," Slater said. "I make extensive use of her gear. If she finds out I'm gossiping with you, she'll cut me off."

"Who am I going to tell?"

"That's the problem. I don't know. Svetlana says, 'Two people can keep a secret if one of them is dead.'"

Pike chuckled. "Of course she'd say that, if she's doing shady stuff."

"I'm doing shady stuff too."

He ran a hand into Slater's hair. "This is the trust part. You have to let go, and trust that I won't mess things up for you."

"Mmm," Slater said, closing his eyes to luxuriate in the feeling of his fingers on his scalp. "I'm trying."

"What happened here?" He tapped below Slater's eye.

"Damn it. Is it bruising?"

"It's just a little red."

"But you need all the details, I suppose, as part of your 'trust' agenda." He lifted his hands and waggled his fingers to put air quotes around the word.

"It looks like you got punched."

Slater told him about following Mauricio into the bar, and getting called out, and getting jumped.

"What kind of place was this?" Pike said.

"It looked like a regular old dive bar, but there's definitely some bunco going on. I think it's somebody's clubhouse. They thought I was a spy from a rival gang."

"You're lucky they didn't cap you."

"That's what I was thinking." He took hold of Pike's arm. "I need to eat."

"Doris is on her way over. She made a faux-tuna casserole. She said if it's a disaster, we can order in."

Slater sat up. "Why are you doing stuff with her behind my back?" he demanded.

"I have a relationship with her. It's part of the deal."

"How did you even get her phone number?"

"She gave it to me."

"Well, I need to know who's coming and going around here."

Pike chuckled. "I just told you."

"There needs to be boundaries, man. She can't just drop in unannounced."

"She did announce herself. I invited her."

Slater sat scowling at him, his heart pounding. There was nothing he could say to that.

"Why are you upset that I talk to Doris?"

"I get the feeling that the pair of you are up to something."

"Like what?"

"A nefarious cabal."

Pike laughed.

"It's not funny."

"I'm not laughing at you. I'm just amazed at how your mind works. What do you think our secret cabal is up to?"

"In the middle of the night a crew of armed gunmen is going to bust in here," Slater said, waving an arm, "and put a sack over my head, and load me into a van, and I wind up in lockdown rehab. Then once a week you and Doris will come and peer in through the little bulletproof glass window and say, 'It's for your own good.'"

Pike shifted closer and stretched his arm around his back. "I would never sign off on something like that."

"I hope not."

"I could do it on a much smaller budget. I'd only need one gunman and two burly orderlies."

Slater eyed him sidelong. "You're a regular laugh riot. You wouldn't need any gunmen if you just tased me again." He poked his thigh with two fingers. "Zap."

Moving in to nuzzle his neck, Pike murmured, "I'm not plotting against you, and I'm not going to shanghai you."

He leaned back to expose his neck, relishing the electric feel of Pike ravishing him, his mouth on his skin. "You can do it if you want to. Do anything. Gut-punch me. String me up. I'd still love you."

Pike pulled back and briefly met his mouth.

"You need to watch yourself around Doris," Slater said. "You don't know what she's capable of."

"I guess I'll find out when she dishes up the vegan tuna casserole."

SEVEN

NOT LONG AFTER, WHEN the doorbell rang, Pike rose. "Showtime."

Slater followed him down the stairs, and Doris greeted them when he opened the front door. Petite and wearing jeans and a knit sweater for the evening cool, she was letting some gray show in her dark hair. She handed Slater a casserole dish, still warm through the towel it was in, and pulled the door closed.

"What happened to your eye?" she said.

"Of course that's the first thing you'd notice. It was a work thing. I didn't think it was going to bruise."

Doris peered at his face, and put a hand on his cheek, brushing it with her thumb. "It might. It looks red."

Slater pulled back. "Pawing at it won't help."

"Sometimes I wish you'd stuck to horticulture," she said, dropping her hand.

"Gardening wouldn't have bought me this obnoxious house." He started up the stairs.

"I parked behind a beat-up SUV with New Mexico plates," Doris said, her tone brighter, following Slater. "Is that yours, Pike?"

"If it's dark green with a turquoise tag, that's me," he said, trudging up behind her. "You could be a detective."

"Everybody in Albuquerque drives a ratty car," Slater said. "It's not as if they're all poor. I couldn't figure it out. It's like it's part of the local culture."

Doris stepped into the kitchen after him. "Maybe they're not as superficial as we are."

"I wouldn't say that's a universal truth," Pike said, and added, "I love that sweater."

Setting the casserole dish on the counter, Slater gritted his teeth. She already liked the guy. He didn't have to oversell it.

"Do we need to warm this up?" he said, waving at the casserole.

"Just nuke it for a few minutes," Doris said. "It's ready to eat."

While Slater loaded the dish into the microwave, Pike pulled wineglasses out of the cupboard.

"I've got chardonnay," he said to Doris. "Would you drink that?"

"Let's do it."

He opened the bottle, and Doris set plates on the dining table. Pike insisted she sit at the end, and each of them sat adjacent. They soon got into the casserole. It was actually pretty good.

After she'd eaten, setting her fork down, Doris eyed Pike. "So what's it like bunking with a vegan?"

"It's less work than I anticipated. I'm embracing it. Oat milk tastes the same as milk-milk."

"He's not belligerent about his food," Slater said. "Unlike some people."

"I can't eat that way when I'm on the road for work, though," Pike said. "I'm in lots of small towns. That means diners and quesadillas and burger joints."

"But you can eat well at home. Speaking of that," Doris said, and gestured with her wineglass toward the French doors, across the big empty room. "Unless you're going to host ballroom dancing, you need some furniture in here."

"I like it spare," Slater said.

"It's your home too, Pike. You could put a desk in here."

"I've already got one. In the back bedroom. It's under the window, so I have a view of the neighborhood."

"I'll have to take a look," she said. "Maybe you could put a rug in here, at least, and a second set of lounge furniture. You could do two sofas facing each other."

"You don't need to be decorating for me," Slater said. "My life is never going to be all heymish and cozy like yours."

"It's a lot more heymish than it was before you moved in here. You own an actual bed, and more than one towel."

As he poured her more wine, Pike chuckled. "You make it sound like he was camping at his old place."

"I didn't want to get all bogged down," Slater said.

Doris eyed him. "So did you get your invitation to Andy's wedding?"

"I did. I was shocked to see that I'm allowed a plus-one."

"Of course there's a plus-one," she said. "He's not going to invite you alone when he knows you're in a relationship."

"Are you bringing that old schnorrer who's been hanging around your place?"

Doris set her glass down and frowned at him. "He's not schnorring off me. And yes, Albert will be my arm candy."

"I'm supposed to be the best man."

"Oh, that is so sweet," she said, her tone rising. "Andy asked you?"

"His dirtbag fiancé certainly didn't. If Kyle had his way, I wouldn't even be invited."

Her eyes narrowed. "Maybe don't call him a dirtbag in your best-man speech."

"I can't believe Andy's marrying that guy. It seems hasty. Like he didn't really think it through. Or maybe Kyle tricked him into it."

Doris waved a hand. "Andy's no pushover."

"You don't think they're compatible?" Pike said.

Slater gestured helplessly with his glass. "I don't know."

"How does he treat Andy?" Doris said.

He pursed his lips, considering that. "Like he's interesting," Slater said finally. "Like he's important. Like he's worth listening to."

"That sounds like a keeper to me," Doris said.

"Do you think I'll have to do that? Make a speech?"

"You'd better find out. The best man usually has responsibilities. A speech, or at the very least a toast."

"When is this?" Pike said.

"Next week." Slater waved a hand. "It's after you get back, but you don't have to go if you don't want to. It's not that important."

"Oh, I'm going, forty-niner," he said, raising his eyebrows. "I know that guy. I wouldn't miss it."

"Why do you call him forty-niner?" Doris said.

"He'll only wear jeans that are authentic to the nineteenth century. Like when they were invented during the gold rush. Like a miner forty-niner."

"That's a distortion," Slater said. "But I do prefer real clothes."

"He doesn't like stretchy chinos," Pike said.

"Stretchy pants are the best thing about this century," Doris said. "I remember the first time I tried a pair. It was like a revelation."

Pike tipped his wineglass toward her. "That's what I'm talking about."

"Stretchy pants act like they're not really there," Slater said. "Or like they're phasing in and out of existence. They weigh nothing, and you can't feel them. Maybe they can use them for space exploration."

"What does Slater call you?" Doris said.

"Reddy Kilowatt."

She nodded. "Because the day you met, you tased him. I've heard that story."

"To be fair," Pike said, "at the time I thought he was working for a terrorist."

Slater folded his arms and raised his eyebrows. "Zap."

"Did you get Andy and Kyle a gift," Doris said, "or just cash?"

"I figured I was working as the best man. My

time and effort are gift enough."

"You have to give them something," she said intently. "It's not optional."

"Damn it." He huffed. "How much?"

"I'd say for a good friend, five hundred. But I know you broke his heart, so you should probably give them a grand."

"That's a lot of lettuce."

Pike sat up in his chair. "You broke his heart?"

Slater eyed Doris. "Who told you that? Andy chose that trash-can twink. I had no say in it."

"It could have been you putting a ring on it, but you wouldn't commit."

"I'd be terrible for Andy. I'd ruin his life."

"Can we back up here?" Pike said. "How exactly did you break his heart?"

"You know we were sleeping together." Slater gestured dismissively. "That's all there was to it."

"Andy had a crush on him," Doris said. "It's hard to shake that kind of feeling when there's an ongoing degree of intimacy. It's like a wound that won't heal because the knife is still there."

"He told you that?" Slater demanded.

"He may have mentioned some of it. The rest is just logic."

"He's a gossipy little costermonger. And he did shake the crush. When he found a sweet little tooth-ache-inducing cupcake named Kyle. That guy has been in his life as long as I have."

Pike folded his arms. "See, this is why I have to talk to your mother. It's the only way I get the whole story."

"I never concealed anything from you."

"Except that the guy was in love with you, and now you're the best man at his wedding."

"It wasn't mutual." Slater waved a hand. "I didn't know what love was until you came along. You're the sunlight that parted the clouds and brought the world to life. The summer monsoon to spark the growth of my dormant soul. My Heracles to rescue me from the rock." He held his gaze. "I love you, and only you. You know this."

"I guess I buy that," Pike said, and cracked a smile. He eyed Doris. "What do you think?"

She squeezed Slater's arm. "It makes my heart swell up to hear him talk about love."

Grabbing his wineglass, Slater shifted in his chair. "You can just tune that stuff out, woman. I'm in damage control mode here."

"So you would have ruined Andy's life," Pike said, "but that doesn't apply to mine?"

"You can handle me," Slater said. "So far, anyway. I don't think Andy could have. Not for long. You know firsthand that I'm trouble, and yet you're here anyway. Andy's a civilian. He never figured that out."

"He's inscrutable, your son, isn't he?" Pike said, eyeing Doris. "He doesn't quite trust me yet."

Slater waved his glass. "You have a key to this place. How much more trust do you need?"

"It's more than that," Doris said. "Honesty and openness are the foundation of a stable relationship."

"You sound like a shrink." He eyed Pike. "That was her hobby, back in the day. She'd send me to shrinks. I must have seen dozens of them."

"Whether it's shrinky or not," Pike said, "she's right. Openness is kind of fundamental."

He suppressed a retort, and took a breath. "I'm used to working on a need-to-know basis. This is all new to me. I'm learning it on the fly. As we evolve our narrative complex."

EIGHT

G RADUALLY SWIMMING UP TO consciousness, Slater knew he was in his own bed, knew it was morning by the daylight outside. His head didn't hurt. Where was Pike?

Forcing himself to get up, he pulled on a pair of skivvies and went upstairs. Pike was at the dining table, dressed for an office day, a coffee mug in one hand and an empty plate in front of him.

"There's some decent bread if you want toast," Pike said.

"You used to make me pancakes for breakfast."

He chuckled and leaned back. "That's what we call the old bait and switch. You let me move in, and I got my own key, so you can kiss your pancakes good-bye."

Kneeling next to him, Slater massaged his thighs, and pressed his face into his dress shirt to kiss his belly.

"I don't need pancakes. I just need to smell you. It makes me high. It's like dope. Opium, or tranquilizers, or MDMA." He pressed his nose into Pike's crotch and inhaled.

With a hand on his cheek, Pike pulled him up. "I have to go to work."

Slater leaned in and met his mouth. "I could be fast. A snappy blow job. You won't even be late."

"That's your version of the bait and switch. It'll have to wait till tonight."

As Slater stood up, Pike rose too, embracing him tightly and kissing his neck. Once he'd gone, Slater made some toast and had coffee. He needed to hustle, he realized, checking the time on his phone—he had a meeting.

Downstairs in the bathroom mirror he saw that the mark around his eye was darker now, with just a hint of a bruise. He'd avoided the worst of it. Once he was dressed, he drove downtown, and found a street space for the Polara on Broadway.

It was still cold, the sun not yet reaching into the canyons created by the neighborhood's tall buildings. Walking up the street, he navigated around the sleeping bags and blanket piles and cardboard barriers of the people still crashed out in doorways and niches. When the shops and storefront businesses opened they'd all get evicted, but for now they could sleep unmolested for another hour or so.

He stepped over the puddles of urine running toward the gutter, and breathed through his mouth when he got a whiff of the tang of homelessness. How had things gotten this bad? Not that long ago the neighborhood business association's private security guards had managed to keep them east of Main Street at night, in Skid Row proper, but with more and more people sleeping rough, the problem had become uncontainable, and spilled beyond those lines. Every street, every part of town had become subject to this unmanageable mess.

It was a short walk over to Fort Ronnie. An out-of-place pink slab built in the worst part of the 1980s, its narrow windows and alienating street presence made it look like a hulking fortress, or a prison, or the lair of some disdainful autocrat. It was officially named after a long-dead governor, but the people who worked in it had coined that moniker, and it fit.

Slater followed a guy in a suit into the lobby, and put his phone and his keys in the little tray at the security checkpoint, then waited while the suit stepped through the metal detector. On the other side the guy grabbed his stuff and walked away. When Slater stepped through the machine, it emitted a series of angry beeps. Eyeing the uniformed guard, a chubby man with his gray hair in a buzz cut, he stood next to the machine.

While he waited for the guard to get up and retrieve the hand wand, two women breezed through the frame of the metal detector, one after the other, neither of them setting it off. Ignoring him and the guard, they collected their phones from the tray and walked to the elevators. The guard came over, and Slater stood with his feet apart and his arms outstretched while he ran the hand wand over his arms and legs. When it got to his fly, the device emitted a high-pitched squeal.

The guard heaved a sigh, seemingly already worn out from his duties, even though it was still early in the morning. "Sir, can you lift your shirt?"

It was tucked in, but it was a little loose, with the fabric folded over his belt. Slater smoothed it upward, revealing the buckle. The guard's eyes narrowed, and he pressed on it with two fingers.

"You like what you see?" Slater said. "Poke a little lower and we can get something started."

The guy frowned. "Settle down, now." He waved the wand again, and it shrieked as it passed. "It's just your buckle. Move along."

Slater grabbed his phone and his keys, and as he waited for the elevator with the office drones, checked the suite number Claudine had texted him. When he got to the right floor, there was no front desk, just a sign on the wall that said FOOD AND AGRICULTURE. Down the hall he found the right office, with a plaque beside the door that read ALEJANDRA MACDOUGALL. He rapped on it with a knuckle.

From inside he heard a muffled "Come in." As he stepped in, the woman behind the desk rose. She was slight, with wavy dark hair, and wore a warm-yellow dress with a chunky necklace.

"I'm a friend of Claudine," Slater said, and handed her his business card.

"Ibáñez," she said as she glanced at it, and got the pronunciation right, "ee-*ban*-yez," rather than the mangled Anglo rendition he often heard, "*ee*-buh-nez," or worse, "*eye*-buh-nez."

"Have a seat."

It wasn't a big office, and there was paper everywhere, books and files stacked on the desk and the credenza behind her, spilling out of an open file cabinet. He took the chair in front of her desk.

"What happened to your eye?" she said.

"A stray ground stroke on the tennis court," Slater said. "I lunged for it and missed, and then *bam*. I was already down thirty-love."

"OK," she said evenly, and set his card on her blotter. "You work with Claudine?"

"We were at school together."

"I took a seminar on invasive grasses that Claudine taught at ELAC. I learned a lot."

"I run into that *Pennisetum* fountain grass all the time," Slater said. "It's truly a nightmare."

"That's exactly the word for it." She cracked a smile. "You know your stuff."

"I didn't know Claudine was teaching."

"She said you were a landscaper." Alejandra tapped his card. "This says you're an insurance investigator."

"I do a little of both," he said, and shifted in his chair. "I wanted to ask you about an outfit I'm looking into. They talked about a protected appellation."

"That's definitely in my wheelhouse."

"It's a tequila producer here in town. It's called Eastside Lightning."

Alejandra's expression shifted, her brow furrowing. "I know all about that company. What's your interest in it?"

"I can't talk specifics, but I suspect some of their inputs have been acquired illegally."

She scoffed. "What inputs? The bulk ethanol, or the labels on the bottles?"

"The plants that they use."

"No surprise that they're stealing. Can you get the DA to charge them for that? It sounds like a great way to shut them down."

"Why do they need to be shut down?"

"They're running a con, Slater. Calling their product tequila is illegal. Tequila is a protected name under appellation control."

"How does that work?"

She sat back. "Under international trade agreements, the pacts we've set up with other countries and signed on to, governments on all sides agree to protect each other's appellations. Appellation is kind of like copyright. You can't legally call something tequila if it's made outside Jalisco. It's the same with bourbon. It doesn't come from anywhere but Kentucky. And champagne only comes from Champagne."

"Why haven't you or some other arm of bureaucracy shut them down?"

"Do you have your phone on you? Take a look at the label on their bottle."

Slater pulled it out, and tapped at it to find the company's website, and brought up an image of the Eastside Lightning bottle. When he zoomed in, he saw that under the brand name, the label was marked "distilled spirits."

"I get it. The label doesn't actually say 'tequila.'" Zane had pointed that out, he remembered, when he'd thought Slater was important: *The word doesn't appear on the label.*

"And yet you just called it tequila," Alejandra said. "The company's online marketing material says it's 'artisanal American tequila.'"

"Is it not a clear legal violation to say that in their marketing?" he said. "Does leaving it off the label make it some kind of gray area?"

"It's not gray to me, or to the Mexican agricultural appellation people." She waved a hand. "We send them cease-and-desist letters, but we can't prosecute them criminally. The Mexicans are going to sue them eventually, and when that happens, they'll just take the word *tequila* off the website, and that'll satisfy the courts. But the damage is already done. Consumers already identify the brand as tequila, and they'll still do that even after they stop saying it."

"Do you know anything about their production?"

"I've looked into them," Alejandra said. "I know they don't import agave, which means they're not using agave to make their product. That's the definition of tequila—it's made from *Agave tequilana*."

"The blue agave," Slater said.

"What plants were you talking about?"

"*Agave tequilana*."

"They're stealing them? From who?"

"I'm still looking into it. Do you know anything about the business owners?"

"My impression is that those two are serial entrepreneurs. One shady business leads to the next. It's a pattern you see sometimes: start a business, get some attention, sell it to somebody bigger before you get sued. The legal problems fall on the new owners."

Slater nodded. "Those are really good insights."

"So you know what Eastside Lightning is up to, but what exactly is your company going to do about it?"

"I'm not sure yet." He stood up. "I want those birds to stop stealing. But I need to dig into it more."

"If you get anything to nail them with, let me know." She rose, and grabbed a business card from the tray on her desk, and handed it to him. "So—are you single?"

Slater frowned. "I appreciate the direct approach, sister, but I'm on dick."

"Well, that seems narrow-minded." She put her hands on her hips. "Do you have a boyfriend?"

"In a way. That term is a vast oversimplification. I'm deeply involved with a guy in a multidimensional romantic narrative complex."

"It sounds intense." She raised her eyebrows. "Have fun with that."

Slater rode the elevator to the lobby and walked out to the street. Back at the Polara, he dropped some coins in the meter, then walked to Andy's building, a single long block away. It was an old textile warehouse that had been converted to lofts.

In the hallway upstairs, walking toward Andy's door, he passed a guy with a bald head and prominent pecs under a stretchy black athletic top. The expression on his face made Slater do a double-take. The guy was kind of energized, and then there was that subtle grin. He knew that look. This guy had just had sex.

He knocked on Andy's door and waited for him to get there. When he pulled it open, Andy's brown hair was unkempt, and he was wearing boxer shorts and a tank top, revealing his lean musculature. He dressed that way even in the cool spring weather because his CP made his metabolism run hot.

"You should have … called," Andy said, and frowned, but turned to lead him inside, walking with his uneven gait.

His pad was mostly a one-room loft, with tall multipane windows, a bed and a little kitchen table, and a desk in the corner surmounted by an array of monitors.

"Who's the cue ball with the shirt?" Slater said.

"You saw Jimmy? He's my masseur. And most … people wear shirts. You must be talking about … what was under it."

"Don't lie to me. He wasn't carrying a massage table."

"He's still my masseur."

Andy dropped into his desk chair and swiveled toward him. It was a high-backed gaming model, even though he didn't play videogames. He said it was the most comfortable chair he could find for the long hours he spent at the computer—he made his living doing what he called "deep research," a euphemism for hacking.

"That guy had those pecs, and he had sex written all over his face. You do too right now," Slater said, and swirled a hand toward him. "That newly relaxed thing."

"You don't get to … interrogate me about my sex life."

"You told me you were going exclusive with Kyle." Slater raised his voice. "Sing, brother."

"Don't talk to me like … one of your lowlifes."

He put his hands on his hips. "You're dodging the question."

Andy huffed. "We're not exactly exclusive. We're just not … having sex with you."

Slater scoffed, and studied his face, his heart pounding. "Fuck that."

"You're not pissed … about the sex. I know that. You're pissed that I'm … with Kyle."

He took a breath, and closed his eyes for a moment. "I want you to do what you want."

"So let me. You're still my … best man."

"Are you kidding me?" he demanded. "I'm the second-best man. Or third, counting the cue ball. Somewhere way down the list. The one you won't sleep with anymore. The one you tossed aside when something better came along. I'm like the old clothes you dump in the thrift-store donation box. An old tire with no tread left on it that you toss in an alley."

"You know damn well that's not … how it went down."

"I thought Kyle would have vetoed your best-man idea in a hot second. Are you sure he even wants me there?"

"We talked it through. He wants it … too. His sister is going to be his … groom's woman."

"Doris says the best man has responsibilities," Slater said. "What do I have to do?"

"We're not doing any engagement party or … stag night," Andy said. "You can just dress up, show up, and … stand up there with me. Hold the rings until we need them."

"Is there a speech or a toast I have to do?"

"That's traditional."

"What the hell am I supposed to say?" he demanded.

"Well, you can't air your … grievances, and you can't say how much you hate … either of the grooms."

"So I just have to make stuff up," Slater said. "Pretty words and lies."

"I know you know how to … do that." Andy grinned. "You'll do fine."

"I guess we'll see."

He tapped near his own eye with an unsteady

finger. "Will your shiner be … gone by then?"

"I was hoping it wouldn't bruise," he said, and absently rubbed at it.

"It looks like it … might not. Should I even ask?"

"I had a difference of opinion with a lowlife." Slater waved a hand. "Listen, I have some work for you. I want you to look into a couple of people. They run a booze company called Eastside Lightning."

As he recited the website address, Andy swiveled toward his desk and pulled on his black plastic gauntlets. They were an input device that somehow compensated for his lack of fine motor control. One of the screens came to life, and he pulled up the Eastside Lightning website, and clicked around it.

"These two?" Andy said, when he'd found the page with the portraits of Zane and Kim.

"That's them."

"What do you need to … know? Just general background, or something … specific?"

"I think they're crooks. Maybe you can find out if they've been sent up, or gone broke, or got sued, that kind of thing."

"So public records." Andy swiveled to face him. "I'll let you know."

"Can I kiss you good-bye, or is that only for your masseur?"

"Are you serious right now?" Andy frowned. "You need to stop pushing that boundary."

Slater held his gaze for a moment. "Bye, beautiful."

NINE

As Slater walked up the block to the Polara, the sun finally felt warm, high in the late morning sky. Traffic was light on the short drive east to the tequila factory, and soon he was cruising past the gate, and parked around the corner.

He had zero interest in the actual work, but he needed to find out how high up the racket went. Was Mauricio just a supplier who lied about his sources, or had Zane and Kim actively recruited a landscape thief?

Instead of walking into the office, he went back to the loading dock, and mounted the few steps to the adjacent door, and pulled on the handle. It was unlocked, and he stepped inside. Hester's blue agave was still intact, sitting in the same spot on the worktable and looking abused, its roots twisted and broken. On the floor just inside the loading dock sat a pallet, laden with a single layer of the white cartons.

"Slade," Rogelio called to him. He was over by

the vats and the pipes and the stainless-steel equipment.

It was a great alias, close enough to his own name that he'd never miss it. Slater called out a greeting as he pulled the door closed behind him.

"I thought you bailed on me," Rogelio said, walking over.

"We didn't actually set a time."

"Most people think the workday starts at eight."

"So I'm a couple hours late."

His brow furrowed as he looked him over. "What happened to your eye? Have you been fighting?"

"I walked into a door."

"You walked into a bouncer's fist before you got through the door, I bet. Are you hung over?"

Slater scowled. "Do I look hung over? I'm here, aren't I? Put me to work."

Rogelio waved at the pallet. "You need to load these onto a truck. It'll be here any minute."

Stepping over to the loading dock, Slater hit the switch to roll up the shutter. There was a box truck in the yard already, making a slow turn, and it started to beep as it backed toward the dock. When it stopped, Slater squatted to grab the handle on the back door and roll it up. The interior was empty. Lifting a carton from the pallet, he carried it inside and set it down against the wall of the truck, then went back for another.

The driver, a squat guy with a pot belly, stepped in through the pedestrian door and stood talking to Rogelio. Once he'd lifted the last box into the truck, Slater called to him.

"Is that all of it?"

"Don't close it up yet," Rogelio said.

They both walked over, and after briefly surveying the interior, the driver rolled the door down and snapped on a padlock. Rogelio handed the guy a clipboard, and he signed it, and said something in Spanish as he walked out. As the truck started up and pulled away, Slater rolled down the shutter on the loading dock.

Rogelio waved him over to the computer that sat at the end of the worktable closest to the dock.

"There's a list of what's happening," he said, gesturing to the screen. "This is the pickup time, and this is how many cartons. Sometime before pickup you should load the right number of cartons on a pallet and move it to the loading dock. These are all the ones for today, see?"

It was set up like a simple spreadsheet, a row for each order, the numbers in big type.

"You have to get the driver to sign for it," Rogelio went on. "Kim makes a clipboard for each of the day's pickups."

"I'm surprised she even comes back here."

"She doesn't. If you don't see the clipboards here, she leaves them in the wall rack just inside the office door."

"What do I have to do to find this list?" Slater said.

Rogelio showed him where to click. "You can look at what's coming up in the next few days. It goes faster if the pickups are close together."

"Can you show me how to drive the forklift?"

"It's not that hard," Rogelio said, and walked over to it, and climbed on. He demonstrated the controls, explaining how they worked. "Most important is don't lift anything too heavy. If you ever have to move the barrels, only do one at a time."

When he stepped off, Slater took his place, and drove ahead a few feet, then shifted into reverse. The controls were peppy and responsive. Next he tried driving it in a circle, and found it had a tight turn radius. He spent a minute raising and lowering the forks, experimenting with the tilt and the speed.

With Rogelio watching him, he drove the forklift into the storage room. It was easy to maneuver, and quiet—the motor had to be electric. At the stack of pallets he practiced maneuvering the forks to the right level, and easing them into the gaps in the wood, and lifting the pallet.

Loading the cartons of product onto the pallets would still require grunt work—multiple layers of the white boxes were stacked the length of the storage room wall. He parked the forklift near the empty pallets and walked back to Rogelio.

"So when do you do the bottling?" he said.

"When the flavoring batch is finished brewing." He gestured at the tall vats. "I need to start one today. It brews for a few days."

"What are the steps in the production process?"

Rogelio groaned. "Real tequila uses the piña from a blue agave. They mash it up to make juice, and ferment it, and distill it twice. That takes forever. This stuff uses just a little agave to get the flavor right. The base is alcohol." He gestured to the blue barrels along the wall.

So that's what Alejandra meant about bulk alcohol. That's what was in the barrels. They didn't distill anything—this wasn't really a distillery. Kim hadn't used that word either, he remembered. She'd called it a factory.

"So you don't need a whole field of blue agave," Slater said. "Just a few plants."

"It's also not really tequila." Rogelio raised his eyebrows. "But you didn't hear me say that." He pulled out his phone to glance at it. "It's lunchtime. Did you bring food?"

"I thought I'd buy a burrito somewhere."

"Come with me."

He pushed open the door next to the loading dock, and once Slater was outside too, locked it with a key. They walked to the front of the building, and Rogelio went to the maroon pickup with the utility rack, and they both climbed in. When he started it, the engine sounded healthy and well-tuned.

"I like your ride," Slater said.

"It's old."

"You keep it in good shape."

He drove out to the boulevard, then a few blocks farther, to a wide corner where a food truck had set up at the curb. It was that time of day, and several people were hanging around, eating or waiting on their food.

Slater ordered a burrito with beans and rice, and got Rogelio to order, then paid for both of them. Once they had the food in hand, he sat at the end of one of the benches the truck had put out on the sidewalk, really just a two-by-six set on cinder blocks, and Rogelio sat on the other, facing him. He spread his feet apart and leaned forward so that anything that dripped out of his burrito would hit the concrete, not his clothes.

As he ate he could feel Rogelio's eyes on him, could see the wheels turning.

Finally Slater spoke. "Do I have salsa on my face or something?"

"I can't figure you out," he said, gesturing with his burrito. "You didn't have to buy me lunch. You're a *pocho*. Why do you want to work for minimum wage?"

"*Pochos* are assimilated Mexicans," Slater said. "I'm not Mexican. I was born here."

"So why don't you have a better job?"

He scoffed. "You sound paranoid. Like Zane and Kim. They thought I was somebody's goon when I walked in there. I wondered what they were afraid of."

"The tequila producers in Mexico have been hassling them," Rogelio said. "They thought that was you. You could easily be a professional Mexican thug."

"I've been called worse. Do you know what the bearded beatnik did before they set up this business?"

"You mean Zane? I don't know him that well. He's just the boss."

"What's he like?"

"An entitled white guy. The kind of person who freaks out in a restaurant when their steak is cooked wrong. The guy who starts shouting when the valet revs the engine of his fancy car."

"I could see that. What about Kim?"

"I know her even less," Rogelio said. "I usually deal with Zane, except to get paid. With me she's all business. I think she's a *fresa*."

Slater frowned. "She's a raspberry?"

"*Este pocho,*" he said, his tone rising. "*Fresa* means strawberry. It also means kind of stuck-up. Kim is too good for the factory. She wipes her hands after she's been in there, even if she didn't touch anything."

"So if you think this isn't a good job, why don't you have a better one?"

"I don't look like what I've been through."

"What the hell does that mean?" Slater demanded.

He chuckled. "They say that at my church. I can't really do much better. I'm Mexican but I'm also black. That's two oppressed minorities right there."

"Bullshit," he said flatly. "I know lots of black guys who have decent jobs. And Chicanos run this town."

"I've been in trouble."

"Have you been inside?"

"Briefly."

"But you're out now. That means your debt is paid." Slater waved a hand. "No one is beyond redemption."

"Tell that to all the people who won't hire me once they've run a background check."

"I met a guy once who changed his name. Not legally, but it meant some of those checks missed his record."

"That sounds like a whole new kind of trouble."

Rogelio rose, and dumped his food wrapper in the barrel. Slater followed him back to his truck. Back at the factory, as they walked in the side door, Rogelio gestured to the computer monitor.

"The next truck will be here in half an hour. Then there's another truck."

Slater stepped over and looked at the screen. The next order was twelve cases. The earlier pickup had been just a few cases too. This stuff didn't seem to be selling in big quantities. But you didn't need quantity if it was expensive, he knew. He wondered what it wholesaled for.

In the back room he started to load the white cartons onto a pallet. The damn things were heavy, and he wasn't used to this kind of labor. After he'd shifted the dozen cases, he stood at the gap in the wall to stretch his muscles and rotate his back. Rogelio was at work at the table with Hester's agave, and he'd already hacked the leaves and roots off, down to the piña. It looked like a bulky underripe pineapple. Wielding the machete, he chopped it into pieces, and loaded the chunks into a basket, and carried it over toward the vats and the production equipment.

Climbing on the forklift, Slater rolled over to the pallet he'd just loaded, and carefully lifted it, then reversed and drove out toward the loading dock. Pausing near the vats, he climbed off and watched as Rogelio transferred the chunks of the piña into a big stainless-steel vessel. The lid, at waist height, had tie-down bolts around its rim. There was a control box next to it, studded with a grid of buttons and LEDs.

"What does that thing do?"

"It's a pressure cooker," Rogelio said. "It steams the agave until it's just juice. We use that to flavor the product."

"How long does it take?"

"A couple of days."

They both looked toward the office door as it swung open. Kim stood there and beckoned.

"Rogelio," she called, then stepped back into the office and let the door swing shut.

Rogelio strode across the space and through the door. Outside Slater heard the double-tap honk of an air horn—the truck was here for the pickup.

Striding over to the loading dock, he pressed the

switch to roll up the shutter. As it rose, the driver came in the pedestrian door. Beefy and barrel-chested, he was wearing green coveralls.

"You're not even ready for me," he said, and scowled at him. "What the hell? I've got places to be."

He should have had the pallet at the dock already, but it was almost there, still on the forklift, just a few yards away.

"Cool your jets," Slater said, jutting his chin at him, then walked over to the forklift. Rolling toward the dock, he set down the pallet, then reversed, driving the forklift back to the storage area.

When he walked back to the dock, the driver stood there, arms folded, glaring at him.

"Are you going to unlock your truck?" Slater demanded, waving at the padlock on the cargo door. "I thought you were in a hurry."

"You want to waste my time?" he said. "Fine, pal, I can do that too."

The right thing to do—the high road—would be to walk away. He knew that. But Slater didn't usually take the high road. Stepping over to the guy, he saw the look of alarm on his face as he approached. But he wasn't fast enough to fend him off. Slater delivered a rapid kovac, left and then right.

"Why do you make me do this to you?" he shouted.

Before he could land another slap, the guy shoved him hard, and Slater stumbled back.

"Fuck," the driver roared, rage in his eyes, and lunged at him.

It was predictable, the way he flung his right fist at Slater's face, the way untrained pugilists always did. He easily sidestepped the fist and landed a punch of his own from below, striking the driver's chin and snapping his head back.

"Break it up," Rogelio shouted. He was hustling toward them from the direction of the office. "What are you doing?"

Slater took a step back and flashed his palms. The driver shook his head to regain his senses, then fixed Rogelio with a dazed look.

"This asshole has an attitude problem," he said, jabbing a finger at Slater.

"He won't open the back of his truck," Slater said. "It's blocking the dock. I'm going to call a tow truck."

"Don't do that," Rogelio said, scowling at him. He gestured to the driver. "You don't get to treat my people that way. Either you open the truck or you get the hell out of here."

Red-faced, the guy scoffed, and stepped over to the dock, and crouched to unlock it, then thew up the door.

"You can wait outside," Rogelio told him.

There was already stuff inside the truck, cartons and shrink-wrapped boxes on a pallet. Slater lifted one of the white boxes and set it inside, and went back for another. Rogelio lifted another one, and with both of them working it didn't take long to shift them all.

Grabbing the clipboard from the worktable, Rogelio stepped outside. The guy came back in, avoiding Slater's gaze, and checked that the cases were all there, then locked the back door and walked out. As the truck was pulling away, Rogelio hit the switch to lower the big shutter, then eyed Slater.

"You need to try to get along with people."

"He was acting crazy," Slater said. "There's really no way to accommodate for that."

"Did you really need to punch him?"

"He was asking for it."

Rogelio threw up a hand. "You can't be doing stuff like that."

"Thanks for backing me up, by the way."

"I didn't actually see what happened. But I need you more than I need him."

Slater nodded. "Bros before schmoes."

Rogelio scoffed and walked toward the vats. Retrieving the forklift, Slater moved the empty pallet into the storage space, then went back to the computer screen to check on the next order. The faint smell of alcohol was starting to suffuse the place, and the humidity was definitely going up. That had to be about the pressure cooker. If it got much thicker in here, they'd have to leave the dock open.

In the back, Slater started to heave the white cases onto a pallet for the next order. His muscles were definitely going to be sore tonight.

"Slade," Rogelio called to him from the gap in the wall. "I'll be back in a minute. Are you OK alone?"

"I've got lots to do."

Slater picked up another case, and set it on the pallet, then heard the office door close and latch. Striding over to the computer, he clicked around, and tried to get into the file system. He couldn't access anything except the shipping details—the rest of the company was walled off.

Besides the list of pickups, he saw, there were freight manifests, like the ones on the clipboards. Then he found the corresponding purchase orders.

They contained mostly the same information, with one enlightening extra detail: the dollar amounts involved. The first one he opened totaled $8,640. That sounded like a big order, but it was only for six cases.

Slater did the calculation in his head. That meant about fourteen hundred a case, over a hundred bucks a bottle. That was what they meant when they called it a premium product—it was absurdly overpriced. Top-shelf real tequila retailed for less than that.

Rogelio stepped in from the office. "What's going on?"

Quickly closing the purchase order, Slater turned toward him. "The next pickup should be happening right around now."

"So roll up the door."

He stepped over and hit the switch to raise the shutter, but there was no truck in sight. Walking back to the storage room, he climbed on the forklift, and gently lifted the pallet, then rolled it out to the dock. He could see why you had to go to school to drive these things. It would be so easy to get rolling too fast. You could cause a lot of damage.

As he was reversing the forklift toward the storage room, a van appeared outside. It wasn't as tall as a box truck—they'd have to lift the cases down into it. Once the driver opened it for them, Rogelio stood in the back of the van, and Slater shifted the cases to the edge of the dock. The driver rolled the van's side door open and helped shift the boxes toward the front.

After Rogelio had the driver's signature, and rolled the shutter down on the loading dock, he went back to the vats.

"I can smell the agave cooking," Slater said.

"It almost smells like tequila, doesn't it?"

"So where does the agave come from?"

"A vendor brings them in. We call him the *jimadore*. He gets them from farmers in the Central Valley."

"The *jimadore* runs a blue agave company?"

"I think he's just a guy," Rogelio said. "He comes here in an old car with the plants in the trunk. We only need one at a time."

"How did you hire someone like that?"

"You'd have to ask Zane. I take delivery but I don't pay him." His brow furrowed. "You don't have to worry about the agave. I'll handle the production. You work on shifting the cases. And on not assaulting the drivers."

TEN

A WHILE LATER ROGELIO LEFT again, through the side door, and Slater walked over to the production area to look at the blue barrels. Under the fire diamond on each of them was a smaller label that said ETHANOL and 55 GAL/208 L. Just like Alejandra had said, they bought it in bulk. Either she knew how they were making the product or she'd made an educated guess. There were four pallets, one with a barrel missing, so fifteen barrels in all. That seemed like a whole lot of ethanol.

In no way was this stuff a premium ingredient, he thought, looking them over. It didn't even look food-grade, more like an industrial chemical. All they were doing here was mixing in some flavoring and bottling it. Even counting the cost of the empty bottles, the labels, and the cardboard cases, it was egregious to mark up Eastside Lightning to over a hundred bucks a bottle wholesale. That had to be dozens or hundreds of times what the inputs cost.

Slater scoffed and walked into the back room to prepare the next pallet. In the late afternoon he loaded another truck, and after he'd shifted the empty pallet back into the storage room, Rogelio waved him over.

"That's the last one today. You can go. Did Kim put you on payroll?"

"Not yet," he said.

"You should talk to her before you leave."

Slater walked into the office and tried the handle on Kim's office door, but it was locked. Across the hall, when he tried Zane's door, it opened, and he stepped inside.

Zane was at his desk, leaning back in his chair, his head tilted back. The angle emphasized his strange beard. He was wearing a red sports T-shirt with a big white number on it. That was a jarring shift from the jacket and ascot he'd had on yesterday. Above his head was a cloud of hazy fumes, and in one hand he held a little glass pipe. As Slater stepped in, he scowled and palmed it.

"What do you want?" Zane demanded.

"Am I interrupting? You should lock your door when you smoke up. Is that crystal meth?"

"Of course not." Eyeing him for a moment, his brow furrowed. "Do you want a taste?"

"I don't do dope."

"It's not dope, dummy. It's a stimulant. To help me focus."

"Do an image search for long-term meth users," Slater said, and put his hands on his hips. "You'll see how focused your future is going to be."

Zane raised his voice. "What are you doing here?"

"Rogelio said somebody should put me on the payroll."

"That's Kim's job. She's already gone. It's not going to happen today."

Slater walked out, closing Zane's door behind him, then went to the front door. It was locked, but he twisted the bolt to let himself out. The Benz SUV was gone from the stalls in front of the office. That meant it was Kim's ride, and the black Bimmer still sitting here was Zane's. He already knew the sweet maroon pickup was Rogelio's. As he walked out to the street toward the Polara, he checked his phone. Andy had texted earlier:

Call me or stop by.

The drive was slow in the sluggish evening traffic, and his muscles felt spent. When he got stopped at a red light he rolled his neck to relieve the tension. Eventually he was downtown, and parked in the surface lot behind Andy's building, and paid the attendant the flat evening rate.

Upstairs, he knocked on Andy's door, and a minute later, when he pulled it open, Andy flashed that easy smile. Such a beautiful man.

"I can't get into their computers," Andy said, walking over to his desk.

"I'm impressed that you tried."

He dropped into his chair. "I did find out that Zane got into … trouble with the feds. He was importing container loads of … rattan furniture from Southeast Asia, then … selling it to retailers. Some of it was covered in … lead paint."

"Is that illegal?"

"Totally. They wanted him to … recall it all and have it properly destroyed, but instead he declared bankruptcy and … shut down the business. That was about a year ago."

"Was that the end of it?" Slater said.

"It looks to me like the feds just … gave up at that point. The address for the import business was … the same as the one for the tequila distillery."

"Good to know."

"I also found out that Kim runs … another business," Andy said. "She's shilling a crypto product."

"Fuck me," Slater snapped. "I hate that field. It's all such bullshit."

"She's marketing it aggressively, but it … looks to be just around here. LA-based newsletters and … ad buys. It's almost all in Korean."

"Kim is totally Korean. If it's all local, I bet she's mining her social network."

"Turn your friends into … customers," Andy said.

Slater gazed out the big multipane windows at the square, thinking it through. "So is it her crypto product, or is she working for someone else?"

"The only person talking about it is … her. There are some breathy interviews on Korean-language blogs, but I can't … figure out the full meaning of what they're … saying using only machine translation."

"Do you think it's a grift," Slater said, "or a legitimate investment?"

"My thinking is crypto is … never a legit investment. But it's all about perception. I can't tell whether Kim … thinks she's selling something real or if … she's on the take."

"Would you be able to tell if I could get you into the company files?"

"Maybe. How will you do that?"

"My Russian tech supplier," Slater said. "I have a dongle I can plug into a company computer. It records every keystroke and broadcasts it to me."

"That's so illegal."

"You don't know that. Maybe I got their permission to do it."

"Plausible deniability," Andy said. "I get it. I don't … need to know. A keystroke logger would … probably give me their logins. If I had that, I could … dig deeper."

"Let me install it, then." Slater shifted on his feet.

"So do you have your … best-man speech written yet?"

"I thought I'd wait. In case you call it off."

"You're funny."

"So you're still going through with it?" Slater raised his eyebrows. "You know you still have options."

"Get out of here," Andy said flatly.

"Bye, beautiful."

When he got to the parking lot, and climbed into the Polara, he texted Etta, an operative who did gig jobs for him and Max, his business partner:

I have some work for you.

Etta had a day job but she loved investigative work, and had a knack for it, and had the requisite sangfroid. Slater started the engine, and before he had time to pop it in gear, her reply came:

At the office? I'll swing by.

He texted a thumbs-up, then drove the few blocks to the Fashion District, and parked in the surface lot across the street from their building. The attendant wasn't around. Maybe they'd gone for the day, but he left his parking pass on the dash anyway. They knew the Thunderbird by sight, but not this ride.

Hustling across the street in a break in the traffic, Slater strode into the lobby, deserted so late in the day, and rode up to the ninth floor, and walked around behind the elevator shaft. He admired their names on the door:

SLATER IBÁÑEZ
MAXIMILLIAN CONROY
INVESTIGATIONS

Twisting his key to unlock the deadbolt, he flicked on the lights. The suite was three small rooms, this one with the reception desk, and an office for Max, and one for him. Slater clicked his tongue to greet Rey Pascual, the plaster statue that sat on the front desk. A skeleton wearing a crown and holding a scythe, Etta positioned him to watch the front door whenever she'd been working there.

Etta had renovated the place for them, making it more livable with some vintage art deco desks and chairs, and old-time light fixtures, and paint on the walls. In Max's office she'd used a rich warm yellow, and in Slater's, dark turquoise. He didn't mind it, and the place felt less utilitarian than it used to. Max said he could charge his clients more now because the place looked so much better.

Slater found a pile of mail on the corner of his desk. It was always mostly trash, but at the bottom of this stack was a padded envelope, with a return address in Hollywood. He ripped it open to find the book he'd ordered from a twelve-step group that dealt with sexual compulsion.

Dropping into his chair, he heaved his boots up on the desk, and flipped through the thin volume. He took a deep breath and started reading.

Keys rattled at the front door, and he heard it swing open. Etta called a greeting and then appeared in his office doorway. Curvy, and with her dark hair cut short, today she was wearing dark pants and a gray vest over a dress shirt.

"Is that what you wear to school?" he said.

"You know it. I just came from there." She paused in front of his desk, her brow furrowing. "Is that a … book?"

Slater sat up. "Don't sound so damn surprised."

"What is it?" she said, waggling her fingers. "Come on, give."

He groaned and handed it over. Etta sat in the guest chair across from him and scanned the back cover.

"Sexual compulsives. I'm so glad you're figuring this out."

"It's nothing to do with me. It's mandated reading by Pike."

"No one ever regretted the descent into the blue dragons' cave," she said, and set the book on the desk.

"Is that code for some sex thing?"

"It means self-examination. Self-exploration."

"I'm not doing that," Slater said. "This is just some due diligence."

"You look like someone punched you in the face."

"More than once, unfortunately. I misjudged a situation yesterday. I thought I was walking into a bar, but I think it was somebody's clubhouse."

"What are you working on?"

He explained the case, about tailing Mauricio and the situation with Eastside Lightning, and that he was working undercover in the factory.

"You know, that name is kind of racist," she said. "The word *eastside* means East LA, Latin LA, and *lightning* implies it's not legitimate. Like moonshine. Put together, it implies that there's something primitive and underhanded about Latin culture."

"Neither one of them are Eastsiders," Slater said. "She's Korean and he's an entitled white bro."

"Predictable. Cultural appropriation with a dollop of disrespect thrown in." She shifted in her chair. "What do you want me to do?"

"Try to connect with Kim, and see what you can find out about her." He explained what Andy had told him about her crypto business, then sat up to grab the mouse and wake his computer. "The Eastside Lightning website has a photo of her, and Andy found a website for her crypto thing."

Once he'd pulled up the photo of Kim and Zane, he twisted the screen for Etta to see.

"At least she's easy on the eyes," Etta said, leaning in. "What's under the gravy?"

"I'd say better manners than the other one."

"You mean Zane," Etta said, reading the image caption. "He looks like a beat poet. Like he's about to bust a rhyme."

"That's just the hip veneer. He's actually a tweaker. I saw him smoking at his desk." Slater waved a hand.

"So much of the crypto world is a grift. Maybe you can get a sense of what Kim is up to."

He pulled up the website Andy had found and clicked to translate it into English. Etta reached for the mouse and scrolled down the page.

"It's a software translation," Slater said, "so it won't have the nuances of what she's trying to say."

"Even translated, I can tell that it's vague. I don't know that much about crypto, but she doesn't even say what coin she's using, or if she's selling her own."

"To me that sounds like a red flag."

"Big time," Etta said. "It also means I can pose as a low-information investor."

"Kim will totally be into you if she thinks you have money to invest. Maybe you can even get some tang."

Her eyes narrowed. "How eloquent. Like I tell my seventh-graders, let's use words that build us up rather than tear us down."

"I'm not sure a little carpet munching is a destructive thing."

"Why would I sleep with her?" Etta demanded.

"Sometimes you can get better intel that way. Although personally, I keep my dick out of my cases."

She frowned. "No you don't."

"Well, theoretically, I strive for that." He shrugged. "It's a blurry line."

"Only for you," Etta said, and rose. "Can you send me that website? Kim's number is right there. I'll phone her in the morning. Tonight is going to be a crash course in crypto for me."

"You don't want to sound too well informed with her."

"I'm running a game here," Etta said, raising her eyebrows. "She'll get the impression that I'm clueless. But if I actually understand the field in some depth, I'll know when she's lying to me about her product."

Slater stood up. "Sometimes I forget that you really do know what you're doing."

She chuckled. "You're going to have to pay me for it."

Once he'd locked up, they rode the elevator down to the street together. It was completely dark out now, and they crossed to the parking lot, where Slater stepped up to the Polara.

"That's your ride?" Etta said. "Where's the T-bird?"

"In the classic-car hospital. I should get it back soon."

"That thing is awfully red. The front end looks like an eighth-grader with new braces."

"It's called a Polara, and it goes like hell. The red serves as a warning: get out of my way."

"You know the rule about cars," she said. "They should be either black or white."

"Says the woman driving a red doll car with a sewing-machine motor."

Etta chuckled. "It gets seventy miles to the gallon. I bet that antique gets about ten. I'll wave to you when I drive past the gas station."

Traffic was lighter at this hour, and soon he was in his neighborhood, and pulling into his garage. He waited for the door to roll down, then hustled up the stairs. Pike was sprawled on the sofa, still in his office drag, awake but with sleep in his eyes.

"Were you napping?" Slater said, and dropped to one knee next to him on the artificial turf.

"I might have drifted off." He grinned and reached for his arm, squeezing his bicep.

"I think I'm really into this grass now," Slater said, and ran a hand into it.

"It's not too weird?"

"It's totally weird. Over the top. And you're totally weird. But I love that. I love that you're not predictable."

He leaned in, and met Pike's taut lips, and spent a minute lost in it, lost in him. When he pulled back, he handed him the twelve-step book.

"I wanted you to see this. It's proof of compliance, officer."

"You got it." Pike briefly glanced at it and smiled. "Let's hope it resonates."

"I guess we'll see."

"Listen—I want to go out tonight." Pike tossed the book on the coffee table. "To see a band."

"What band?"

"It doesn't matter. We'll find a good one. I could do a rowdy dive with cheap beer, or some hotcha place with swanky cocktails." He caressed his neck. "Are you up for something like that?"

His back hurt, and his muscles ached, but none of that mattered.

"If it involves the man with a million volts in his pants," Slater said, "then yes, that's the only thing I want to do."

———•———

AFTER THEY'D EATEN, PIKE found a place with live jazz on Crenshaw, and they drove over in the Polara. They got a table at the side of the stage and ordered beer. The music was good, hot and creative, and they sat through a couple of sets.

Twisting in his chair to look at the bar behind him, Slater saw that it wasn't busy right now. He got up and went over, and when he leaned on the bar top between the stools, the bartender, a guy in a red vest and a bow tie, stepped over.

"Do you have premium tequilas?" Slater said.

He raised his eyebrows. "Lots of them. What are you looking for?"

"Eastside Lightning."

"Sure. That stuff is spendy. Twenty for a shot, twenty-five for a margarita."

Slater nodded. "I'll talk to the server when she comes around."

He sat with Pike again, and sipped his half-empty beer, and got into the music. When the server asked about a second round, Slater shook his head, and Pike ordered soda water. He smiled at the woman, and looked her in the eye, and thanked her. The guy actually enjoyed it, Slater realized. The thing about connecting with people.

When the set ended, Pike waved to Slater's beer. "You're nursing that. I can drive if you want to drink. I only had the one."

"I need to take it easy on the applejack, considering what comes later. I need to be fully present for that."

He raised his eyebrows. "'What comes later.' That sounds kind of nebulous."

"If you need specifics," Slater said intently, "picture me red-hot and rock-hard and deep inside you. I'm going to make you howl like a coyote when the sun goes down."

Pike chuckled. "Do you want to get out of here?"

They went out to the boulevard, and walked down the block to the Polara. Pike zipped up his jacket against the chill night air. The drive back was quiet, Slater with his hands on the wheel, Pike gazing out at the dark city rolling by. It felt right. They were at that point now, familiar enough, comfortable with each other. They didn't need to talk all the time.

Once they were home, and up in the bedroom, Pike pulled the drapes closed and unbuttoned his shirt.

"I was thinking about how you were pissed at me yesterday," he said.

Slater sat on the side of the bed to untie his boots. "It's the other way around. You were mad at me."

Stepping out of his pants, fully naked now, Pike put his hands on his hips. "Are you sure about that?"

He scowled at him. "You were tripping about not getting all the minutia of what I'm doing every day."

Pike jutted his chin. "Maybe you need to reinforce some of those points."

Then it clicked. "Is that what we're doing?" He rose, and pulled off his shirt, and dropped it on the floor. "You're sure you want to go there?"

"You tell me."

Stepping closer, Slater slapped his face, hard enough to turn his head.

Pike gasped and met his gaze. "You're going to need bracelets if you plan to play it that way."

He stepped around to the bedside table and pulled open a drawer to grab a pair of handcuffs. They were chunky, and heavy, hinged rather than linked with a chain, and way more comfortable than cop ones.

Turning back to Pike, he said sharply, "Hands."

"Make me."

Slater grabbed his wrist, and twisted it hard, eliciting a yelp. As Pike stepped sideways, Slater shoved his arm up his back. No way could he ever get the jump on this guy if he really wanted to resist him, but he wasn't doing that. He was into this. Slater grabbed his other wrist, and snapped on the cuffs, then spun him around.

Pike was fully hard now, and Slater slapped his other cheek, then caressed his pecs and leaned in to nuzzle his neck. When he grabbed his cock, Pike moaned and leaned into him. After stroking him for a moment, mouthing his jaw, Slater pulled back and shoved his shoulder. Losing his balance, he tumbled back onto the bed.

"What are you trying to pull?" Pike demanded.

Slater curled his lip into a sneer and grabbed his woody in his jeans. "I'm going to fuck you senseless."

Once he'd popped his fly and stripped off his pants, he climbed up beside Pike, and grabbed the lube and a condom. With their mouths together, one hand behind his neck, Slater worked a thumb into him. Eventually he sat up, and rolled on the condom, then shoved Pike's knees up.

As he gently pressed into him, Pike winced with the intensity of it, his head lolling back.

"Focus," Slater demanded, and slapped him, and gradually pushed deeper. He was soon pounding him, slowly at first, then building up speed.

"Punk," Pike said through his teeth, meeting his eye.

Slater slapped him hard, and pounded harder, shifting up to get closer to him. Grabbing his throat, he didn't squeeze hard enough to cut off his air, just enough for Pike to be aware that he could.

Straining toward him, Pike mock-spit at him, and Slater came, thrusting deeper, then collapsed on him, and buried his nose in his neck, breathing in the heady scent of his hair.

Once he'd caught his breath, he pulled back and grabbed Pike's cock, still rock hard. Stroking him, he leaned close.

"Who's the punk?" he growled.

Pike spit at him again, so Slater shifted position, and with his free hand, covered his mouth with his palm. Pike managed to bite into it, and Slater yelped, then slapped him, and stroked him faster. Straining upward, Pike's face contorted as he climaxed, and Slater kept firm hold of him until he sank back.

Stretching out beside him, Slater put a hand on his sweaty chest, and closed his eyes, listening to Pike's breathing, feeling it gradually slow. When he sat up, he saw a spot of red at the corner of his mouth.

"Damn—you're bleeding."

"I thought I tasted blood."

"I hit you too hard."

"It's just a little nick." Pike grinned. "Totally worth it."

"Are your hands falling asleep?"

"Not yet. But you can unhook me."

"In the morning," Slater said, and kissed his neck. "Your chest looks too good like this."

"I actually wouldn't even mind. As long as you're here, and you touch me like that, and I can smell your skin."

Swinging his legs off the side of the bed, Slater

sat up and grabbed the key from the bedside drawer. Rolling back, he nudged Pike onto his side and unlocked the cuffs.

Once he'd rubbed his wrists and wriggled his fingers, Pike wrapped his arms around him, and pulled him close, and mashed his nose into Slater's ear. Even though they were sweaty, and it was too warm to do this for very long, it felt perfect.

ELEVEN

⌐⌐⌐⌐⌐⌐⌐⌐⌐⌐⌐

SLATER WOKE WITH PIKE's big arm around his belly, his knees notched behind his. When he shifted onto his back, Pike woke and grinned at him.

"What?" Slater demanded, his tongue still thick.

"Waking up next to you. I still have to do a double-take. Every day feels like my birthday did when I was eight years old."

Slater caressed his chest. "Doris pegged you as a charmer. It makes me think you're a dangerous man."

"The words may be sweet, but they're sincere."

"I keep expecting some game show host to storm in here," Slater said, "and say, 'We punked you but good, you big sucker. None of this is real.'"

Pike chuckled, and put a hand on his face, and thumbed his cheek. "Your eye looks better. The color's fading."

"It's too cold to get out of bed."

"Commercial airliners wait for no one."

He sat up and folded the covers to the end of the bed. Slater forced himself to get up too, and pulled on a pair of boxer shorts. As Pike was getting dressed, he went up to the kitchen to start the coffeemaker.

They ate fruit and cereal, and drank coffee together, and eventually Pike got up to put his dishes in the machine.

"I'm out."

Slater leaned back against the counter and folded his arms. "Do you know where to park?"

"I got that figured out. I downloaded a coupon. They have a shuttle to the terminals."

"Is it for one of the hotel parking structures?" Slater said. "At some of them they steal gas."

"Seriously? Which ones?"

"I'd have to ask around. Just pick a spot close to the ramp or to the elevator, not out of sight in the back. Park with your gas tank door facing the aisle."

"This town." He scoffed. "It's going to be strange not to have my wheels there."

"Your mother has two cars. Drive one of those."

"It's not the same," Pike said, raising his eyebrows. "It's not mine."

"You big baby. I'm driving someone else's car all week."

"It's tough out there for the classic car aficionado."

Pike leaned in to kiss him, and lingered in it. Eventually Slater pulled back.

"You have to stop. You're putting lead in the pencil."

"You won't forget about me?"

"Impossible. You're the man with a million volts in his pants." He slapped his butt. "Zap."

Pike briefly mouthed his neck, then pulled back, and went to the stairs, and trotted down.

"Don't forget to bring your tux," Slater called after him.

It was still early, he saw, and he went down to the bedroom to get dressed. He could get to Eastside Lightning on time. Down in the garage, past the nose of the Polara, was his gear cupboard. Designed to stow firearms, it was a heavily armored box built to look like a basic sheet-metal cabinet, the kind of thing they sold at office-supply stores, so it could hide in plain sight. Slater didn't have any guns, but he kept all his illicit tech inside.

Once he got it open, he grabbed the heavy binder of ghost keys and the lock reader, and loaded them into a black canvas duffel bag. It was one of Svetlana's ingenious products: there were only so many standard keys, and this big binder contained most of the iterations, in little numbered pouches.

The keystroke logger was the size of a thumbnail, stored in a plastic sandwich bag so it wouldn't get lost. He scooped it up, along with the relay unit for it, and tucked them into the duffel bag.

Sitting on a shelf at eye level, one of his audio bugs caught his attention. It was built to look like a pocket calculator. Most people wouldn't be surprised to find an unfamiliar one of those lying around the office, and they were easily ignored, but not likely to get thrown out. He might as well plant that while he was at it. He grabbed the calculator and put it in the duffel bag, then locked the cabinet, and loaded the bag into the trunk of the Polara.

Once the garage door had rolled up, he backed

into the street and headed for Soto Junction. He parked the Polara out of sight on the next street again, then walked back to the factory gate. Rogelio was just pulling in as he walked up.

"You're on time, Slade," he said, climbing out of the maroon pickup.

"You sound surprised."

He laughed, and they walked back to the factory door together.

"You take the bus?" Rogelio said. "You can park in here if you want to. Just don't get too close to the bosses' cars."

"You're a morning person," Slater said.

"I guess I am. Why do you say that?"

"You're totally energized right now. It's actually annoying."

Rogelio unlocked the factory door with a key, and they stepped inside. The air was thick with humidity and the smell of warm alcohol and agave.

"Maybe we'll work with the dock open for a while," Rogelio said, and went to roll up the shutter.

Slater checked the pickup schedule on the computer. The first one wasn't for a while. Eight cases. In the back he loaded them onto a pallet, and once he'd finished, walked out to talk to Rogelio. He was working at the production equipment, peering at gauges and scratching on a tablet with a stylus.

"When I came here on Wednesday I saw a guy pull up in an old blue Lincoln. That was your *jimadore.*"

"His name is Mauricio."

"How well do you know him?"

Rogelio frowned. "Why are you asking me that?"

"He didn't look like a farmer. What kind of

agriculture supplier makes deliveries from the trunk of a Town Car?"

"I've wondered about that myself. He's definitely not a farmer. I think he might be a gangbanger."

"Based on what?"

"Just the way he looks, and the way he talks when he comes in here."

"White folks often assume I'm a gangbanger."

Rogelio grinned. "You wouldn't be mistaken for one in my neighborhood."

"So you don't really know where he gets the blue agaves."

"The one time I asked Zane about Mauricio, and where the agave farm was, he told me to worry about my own job." He gestured to the loading dock. "If that shipment is ready, grab a broom and clean up around the worktables."

"I missed Kim last night. I still need to get on the books."

Slater walked into the office and tried the handle on Kim's door. It was locked, so he tried Zane's door across the hall, and stepped in.

Sitting at his desk, clad in the same red sports jersey he'd been wearing yesterday, Zane swiveled toward him. "That's the second time you've done that. What the hell are you trying to pull?"

"I'm not pulling anything, Zane." He frowned. "Settle down."

Sitting up, he reached for his keyboard and locked his computer. But before the screen went dark, Slater got a look at it. He knew that site, the familiar color palette and the grid of fleshy images. It was a hookup site for guys.

"What do you need?" Zane said, and gestured impatiently.

"Where do you get the blue agave plants?"

"Why do you care?"

"Are they sourced locally?"

"Not that it's any of your damn business," Zane said. "I have a guy who buys them from farmers." He waved an arm. "Doesn't Rogelio have anything for you to do? I need to get back to work."

Slater put his hands on his hips. "If 'work' means that hookup site you were on, toots, I could save you some time. I can smoke you right here."

His eyebrows shot up. "You have got to be kidding me."

"You're pretty tits-out about your drug use. Why not your sex life? Roll your chair out." Slater whirled a finger in the air. "You don't even have to get up."

"Oh, man." Zane's eyes narrowed. "You know, I'm not gay."

"Of course not. But you hook up with gay guys. That's a totally different thing."

"Exactly. You get it."

Slater pursed his lips and thought about it. "Normally I don't really put up with closet cases."

"I'm not closeted. I told you, I'm not gay."

"Well, I'm gay." He gestured to Zane's pants. "I can see by the bulge in your crotch that you're not exactly disinterested. Am I going to smoke you or not?"

"You're not going to say I forced you into it because I'm your boss?"

"It would be hard to claim I got assaulted when any objective observer can see I could easily knock your block off. Blindfolded and with one hand tied behind my back. And who am I going to complain to? Your board of directors?"

Zane chuckled, his eyes bright. "Lock the door," he said, and shifted his chair away from his desk.

Once he'd flipped the bolt, Slater walked over and knelt in front of him, pushing his knees apart. Zane unbuckled his belt, and Slater batted his hands away. Holding his gaze, he unzipped his fly and pulled out his junk. He knew the guy was big, and he was already chubby, and getting bigger. Grasping his cock with a hand, he started to smoke him, and Zane slid toward him, closer to the edge of his chair.

As he got harder, he groaned and then spoke, loudly repeating, "Yes, yes."

He worked him with his mouth, and when Zane climaxed, he yelped and strained toward him. Slater sat back, and took a breath, and rested on one knee.

"You're so good at that," Zane said, his face red.

"I've had lots of practice."

Zane sat up and zipped his fly. "I hope Kim didn't overhear that."

"She's not even here." Slater stood up and adjusted his woody through his jeans, willing it to subside. "So am I going to get anything in return?"

Zane pulled his shirt down and eyed Slater's crotch. "It's tempting, but I'm awfully busy today."

"Most people would reciprocate. But I guess it's OK. You probably couldn't get me hard anyway."

His expression clouded. "Are you after money? I don't pay for sex."

"And I don't charge for it," Slater said, and frowned.

"What does that mean? You think you can extort

me?" He scoffed. "There's nobody you could tell that would be upset by my letting a guy blow me. Who would listen to you anyway? You're the help. I buy and sell people like you." He raised his voice. "I'm not going to pay you anything."

"You seem pretty tightly wound, Zane. You should get some of that GI gin to balance out the crystal."

"I don't do that much. Just occasionally when I'm in the flow."

"You're high right now," Slater said. "I can tell. Just don't start mainlining it."

"What's GI gin?"

"It's also called purple drank. In the South it's sizzurp. Codeine syrup."

"Why would I do that?" His lip curled in disgust. "You seem to know an awful lot about it."

"I have to deal with junkies all the time. I'm always amazed at how many people in this town are hopped up on something. In that respect, you're not really a 'pioneer.'" Slater waggled his fingers in air quotes. "Or an arbiter of things we haven't seen before. Junkie town is a very well-trodden path."

Zane jabbed a finger at him. "Fuck you. I don't have to listen to this. You're nothing. Common as dirt. A minimum-wage come-dump."

"We all are."

"What?"

"Common." He flashed his palms. "That was part of the revolution, rejecting the nobility and inherited titles. Remember fifth grade? You might think you rank a level or two up from the rest of us, but the law uses the standard of common sense. That means we're all the same."

"You're a prick, you know that?"

"I know," Slater said, and gestured helplessly, and walked out.

In the hallway he had to smile. The guy was a total yutz, but he knew a lot more about him now. He was so self-involved that he couldn't even see what was going on around him.

His phone had buzzed a minute ago, and he paused to check. It was a text from Etta:

I've got a meeting with Kim to talk crypto.

Slater thumb-typed a response:

Right on. Where and when?

Her reply came a moment later:

Today at 11 at the Baltimore.

Slater wrote back:

Can you get the time off?

He didn't have to wait long for her response:

I scheduled her during my prep time.

Slater had to chuckle. Etta was definitely a striver.

Back in the factory, he went to the computer and checked the time of the next pickup. It was happening soon. Walking into the back, he found the forklift parked next to the wall and plugged in. Disconnecting the cable, he climbed on, and lifted the pallet he'd loaded earlier, then rolled it out to the loading dock.

When the truck arrived, Rogelio came over to help him load it, and dealt with the driver, and got him to sign the clipboard. He didn't have to pitch in, as he had other stuff to do, but he really was a decent guy.

He needed to get into Kim's office, but he had no idea when she'd get here. He couldn't really go in with Zane sitting across the hall either. His phone buzzed in his jeans, and he pulled it out to check. Hester. He did have to talk to her at some point. Striding over to the door to the yard, he stepped outside and picked up the call.

"I wondered if you'd ghosted me," Hester said. "Have you made any progress?"

"I found out who took your agave plants. I'm working on a way to put an end to it."

"Who was it?"

"A low-level hood. I'll put it all in my report. Before I get to that, I'm going to try to disrupt his business model."

"I suppose you'll want more money."

"Tell you what," Slater said. "If I can't shut it down, we'll call it even. If I do, I'll hit you up for another couple g's."

"How long will it take until you know?"

"Give me through the weekend. I won't drag it out beyond next week."

"OK, Slater," she said. "Claudine trusts you, so I trust you. Let me know what happens."

As they talked he'd walked along the wall to the front of the building, and once he'd tucked his phone away, he saw that the only vehicle here was Rogelio's pickup—Zane had left. This was his opportunity.

Striding out to the street, he hustled to the Polara and grabbed his duffel bag from the trunk. Briefly opening the driver's door, he reached behind the seat and grabbed a pair of black latex gloves from the box and tucked them in his hip pocket.

The duffel bag probably looked like burglary tools, he thought, carrying it back to the factory. That's exactly what was in it, but it was broad daylight, and during business hours. Nobody was going to challenge him.

TWELVE

WALKING UP TO THE office door, Slater tried the handle, but it was locked. Leaving the duffel bag on the step, he walked back to the factory door and went inside.

"Where were you?" Rogelio called to him. He was over at the pressure cooker, with steam rising around him.

"Lunch," he said, and stepped over to the office door.

It was still unlocked, and he stepped through, then flipped the bolt behind him. Rogelio probably had a key, but that might slow him down. He walked through to the front office to pull open the door and grab his bag. Locking up again, he pulled on the black latex gloves, then took the plastic paper tray from the front desk and set it on the floor, on edge, just inside the door. It wouldn't slow anyone down, but he'd hear the door strike it if someone came in, and that might give him enough time not to get caught. Kim's office was still bolted, but when he tried the door to Zane's office, it was unlocked.

"Idiot," he muttered, and stepped inside. Briefly scanning the room, he couldn't see any cameras, and nothing that looked out of place that might conceal a hidden camera. Desk clocks were a big one—nobody needed a damn desk clock anymore, but some consumer spy-gear manufacturer had decided they were innocuous enough to hide cameras in, and now he saw them all the time. But Zane didn't have a desk clock. It made sense that if you were up to something, running a game, the last thing you'd want to do would be to create a record of it.

Digging in his duffel bag, he pulled out the calculator. It actually worked as a calculator, with a solar cell and a readout. The only giveaway that it was something more was its excessive weight—the audio bug and its broadcast capability needed a sizeable battery. He peered at the edge of the device and found the barely visible recessed switch, the one that activated the bug, and snapped it on with a fingernail.

Looking around Zane's office, he set the device on a cluttered credenza behind the desk, next to the TV set. It wasn't hidden but it was out of view of Zane's chair, next to a stack of files that obscured it. Zane was unlikely to notice it anyway—that guy had his head pretty far up his own ass.

As he stepped into the hallway, he pulled the door closed, and set the duffel bag on the floor in front of Kim's office. Dropping to one knee, he examined the bolt on the door. It was a standard hardware-store lock. That was very good news. Any kind of exotic lock wouldn't be covered by Svetlana's ghost keys.

Fishing the lock reader out of the duffel bag, Slater connected one end of the wire to his phone. Svetlana's app popped up, showing a black screen and the Cyrillic characters "готов." He didn't know the word, but he knew it meant the reader was waiting for input. At the other end of the wire was a key-shaped probe, and he slid it into the lock. Almost instantly the screen went green and displayed 413. Hauling the heavy binder out of the duffel bag, he flipped to the pouch with that number and extracted the key. He slid it into the lock, but it wouldn't turn the cylinder, no matter how much he wiggled it.

"Damn it," he muttered, retracting the key. He could feel sweat beading his brow. Svetlana's stuff either worked flawlessly or didn't work at all—it didn't make mistakes. He reinserted the probe and eased it out slightly. This time the screen said 329. When he flipped to the page with that key and tried it in the lock, it twisted freely.

Taking a breath, he packed the key binder back into the duffel, and tossed the lock reader in on top of it. Heaving up the bag, he stepped into Kim's office, and closed the door behind him, and bolted it.

She'd left the room lights on, and he scanned the space, looking for obvious and concealed cameras, but nothing looked like that. There was a window, but it faced the steel picket fence and the parking spaces on the next lot. Nobody would be looking in at him. He tried the top drawer of each of the file cabinets, but both of them were locked. It would have been too time-consuming to dig through them anyway.

The computer was on the floor under her desk, and Slater knelt and pulled it partway out, then dropped to all fours to look at the cables on the back. The keyboard was attached to a USB port, and he disconnected it, then fished the keystroke logger out of its plastic bag and slid it into the port. A minuscule LED on the side flashed green, just once—it was working. He plugged the keyboard into it. It only raised the profile of the connector half an inch or so, and it was the same kind of black plastic, meaning it was practically invisible.

Rising to his knees, he tapped at the keyboard on Kim's desk to make sure it was still working. The screen came to life and asked for a password.

He pushed the box back under the desk and brushed away the dust he'd disturbed. As he was about to get up, still on his knees, he heard the sound of hard plastic being struck—his booby trap at the front door.

"What the hell," a muffled voice said. That was Zane.

Slater's heart was pounding, and he stood up, and silently heaved the duffel bag onto his shoulder. Was Kim with him? Treading carefully to the door, he stood with his ear to it, listening. He heard Zane open his office door. It didn't close again. He waited, but there was no further sound.

The longer he stayed here, the worse it would be to get caught. He had to make a move. It was about getting paid—that's what he'd say. He needed to talk to Kim about getting on the payroll, and he'd knocked, and she'd left the door unlocked. There was no evidence he'd picked the lock or forced it. The duffel bag would be harder to explain.

Taking a deep breath, he slowly turned the

deadbolt. It shifted quietly, and he twisted the handle, easing the door open a crack. From this vantage he could only see the empty front office. Whether Zane's door hung open or not, the guy wouldn't see him from his desk. If he was at his desk.

Pulling the door wider, he could see into Zane's office, but the guy wasn't in view, and no sound came from within. Slater stepped into the hall, and pulled Kim's door closed, then eased the ghost key into the deadbolt to lock it, his actions slow and deliberate so as to make no sound.

Once the bolt flipped, he treaded back to the factory door, and peeled off the latex gloves, then gingerly unlocked it and stepped inside.

Rogelio was still focused on the pressure cooker, and the room smelled like hot wet mulch, but with the dock's shutter rolled open it wasn't building up to a nauseating level. The guy was immersed in whatever he was doing and didn't even look up when Slater stepped in.

Even though the key logger was plugged into a computer, it didn't access the network through it, instead broadcasting to the relay box. That was a bigger unit that Svetlana had built to look like a generic plug-in transformer, the kind that came with myriad low-voltage electronics. But it had to be close to the key logger—he needed an electric socket not far from Kim's desk.

The wall of the factory space that abutted Kim's office had a workbench with a tool rack above it, and under the bench was a cylindrical red tank on little wheels. That was an air compressor—it had to be plugged in somewhere. Crouching, he looked under the bench. At the back was a quad outlet, and one of the sockets had nothing plugged into it.

Digging in his duffel bag, he pulled out the relay unit and reached under the bench to plug it in. The indicator lit up red, then a moment later turned amber. That meant it had connected to the USB dongle. As he stared at it, it turned green—it had connected to the cell network. That was it. Svetlana's software would record every keystroke on Kim's computer.

He stood up and pulled out his phone. Both devices had connected: in Svetlana's interface the calculator was marked as "Listening" and the key logger was "Typing." He tapped on that one, and a message bubble appeared that said "нет актив." He had no idea what that meant. The multilingual interface was so damn clunky. He'd worry about it later, once Kim had used her computer.

Tucking his phone away, he walked over to the computer on the table and checked the activity list on the screen. The next pickup was later in the day. Slater went over to the tanks to talk to Rogelio.

"I'll be back in a while."

Rogelio frowned. "I'm your boss, you know. You should ask me, not tell me."

"When you pay minimum wage, you kind of have to roll with it."

"Oh, Slade, *No te hagas.*"

Slater had heard that before. It meant something like *Don't mess with me.* He gestured to the dock. "I'll be back to set up the next pickup."

Scooping up the duffel bag, he walked out the side door. Normally he'd want to punch the guy in the face, talking to him like that, but Rogelio never pushed too hard, and he pitched in to load the trucks.

Once he got out to the street, and around the next corner, he loaded the duffel bag in the trunk of the Polara, and got behind the wheel. Downtown he found a street space on Broadway a block from Andy's. When he got upstairs, Andy opened the door, as usual clad in boxers and a T-shirt, and beckoned him in.

"Don't you have to prepare for your wedding?" Slater said.

"The rehearsal is later today." He sat at his desk. "What have you ... got for me?"

"I installed the key logger. Can we pull it up on your computer?"

"How do you access it?"

"All my surveillance gear has a web interface." Slater pulled out his phone, and planted his feet apart, and looked for the note with his login details.

"Do you have to ... stand like that?" Andy said.

He looked at him and frowned. "What are you talking about?"

"You look hot. You're getting me ... revved up. It's rude."

"I'd fuck you right now," Slater said. "Gladly. You're the one who said no sex."

"That doesn't mean you can just ... stand there like that, in those jeans."

"Next time I'll bring a modesty sarong." He scoffed. "You are so fucking weird."

"Just dial it down a notch. The swagger." Andy swiveled to his screens. "What's the address of ... the server?"

Slater recited the string of numbers that made up the web address, reading from his phone.

"It's asking me something in Russian."

"It wants my user name," he said, and recited it.

"Blank screen," Andy said. "Is that normal?"

Slater leaned in to look. "Usually it comes up faster than that."

In his pocket his phone buzzed, and he pulled it out to check. Svetlana.

"Did you buy a new computer?" she said when he picked up.

"It's not my computer. I'm trying to give access to one of my operatives."

"Which devices does he need to see?"

"Only the keystroke logger. I connected it earlier today."

"Your operative can use a new user name and password. I'll text it to you. They will have access to the keyboard device."

"That works," he said, and ended the call.

"Your Russian supplier," Andy said.

"She wants you to use a different login."

"I know why. She doesn't want just anyone … accessing the gear she built. It increases the risk of her … getting busted."

Slater's phone buzzed with a text, the details from Svetlana, and he recited them for Andy. As soon as he'd entered them on Svetlana's interface, the screen displayed "Typing" along with a line in Cyrillic.

"There won't be any record of anything yet," Slater said. "I don't know when Kim will be back at her desk. I'm not even sure if she works Saturday."

"I'll keep an eye on it," Andy said, swiveling

toward him. "Now get out of here before I … sexually assault you."

"It's not assault if I'm into it. Even if Kyle disapproves."

He walked out, and down to the street, and saw there was a text from Duarte:

> Your baby is ready. I can bring it to you.

At last, he thought, and when he climbed into the Polara, thumb-typed a reply:

> Can we do the swap when I get to my house? This evening or in the morning.

Slater drove back to Soto Junction, and when he walked through the gate of the factory, he saw that the black Bimmer was here, but not Kim's ride. The loading dock shutter was still rolled up, and he walked in the adjacent door.

"That was a leisurely break," Rogelio said.

"I had to wait for the guy to grind pepper onto my salad."

He frowned. "I thought you went for lunch before."

Slater didn't respond to that, and went to the screen to check the quantity of the next pickup. In the back, as he was heaving cases onto a pallet, he heard an engine briefly rev in the yard. The truck wasn't due for a while yet. He went to the dock, but no vehicle was in sight, so he stood at the edge and craned out to look. The blue Town Car was parked up by the office.

"Your *jimadore* is here," he called to Rogelio. "Is he bringing more product?"

"Nobody told me if he is. Maybe he's here to get paid."

Slater strode back into the storage space and opened his surveillance app. When he tapped on the "Listening" entry for the audio bug, he saw that there were two recordings from Zane's office earlier today, but instead of listening to those he tuned in to the live stream. Standing behind the stack of pallets, he held the phone to his ear so Rogelio wouldn't overhear it.

Mauricio's voice was easy to recognize, with his familiar East LA intonation.

"Are you going to offer me some of your *aguardiente*?" Mauricio said.

"Not this early in the day."

Zane's voice wasn't as loud. He must be farther from the bug.

Mauricio scoffed. "I take a lot of risk to get those plants. I could get busted any night I'm out harvesting them."

"You're too smart for that, aren't you?" Zane said. "Besides, you can't renegotiate the terms now. We have a deal."

"I need to get paid more. You're ripping me off."

Zane laughed audibly. "So go to the cops."

"Fuck you, you goddamn frat boy."

Neither of them spoke again—Mauricio must have walked out.

Slater killed the app and tucked his phone away. There it was—Zane knew how the guy was obtaining the plants. He wasn't just an innocent recipient of stolen goods. He was fully complicit.

Climbing on the forklift, he moved the pallet out to the dock. Once he'd set it down, he drove backward to return the vehicle to the storage space. Rogelio was at the tanks, wearing elbow-length black rubber gloves, with the lid of the pressure cooker open. As Slater rolled by in reverse, he met his gaze and raised his eyebrows. Rogelio chuckled and shook his head at his cockiness.

This guy wasn't part of the thievery. He knew that now, could feel it in his gut. It made sense that Zane wouldn't read him in on it if there wasn't a good reason to.

As he stepped off the forklift, his phone buzzed in his pants. He pulled it out to find a text from Etta:

The meeting went well. I have insights.

Slater went out the side door and into the yard, and walked along the wall to be out of earshot, then dialed Etta.

"It sounds like Kim was eager to meet you," he said, once she picked up.

"Eager to take the meeting," Etta said, "but she didn't drop the sales hammer. It felt more like the slow burn. The long game."

"Does she have another office for that business?"

"We met at her club in K-town and had cocktails. I think playing dumb worked. She wants to hang out—I'm invited to her house on Sunday. I'm sure I'll hear more about investing then."

"What's your sense of the product? Is it a scam?"

"So far it's extremely vague. She talks about big returns in a short time. It feels unrealistic."

"Where does she live?"

"Hancock Park."

"That means money."

"I'm thinking I should record everything," Etta

said. "Max has a wire we use sometimes for face-to-face stuff."

"That might be useful. Especially if she's promising something impossible. You don't have to be at work?"

"Schools are actually closed on Sunday."

"Who knew."

Slater ended the call, then stretched his back, and rolled his neck. Just a couple of days of this kind of work and his muscles ached. He could ditch Eastside Lightning now, he decided. He'd learned enough.

THIRTEEN

J UST IN CASE ANDY might have found something that he should stick around for, he dialed his number, but it went to voice mail.

"Idiot," he muttered, and then looked at the phone again when it buzzed. Andy had texted:

Talk later. At the rehearsal now.

Slater wrote back:

What is there to rehearse? You just have to accept that gunsel has conned you into doing this, and say yes, and face the fact that your life is effectively over.

No way would he get an answer to that. He tucked his phone away and walked back to the factory. As he stepped up to the door, he saw Kim's ugly little Benz pull through the gate, and behind it a box truck, lumbering toward the loading dock.

Rogelio was still up to his elbows in the production process, and he didn't come over to help. It was a small order, and it didn't take long for Slater to get it loaded on his own, and to get the driver to check the box and sign off on it. As he was moving the pallet back into the storage space, he heard Kim call for him: "Slade."

He walked out to find her standing in the office doorway. Rogelio was right—she really was afraid to come in here.

"What's up?" he said, walking toward her.

"I need to get you on the books. Come into my office."

She didn't wait for him, letting the door swing closed. When Slater strode into the hallway, he found her office door open, and Kim sitting behind her desk, peering at her computer screen. Slater dropped into the chair across from her.

"You speak really good English," she said. "Not like most of the workers we get."

"Thanks. So do you."

She looked up at him and frowned. "What's your legal name?"

"John Slade. No middle."

"Can I see your ID?"

"I don't have it on me."

"That's a little strange. Who walks around without their ID?"

"I'm afraid of losing it, so I leave it at home," Slater said.

"If you're not legal to work in this country, it doesn't matter. But we pay less."

"How much less?"

She thought about it. "Thirty percent."

"I'd call that wage theft."

Kim raised her eyebrows. "Who are you going to

call to complain about it?"

"I'm actually allowed to work."

"So what's your social?"

He rattled off a number that he used sometimes, as he knew it would come back as valid in the system. He wasn't sure whose it was, but he'd memorized it for exactly this kind of situation.

Once she'd tapped at her keyboard, Kim turned to her credenza and pulled a sheet off the printer. "Sign this."

It was just a standard tax form, he saw, looking it over, and he grabbed a pen, and signed "John Slade."

"So how is it working with Rogelio?" Kim said, reaching for the form.

"He's pretty easygoing. The guy knows what he's doing."

"He's got you on logistics?"

"If you mean moving stuff around, yes."

"What are you doing Sunday?" Kim said. "I have some work at my house I could use help with. I know you guys work as much as you possibly can, what with rents the way they are, and sending cash back to *la familia* in May-hee-co. You can come by after mass."

"What kind of work?"

"I'm clearing out my library," Kim said. "Turning it into a gym. I need all the books gone."

"That sounds like a radical change."

"The books were included when I bought the house. I don't care about them. They were only for decoration anyway. Who needs an actual library?"

"Have you got boxes for them?"

"Plenty."

"Sure," Slater said. "I can box books for you."

"I'll pay you through the company with your paycheck." She scrawled on a yellow notepad and then tore off the page and handed it across to him. "That's my address. It's near Larchmont and Third."

"How did you get connected with Zane?" Slater said. "You two seem like very different people."

She met his gaze. "In what way?"

"You know exactly what I mean. Different ethnicities, different generations."

"His mother and I did Pilates together. I heard Zane wanted to pioneer tequila production in LA. I know people love spirits, especially artisanal hand-crafted spirits. He had the plan, and he owned this building from when he was doing import-export, and I had the capital to make it happen." She waved a hand. "Why do you care?"

"Just curious about the company, since I'm working here."

"Well, there you have it." She flashed a thin smile. "Bye, now."

Slater rose and stepped to the door.

"Don't forget about Sunday," she called after him.

Back in the factory, he walked over to Rogelio.

"I'm going to head out."

"It's not quitting time yet."

"There's no more pickups today."

"I saw you shifted some cases in the back," Rogelio said. "That's a good idea. Make them more accessible. You can spend an hour doing that."

"No thanks."

He laughed. "*Huevón*, I'm not sure you have a firm grasp on how employment works."

"Later, big guy," Slater said, and walked out to the yard.

On the way to the street, he texted Etta:

We need to talk before you go to Kim's place.

Her reply came as he was climbing behind the wheel of the Polara:

I'm meeting Max at the office tomorrow on my lunch break. That guy owes me money. Talk then?

Slater had to grin. It sounded like tough talk, but she'd never actually have to shake Max down. Both of them were happy to pay her. She was competent and did things they couldn't. Because Etta's daily habitat wasn't the cesspool that Max and Slater swam in, she often had alternative perspectives on people, and on their motives. He sent her an acknowledgment, then texted Duarte:

I'll be at my place in 20.

The navigation app sent him through downtown, and on surface streets. At this hour the 101 would be jammed. He parked the Polara on the street in front of his place, and grabbed his stuff, and used the garage opener to roll up the door.

The duffel bag, he remembered. He went back out to the Polara and took it out of the trunk, then loaded the key binder and the probe into his armored cabinet. There was a small bag of cash stashed in here, just a couple of racks, and he opened it and took a sheaf of C-notes, half a rack, and folded them over, and stuffed them in his hip pocket.

He was locking up the cabinet when the Thunderbird nosed into the garage. It gleamed like it had just been waxed. Duarte killed the engine, and stepped out, and called a greeting. He was wearing cargo shorts and a nylon jacket over a T-shirt.

As Slater stepped around the front end of the car, he saw Duarte pull off the puffy blue paper covers that he was wearing over his work boots.

"Crime-scene booties?" Slater said.

"You don't need my dirt in your vehicle."

"You were able to get the parts?"

"It took a while," Duarte said, "but it's running like new."

"The engine sounded great when you pulled in. What do I owe you?"

"Three g's will cover parts and labor."

"What about the Polara? I have to pay you for that. It's a great ride, by the way."

"It's covered in the three."

Slater handed him the keys to the Polara, then dug out the wad of cash, and riffled through it, quickly counting out thirty C-notes, and handed them over.

"You're not going to bargain?"

"You take good care of me, Duarte. There's no discounting that. Vera had a beneficial calming effect too."

"Isn't she the best?" He tucked the cash away, not bothering to count it. "If you cross her, she'll take your head off. Like, literally, with her bare hands. But she has that amazing compassion too."

"You make a great team."

"People who've seen crazy stuff happen are good in tense situations. She's seen some stuff." Duarte waggled the Polara keys. "Later, Slater."

Once he'd walked out, Slater climbed into the Thunderbird to deposit his garage door opener, and his binoculars, and his phone charger. They'd cleaned the interior too, he saw. The carpet looked immaculate. As he hit the button to close the garage door, he saw the Polara roll by, back toward the boulevard. Such a sweet ride.

Climbing the stairs, he ditched his boots and his work shirt, and pulled on a T-shirt, then shook some ibuprofen into his mouth from the bottle in the bathroom, hoping it would relieve his aching muscles. Climbing the stairs, he made his way to the sofa.

He still wasn't used to the fake grass. It looked so real. Just seeing it made him smile. Pike was so odd sometimes. It was the best possible kind of odd. Stretching out, he looked at the sky outside. Twilight was starting to descend, the light shifting from golden to gray.

When he looked at Svetlana's app, the bug in Zane's office had generated another recording. He tapped on it and turned on the speaker.

"Are we going to pay the ethanol guy?" It was Kim's voice, tinny and muffled but still clearly recognizable.

"I think we can string him along a while longer." That was Zane.

"We have the cash. If we pay him, he'll quit bugging us."

"The downside is if we pay him, it makes the spreadsheet balloon up," Zane said. "All that green looks bad if there's ever an audit. If we don't pay him, there's no record of that money."

"When did he deliver the product?"

"I checked. It's been eight weeks."

"The voice mail he left me sounded like he's pretty upset," Kim said.

"So what do you want to do?"

"Let's pay him twenty percent. That way he won't try to repossess the product. That'll buy us a few months."

The recording ended, and Slater sat gazing out at the corner of the hillside in the distance. It was green after the winter rains, turning gray now as the daylight faded. He couldn't see the baseball stadium but he knew it was up there, beyond the towering light stands aimed down at the sprawling acres of parking.

These two were trying to rip off their ethanol supplier, the same way they were ripping off Hester. Actively not paying him even though they could afford to, giving him just enough that he wouldn't make trouble. They really were lowlifes. That was unequivocal now.

Even with the French doors closed he could hear the dull roar of the city outside. Even in this quiet residential neighborhood. It was out there, persistent and relentless, and overwhelming if you let it be. Piss-stained sleeping bag–strewn Broadway, once a glittering entertainment strip, now emblematic of the metropolis in its dysfunction. Grifters ripping off their suppliers. Kim trying to pay him illegally low wages. The never-ending grind. He hadn't noticed it for a while. Pike had distracted him from all that.

But Pike wasn't here, and it was easy to fall into the old patterns. Under the sex rules, he could find a hookup when Pike was away. He thought about that. It was as easy as opening the hookup app on his phone. But maybe he didn't need to. He'd messed around with Zane today, and he was wiped out from all the manual labor at Eastside Lightning, all the work that he was never going to get paid for.

Rising, he went into the kitchen, and pulled the fifth of bourbon from the cupboard. There was much better booze in here now thanks to Pike's civilizing influence. Good scotch and even high-end bourbon. But Slater drank so much of it that he had to stick with the cheap stuff. The booze rules said his ration was half an inch, and he poured that much in a tumbler, scowling at the paucity. It had been a long day. He added another finger. He deserved it. Plus Pike wasn't around to behave for.

After a first satisfying heady slurp, he walked back to the sofa, relishing the burn in his throat, the vapor in his nose. The twelve-step book was here, just about the last thing he wanted to read, but he grabbed it anyway.

He turned on the lamp on the side table, and stretched out with his back to it, and got comfortable. Right up front was the list of the twelve steps, similar to AA and NA. You have to admit you're powerless, and admit that things are unmanageable, and then you have to take a personal inventory. Instead of boozing or shooting up, the issue for these people was about having compulsive sex. It wasn't about quantity, it seemed, but about the tone of it.

Why was Pike so insistent that he read this? His life was in no way unmanageable. He liked sex and he had a lot of it. That meant life was good, not that it was messed up. And admitting you were powerless sounded like exposing a weakness. Like strolling into a gang clubhouse unarmed. That was a great way to get taken out. He took a breath and flipped the page.

Sometime later he started awake. It took a moment to realize his phone was ringing. It was completely dark outside now, and he scrabbled for the phone amid the blades of fake grass. It was Pike.

"Hey, forty-niner. What are you up to?"

"I must have been squeezing the artificial grass between my toes," Slater said. "It's so luxurious it sent me straight to shluffy ville."

"It's great, isn't it? I hope Rosa doesn't shred it with the vacuum cleaner. She seems a little cavalier sometimes."

"My little blue twelve-step book says you can't control other people's behavior. Only your own."

"You know," Pike said, "With a sidearm and handcuffs, I actually manage to control people pretty effectively."

He chuckled. "You can't pull a gun on Rosa. It'd be impossible to find someone else with her skill set."

"You mean you don't want to pay someone else to do your laundry," Pike said. "I'm so glad you're reading that book. Not fucking some rando."

"You're the only rando I want to fuck. You know, you should probably be envisioning that right now. Imagining me with my arms around you, sweaty and hard, deep inside you."

Pike groaned. "Man, such big talk. I would really, really like to get into it, but my mother is in the next room."

"High-test sex is worth waiting for. We'll double down when you get back."

FOURTEEN

W HEN SLATER WOKE, HE was in his bed, with daylight streaming in the sheers. He wasn't sure how he got down here, or when, but his head didn't hurt. That meant he hadn't reupped on the bourbon last night. His phone had just buzzed, he remembered, and he grabbed it from the bedside table. It was a text from Andy:

I got some stuff. You can drop by.

"Dick," he muttered, and pushed himself out of bed.

The gatekeeping thing was fairly new, telling Slater when he could and couldn't be there, like he was a bad penny. It had to be more of Kyle's nefarious influence.

Once he was caffeinated and got dressed, he headed down to the garage. It was remarkable how clean the Thunderbird was. Duarte must have a powerful shop vac. The engine started on the first twist of the ignition, and it sounded brand-new.

Backing into the street, he waited for the garage door to roll down, then drove to Andy's, and parked in the lot behind his building. Upstairs he knocked on the door. When Andy pulled it open, he was in his boxers, his hair a perfect tousled mess. Slater followed him inside.

"How was rehearsal?" Slater said. "Have you finally decided it's not worth it?"

"I'm not even sure why we … did that. It's all common sense. Stand up there, say a few … words, put a ring on it." Andy dropped into his desk chair. "Maybe it was so our parents could … all get comfortable with each other."

"That's basically what you're signing up for: living your life for other people. What have you got for me?"

"Kim used her computer yesterday. The keystroke … logger was useful. Unfortunately I couldn't get into the … Eastside Lightning files. I assume she was already … logged in, so she didn't type any passwords to … give me access. But she logged into her … crypto business from her desk."

"You were able to get into that?"

"It's lots of marketing stuff. But I found … a client list."

"Her investors," Slater said.

"She keeps track of them in a detailed spreadsheet."

"Right on."

"I'll share the files with you," Andy said. "It seems thin on what she's actually selling. I can't find … anything about her crypto product. I did get onto her videos. The stuff she uses to attract customers. They're in ... Korean but I had them machine translated. She talks about her platform, and says it's a money-generating system, but then she ... doesn't actually explain the mechanism that makes it work. She also claims that it doesn't matter if the ... wider crypto market is doing well or doing poorly: you're always going to be ... making money."

"So it's snake oil."

"That's my assessment. If it were possible only to ... make money and never lose it, everyone would do it. Everyone ... would be rich."

"This is really useful."

"It's broad strokes," Andy said, his head gently wavering with his rhythmic random muscle movements. "I'm going to dig some more. I have time ... tomorrow. I'll let you know what else comes up."

"I guess I'm not allowed to even suggest that we mess around."

He frowned. "You're such a dick hound. How many times do I ... have to spell it out? It's not going to ... happen, Slater. You have to leave."

Slater held his gaze for a moment before he walked out. "Bye, beautiful."

Retrieving the Thunderbird from the lot behind Andy's place, he drove to his office, and parked across the street. Upstairs the lights were on, and the statue of Rey Pascual was facing the front desk instead of the door.

"Hey, Rey," he said as he flipped the deadbolt behind him.

Etta craned her head out the door of Max's office. "Did I just hear you say hello to Rey?"

Slater stepped over and stood in the doorway. Max was wearing his gray checked suit, a yellow necktie loose at his collar, the butt of his sidearm visible under his jacket. He had that mousy brown hair that seemed to be the default setting for white guys, and a gut hanging over his belt.

"One of the shrinks Doris sent me to in middle school told me I needed to be more civil," Slater said. "'Use your words, not your fists,' they'd say. And now you're calling me out on it."

"I'm not sure if civility counts with inanimate objects," Etta said.

Max leaned back in his chair. "Almost every client that comes through here asks me if Rey is the narco saint. I like that he makes us look badass." He waved at the room. "Combined with Etta's decorating, it strikes the right tone: we're classy up in here, but also deadly."

Slater chuckled. "That's totally who we are."

"The narco saint is La Santa Muerte," Etta said. "She's female and Catholic. Rey Pascual predates the conquest, and he's a boy, like you two chuckleheads."

"Why do the drug runners love her?" Max said. "She's dead. I doubt they want to be like her."

"It's because she doesn't judge. She's the opposite of the holy virgin. The virgin expects you to behave, or else. La Santa Muerte encourages people to think about the well-being of everyone, without exception, without judging what you've done."

"Couldn't she do that without being dead?"

"The reason she's dead is to remind us that we're all equal. Because all of us are destined to die."

"Good god, woman," Slater said. "You're such a teacher."

"Did you know this goon was on channel 6 yesterday?" Etta said, waving an arm toward Max.

"I was babysitting that rapper," Max said. "Guiding her through the scrum into the courthouse."

"The one who shot her boyfriend?" Slater said. "That was in the news."

"Allegedly," Max said. "And it wasn't her boyfriend. She shot her manager."

Slater waved a hand. "You have to show me."

Max chuckled and sat up, grabbing his computer mouse with a big meaty hand. "We were just reviewing the footage."

Slater leaned in to see the monitor. The video had a TV station logo in the corner and showed a view of a set of broad steps and the street in front. He knew that place—one of the courthouses on Hill Street. Dozens of people crowded around, many of them with cameras. A black SUV pulled up and stopped short, and Max stepped out of the back, wearing his sharp gray suit. He took the hand of a woman wearing a pink suit, in dark sunglasses and soberly coiffed hair, and guided her out of the vehicle. With one arm protectively around her shoulder, he extended the other to clear a path.

"Come on, people," Max said intently. "Make way."

The woman was barely as tall as Max's shoulder, and he deftly sheltered her as he pushed through the crowd. The pair of them finally stepped through the courthouse doors and out of view.

"I bet she doesn't dress like that in her rap videos," Slater said.

"Doesn't he look professional?" Etta said. "Like, don't mess with me."

Max guffawed. "That's about as good as it gets on a babysitting job."

"How did you get into the courthouse?" Slater said. "You were wearing your sidearm."

"The lawyers took over once we were inside. I didn't make it past the metal detector."

Slater eyed Etta. "So did you get your money from this goon?"

"We're all square."

"I need a minute, and then we can strategize."

He stepped over to his office and dropped into his chair. Once he'd woken his computer, he pulled up the documents Andy had sent. Kim's client list was a lengthy spreadsheet, and it had lots of biographic detail for each entry—age and gender, contact info, where they worked. Whatever her flaws, at least Kim was meticulous and well organized. There were dozens of names, he saw, scrolling through it. This was pure gold. He could talk to these people directly and find out what Kim had been promising them. He sent the list to the printer at the side of his desk, and it came to life with a low hum.

When Etta stepped in, she took the guest chair, and picked up the little statue that sat at the base of his monitor. An image of Pollux, naked and standing with a horse, it had been a gift from Pike. She took a minute to look it over, even though he knew she'd seen it before.

"This guy predates Catholicism too," she said. "Did you ever find out where Castor is?"

"On Pike's desk."

"That actually makes sense." She set it down. "How is that hunk of man?"

"I have no idea. I see him all the time but I can't be objective. It's like looking at the sun. I can't really see anything except the intense blinding rays of Pikeness."

She chuckled. "It sounds like you've got it bad."

"So Kim asked me to come over tomorrow and clean out her library," Slater said. "It must be a big house."

"I checked out the overhead view of her address. It's not an estate like in Bel Air, but it's definitely a mansion. More like in Beverly."

"So there's lots of space. If we're both there at the same time, you can keep her busy talking crypto while I poke around."

"You're going to clean for her? She thinks you're grunt labor."

"I already work for her as a grunt, and I suspect I'm as rare as a unicorn. Who else is going to work for minimum wage these days?" He waved a hand. "What did she tell you about this meeting? Do you think there'll be other investors? Will there be staff around?"

"I have no idea." Etta furrowed her brow. "My impression was that it was just going to be her and me. She was being all chummy like that. I think most of her clients are Korean, so I'm an outlier. To be handled separately."

Slater nodded. "It's unlikely she'll entertain you in the library if I'm in there doing manual labor. Probably not in her office either. If she has an office, or even a desk, I'll try to find it and rifle it."

"That'll work if no one's around. Like you said, there might be staff, or her family. Maybe I'll try to talk loud so you'll know where we are."

"If the place is quiet, and you're going to change locations in the house, you should warn me. Laugh loud or drop something heavy."

"I can do that. Once I'm there, do you want me to text you our location?"

"If you can get away with it." Slater half-rose to pull the pages off the printer. "Another thing. I got a list of Kim's investors. It has their contact details and where they work. Do you have time to talk to some of them today? We could split this list."

"I can't." She slowly shook her head. "I have to be at school."

"Since when are public schools in session on Saturday?"

"I'm doing after-school intramurals. I can't really get out of it." She waved a hand. "Don't you technically have a job now too?"

"The counterfeit tequila? Do you think a factory like that works on Saturday?"

"The factories in this building are working today." Etta raised her eyebrows. "It might be something you ought to know, seeing as you work there."

"I don't think I'll be going back. I was only there to surveille them. It's freaking hard work, and they're never going to pay me. Although I did get to drive the forklift."

"Didn't the woman who lost the agave plants pay you? I bet you billed her way more than the wages in a tequila factory."

"That's actually true," Slater said. "She paid me up front."

"It's weird how money is attracted to you. It seems to pool around your feet."

He frowned. "I work hard for what I get."

Max appeared in the doorway. "So I'm sitting over there eavesdropping."

"It's hard not to," Slater said. "We left the door open."

"You're doing interviews today?" Max said. "I'm done with the pistol-packing rapper. I can pitch in."

"Oh, man, that would be great."

"You've skulked around peeping in windows on my cases. I can burn some shoe leather for yours."

"This is the list of Kim's investors," Slater said, and split the sheaf in two, and handed half to Max.

"Can I see?" Etta said, and Slater gave her the other half.

She shuffled through the pages. "These work addresses are all in Koreatown," she said finally.

"Koreans are her target victims."

"You're sure it's bunco?" Max said.

"Not completely." He looked to Etta. "What's your estimation?"

She looked up from the pages. "I'd say I'm seventy-five percent sure it's a scam." Flipping to the next sheet, she added, "The workplaces listed here are mostly consumer-facing businesses. Shops and restaurants and services. I'd say Kim's marks are mostly petite bourgeoisie."

Max eyed her. "Petty what now?"

"It means small business owners," she said. "People who don't have to sell their labor in the capitalist system but who don't own the means of production either."

"You sound like a pinko. You know you're functionally a capitalist, right? I just paid you cash money for working that stakeout."

"That makes you petite bourgeoisie."

He looked to Slater and raised his eyebrows. "It's not every day I get called petite. What do you need from these people?"

"I want to know what Kim has been selling them. I know she calls it a crypto investment, but do they know what it is specifically? Have they been told that Kim's product runs on blockchain? Do they even know what blockchain is?"

"Why does blockchain matter?" Max said.

"If she's not using blockchain, it's not really a crypto product."

Etta stood up. "I have to get back to school." Turning to Max, she said, "Can I get the wire? I'm going to record my meeting with his target tomorrow."

Max stepped over to the boxy black safe that sat in the corner behind Slater's desk. It was probably a hundred years old, contemporary with the building, complete with faded gold lettering on the door. Dropping to one knee, Max dialed in the combination, and twisted the handle, and pulled it open. He didn't bother to shield the combination from Etta, as there was no way she could read the numbers on the dial from where she was standing. They were building trust with her, but not to the point yet where she had access to the safe.

Max took out the wire, literally a length of wire with a small mike at one end and a slim black box at the other, and handed it to her. Closing the door, he gave the dial a spin and stood up.

"You remember how it works?"

"No sweat," Etta said.

"Tomorrow, don't call me Slater," he said. "I'm using an alias with these lowlifes. I'm John Slade."

"I won't call you anything. If I even see you. The game I'm running is that we've never met." She walked out, calling back to them, "Later, fellas."

Slater heard the front door close, and her key flip the bolt.

"She'll be running a game tomorrow," Max said. "Today she was referring to our target as 'the square.'"

"I feel like such a bad influence." He frowned. "At least I didn't teach her how to shoot."

Max chuckled. "Some time at the range doesn't mean she's going to start packing. In this business you need to know your way around weapons."

"I can't argue with that."

They took the elevator down together, and crossed to the parking lot. Max climbed into his matte-gray Challenger, and Slater followed him out onto the street. They were both headed to the same neighborhood, but he soon lost sight of the Challenger in the traffic.

FIFTEEN

SLATER'S FIRST STOP IN Koreatown was a restaurant. The name on the client list was Park Su-ho. He sighed. There were a lot of people named Park in this town. Pulling up on the joint, it looked open. He found a meter, and pulled in, then walked back. There were only a few diners in the early afternoon, sitting at the tables farther back, and at the register near the door was a woman about Kim's age, her hair tied back. When he stepped in, she smiled in greeting.

"I need to talk to Park Su-ho."

Her expression shifted. "That's me. What can I do for you?" Her English was clear but it wasn't her first language, as she had a subtle accent.

"I'm investigating a financial product sold by a woman named Kim. I understand you bought in."

"Who are you?"

He dug in his hip pocket and handed over a business card. She looked it over, then met his gaze.

"Why is an insurance company investigating Kim's business?"

"We need to know what you were told when you signed up," Slater said.

"Just that Kim had created a new cryptocurrency. I know there are a lot of them, but hers is doing really well. It hasn't lost value when others have crashed."

"She told you it was doing well, or you actually got interest payments, or dividends?"

"Why is your company interested in this?"

"We need more detail on the crypto product, and how it works."

"I'm not a technical person. Why don't you talk to Kim? She's a real spark. I know she'd be happy to explain it."

"Thanks for your time," he said, and walked out.

Next was an autobody shop, not far away, on a busy boulevard. Slater drove over, and found a street space up the block, and fed the meter. The name on the client list was another Park. As he walked up to the place, he found a mechanic in coveralls standing at the open hood of a Toyota.

"Is Park here?" Slater said, approaching the guy.

The mechanic turned and gave him a pointed once-over. "Are you a customer?"

"I'm the guy who's going to rough you up unless you tell me where Park is."

He scowled. "A bill collector, is that it? Piss off."

Slater stepped closer and slapped him hard, a firm kovac, right and then left. "Why do you make me do this to you?" he said through his teeth.

The guy moved fast and punched him in the gut, but Slater managed to get in a left, snapping his jaw.

Planting a hand on his shoulder, the guy shoved him away. Slater stepped back, and straightened up, and massaged his stomach with a hand.

"That really hurt."

Fists balled, teeth set, the mechanic stepped toward him, and Slater quickly took a defensive stance. A guy with gray hair stepped out of the office and shouted at them.

"What is this? Stop it."

The mechanic instantly froze, and dropped his hands, and glared at Slater.

"You must be Park," Slater said.

"Are you OK?"

"I will be." He massaged his belly and jutted his chin at the mechanic. "You should teach your grease monkeys some manners."

"What do you want?" Park said. He spoke with an accent.

"To talk about your investments with a woman named Kim."

His eyebrows shot up. "OK. Come into the office."

It was a cramped space, grimy with years of machine oil tramped in on work boots and greasy hands. Park sat behind his cluttered desk, and gestured at the pair of chairs in front.

"Are you from the authorities?"

"I'm not the police or the government," Slater said, and pulled out his business card, handing it over before he sat down. "I'm private. We're looking into Kim's financial product."

"Insurance," Park said, half to himself, gazing at the card. He looked up. "Kim made a cryptocurrency."

"How do you know that?" Slater said.

"What do you mean?"

"How do you know what she's selling is a crypto product?"

"Because it is," he said, and waved a hand. "She said it is. I know her well."

"When did you buy in?"

"It's been a few months. What is the insurance industry's interest in her?"

"I want to know how much information you had when you bought in," Slater said. "Did she give you a prospectus?"

"What's that?"

"A document explaining what the product is, and what's going to happen with your investment."

"There's nothing like that. She's a smart woman. She makes a lot of money. Lives in a big house."

"Have you received statements about your holdings?" Slater said. "What about interest, or dividends? Have there been any payouts?"

"I'm not going to talk about that." He sat up. "Unless you can be more specific about why you're asking, Mr. Ibáñez, you'll have to leave."

Slater got up, and glanced around the garage as he walked out, but the mechanic wasn't in sight.

The next place on the list was just a couple of blocks farther up the boulevard—he could walk. It was a retail shop, and the door was unlocked. He looked around as he entered. It was all handbags, on racks and tables and hanging on the wall behind the counter.

The place was devoid of customers, and when he stepped in, a clerk came out of the back, and stood at the register. In her twenties, she had long hair, and a knit sweater, and beamed at him.

"Are you shopping for yourself, or for a girl-friend?" she said.

This woman was clearly a native speaker. Slater stepped up to the counter.

"I'm looking for a woman named Jung."

Her smile faded. "I'm Jung. We all are. It's our family name."

"Jung Ji-young, specifically. Is that you?"

"I'm Ellen. Why are you asking about Ji-young?"

"She invested in a financial product with a woman named Kim," Slater said.

She scowled. "Ji-young is my mother. Do you work for Kim?"

"I'm an insurance investigator." He handed over his card.

"What does Kim have to do with insurance?"

"We're trying to ascertain what her investors knew before they bought in."

"That makes it sound like you think it's a racket."

Slater raised his eyebrows. "Is it a racket?"

"I'm convinced it is. My mother knows Kim from the community, and she trusts her. But I think she's getting scammed."

"What evidence is there of that?"

Ellen watched him for a moment, her expression thoughtful. "What's your end game?"

"I need to know whether it's a legitimate investment or not."

"Why? And if it's not, will you try to shut it down?"

"Not single-handedly," Slater said. "But the more information I have, the better."

"I have a file on Kim. Give me a minute." She turned and stepped into the back.

While he waited Slater glanced around the shop, and lifted a little black purse from a table. The price tag on it said $1,200. He set it down again. If that was on the dollar rack in a thrift store he wouldn't even look at it twice.

When Ellen returned, she had a file folder in hand, and set it on the counter, and folded it open.

"This is Kim's portfolio."

"She gave your mother this?"

Ellen nodded, and he pulled it closer, and flipped through the pages. It was mostly in Korean, and it looked like the same material as on her website. There was a color printout of a magazine article in English that he hadn't seen before.

As Slater pulled it out of the stack and set it aside, Ellen tapped it with a manicured nail. "Look at this clipping. It was prominently placed in the sales package. It makes you think it's from this magazine, right?"

Slater leaned in to look closer. The masthead *Wall Street Tonight* spanned the top of the page, and below it was a smiling portrait of Kim, sitting in a wing chair and looking heavily styled, with columns of text around the photo. He'd seen this glossy weekly. It was the kind of thing that got stacked with the fashion magazines and copies of *National Geographic* at the barbershop or the dentist's office.

"It's not from the magazine?" he said.

"It was in the magazine, but it wasn't written by anyone there. If you read it, the copy is full of grammatical errors. And see this?" Ellen pointed to the fine gray print in the corner of the item. "It says 'featured partner.' That means it's advertising, not editorial. She paid them to print this."

"I can see how that makes it look like a con," Slater said. "She's surfing on their reputation, not her own."

"At first glance, you think, oh, Kim has been featured in a big business magazine. It's enough to convince people with no understanding of crypto that she's savvy and could make them rich."

"Your mom isn't a crypto person?"

Ellen scoffed. "Beyond getting her cell phone to work, she's not technical at all."

"I've talked to a couple other investors. I'd say so far none of them are experienced with crypto."

She shifted on her feet. "Think about who Kim is going after. I'd bet most of the people are first generation, so English isn't their first language. They don't know that 'featured partner' means paid advertising. It's easier to mislead them. Like how she fooled my mother."

"Can I take this?"

"I'll make copies for you." She met his gaze. "Maybe you can return the favor. Can your company share whatever information you have?"

"Are you going to try to shut Kim down?" Slater said.

"How would I even do that? My mother still trusts her, even though I know our money's gone. But I bet Kim is still recruiting. Maybe I can spread the word, and slow her down, and save someone else the headache."

She scooped up the folder and stepped into the back. Gazing out at the street, Slater saw that the afternoon traffic was slowing down. He could hear the distant sound of a copier shuffling paper.

When Ellen returned with the photocopies, he pulled out his phone. "What's your cell number?"

Once he'd thumb-typed it into his contact list and scooped up the sheaf of copies, he walked out and headed back to the Thunderbird. Setting the paperwork on the passenger seat, he drove the few blocks to the workplace of the next name on the list.

Slater hit four more businesses, with varying degrees of success, unable to communicate with one person at all, and rapidly getting eighty-sixed from another. Eventually he was walking up on a work address for a woman named Lee.

The name of the business didn't give away what it did, but when he pulled open the door, he saw that it was a dry cleaner. A big rolling rack of hanging garments shrouded in filmy plastic stood idle behind the counter. Max was standing at the register, talking to the clerk, a skinny guy in his teens or early twenties with a dark mustache and round glasses, wearing an argyle sweater. Pausing inside the door, Slater listened to their interaction.

"I don't think my name will mean anything to you, but here's one of my cards," Max said, and palmed a bill, and let the guy get a glimpse of it. "Where's Mr. Lee?"

The clerk reached for his hand, and the bill quickly disappeared. "He'll be back tomorrow."

"You could have told me that for free," Max said.

He glanced toward the doorway and noticed Slater standing there. Briefly meeting his eye, Slater raised his eyebrows and stepped out to the sidewalk.

"Is Mr. Lee a duplicate?" Max said, stepping

outside. He pulled the sheaf of paper from his inside jacket pocket and folded it open.

"I probably had the wife," Slater said. "I've got a Lee at this address too. A woman."

"It's K-town, Slater." Max folded the list and tucked it away. "Everybody's named Lee, or Kim, or Park."

"Those names definitely cover a lot of people."

"Are you ready to knock off? I've got some ideas."

"I've seen enough too."

"Do you know a diner or a coffee joint around here?" Max said. "We can debrief."

"Let me check where it is." Slater stepped toward the curb to get out of the path of a pedestrian and looked at his phone. Finally he gestured up the block. "It's right up there. We can walk."

As they set off, a prowl car passed on the street, moving fast, its light bar flickering but with no siren. It pulled up at the red curb in front of the dry cleaner.

"That's odd," Max said, and paused to look back. "I didn't see anyone else go into that place. I know they're not getting robbed."

A lone uniform climbed out of the car and hustled inside, and they kept walking. When Slater glanced back a moment later, the cop was striding toward them.

"Heads up," he said. "There's a boy in blue headed this way."

"He's definitely coming for us," Max said, and they both stood and watched him approach.

It was just the one cop, around thirty, maybe, his black hair slicked back. He was buff, and had a determined look in his eye.

"Do you know what white privilege is?" Max said quietly.

"Of course I do. I'm surprised that you do."

"I'm dating a black woman. I've heard all about it. Just keep your mouth shut and let me work my privilege."

Slater glared at him, but the cop was already on them, his brow furrowed.

"What can we do for you, officer …" Max said, his tone jovial, and looked pointedly at his nameplate. "Officer Lee. I should let you know I'm armed."

He had to tell him that, Slater knew. It was one of the rules of having a gun permit. Max sounded more glib than privileged right now, but maybe that's how it worked.

"What's your game, exactly?" the cop said. "What did you want with the dry cleaner?"

"I know you're sharp, officer." He gestured to the shoulder of his uniform. "They don't give the stripes away to dummies. Did the dry cleaner call you?"

"I've got a better one for you. Who the hell are you?"

"Let me show you my ID."

Max reached into his jacket, and pulled out a black folding wallet, and handed it over.

"You're a PI," the cop said, studying it. "That explains the sidearm. Are you working for Kim?"

"I'm investigating Kim."

His expression softened. "The clerk thought you were there to shake more money out of him."

Max took his wallet back. "I'm just asking some questions."

"The clerk said you slipped him cash. A bribe. He

assumed you were a crook."

"The other side of that," Slater said, "is that the clerk was happy to take the dough. I watched it myself. If you're going to call it a bribe, the clerk was complicit."

The cop looked at him, his brow furrowing. "Who are you, exactly?"

"I'm Max's operative."

Max waved a hand. "Cash greases the wheels, Officer Lee. Loosens lips. It was just a small gratuity."

The guy shifted on his feet, watching Max. "He's my little brother. He wasn't sure what you wanted."

"Is he the one who invested with Kim?" Slater said.

He glanced at Slater, then eyed Max. "Why are you investigating Kim? And who are you doing it for?"

"Unfortunately, officer, I can't really disclose my clients and their motives."

"We can tell you it's somebody in the same situation as your brother," Slater said. "One of Kim's investors."

The guy eyed him for a moment. Slater could see the wheels turning.

"It wasn't my brother," he said finally. "It was our parents. They went hard for Kim's flimflam. Are you working toward a civil suit? I would love to get them into something like that."

"We're not there yet, but I can give you a contact," Slater said, and dug out his phone. "A woman named Ellen Jung. Her mother also invested with Kim. Ellen thinks Kim is using her social connections to prey on first-gen Koreans."

Stepping closer, the cop snapped a photo of Slater's screen with his own phone. "That's exactly who my parents are. I'll talk to her." He looked to Max. "If you learn anything significant that you can disclose, can you share it with me?"

"Give us your cell number," Slater said, and thumb-typed it into his phone as the guy recited it. Looking up, he met his eye. "What time does your shift end?"

"Why?" His eyes narrowed. "Are you hitting on me?"

"I'm glad you can tell."

"It's not going to happen." He scoffed. "Thanks for the contact." Turning, he walked back toward the prowl car.

As they started toward the diner again, walking abreast, Slater noticed that Max had a stupid grin on his face.

"What's so damn funny?" he said, eyeing him sidelong.

"You think I'm all smooth with women," Max said. "And here you managed to seamlessly lay your mack down."

"It didn't get me anywhere. With you, they flirt back."

"Aren't you in a relationship?" Max said.

"Yeah, there's that."

When they stepped into the diner, the place was busy, most of the tables occupied, the din of conversation filling the room. A woman standing at the register waved them to an open table along the wall. Once they'd sat down, a woman in her fifties in a dark-red apron stepped over.

"The basic bibimbap," Max said, raising his voice to be heard.

"Same," Slater said, and to Max, "Will you eat my egg?"

"No, man, I don't want your damn egg. One's enough."

Slater handed the menu to the server. "Hold the egg on mine." As she stepped away, he eyed Max. "So what's the dope on Kim's investors?"

"I went to nine places. All in K-town. Etta was right: they're all small business owners."

"Mine too. And everybody's working on the weekend."

"You have to admire that work ethic." He reached inside his jacket and pulled out the client list. From the back of the sheaf of paper he extracted half a dozen pages. "I got this from one of them."

It was the colorful promotional stuff in Korean as well as the bogus business magazine article, Slater saw, leafing through them.

"I saw this today too."

"A couple of them spoke no English," Max said, "so it was a very brief interview."

"The ones I talked to had zero understanding of what they were investing in. That was universal."

Max nodded. "Same. Nobody even had a concept of what crypto actually is. They just knew what Kim told them."

"So they're patsies."

"It looks that way to me."

Max sat back as the server set down their food, then stirred in his egg, and shoveled in a few mouthfuls with his chopsticks.

"What happens if one of these birds reports back to Kim that someone is sniffing around?" he said. "I gave some of them my card."

"I had to smear mine around too." Slater gestured with a chunk of pink pickled radish gripped in his sticks. "But the name on it is different from the one I'm using at the factory, so Kim won't connect it to me."

"Do you think she'll skip the country?"

"I suppose she might be worried that there's suspicion of her. But that cop was talking about a civil suit. It makes me think Kim is careful enough with her grift that she won't be arrested for fraud. If there was any chance of criminal charges, the cop would have gone there already."

"Nobody's paying you to look into Kim, are they?" Max said. "Didn't it start with some pilfered landscaping?"

Slater groaned. "I probably need a reality check. I already figured out what I needed to. That Zane and Kim are both multilevel scammers. I should probably focus on how to shut down their thievery."

"But it doesn't feel right to just walk away from the crypto grift."

He scraped together the last of his rice and eyed him. Max knew him better than he thought. "You called it."

SIXTEEN

T WILIGHT WAS FADING TO darkness as Slater got to his house, and parked the Thunderbird, and climbed the stairs. It felt empty without Pike. The place wasn't complete without him in it. Like it was just waiting for the guy.

Not bothering to turn the lights on, he stepped over to the French doors, and looked out at the glittering towers of the Financial District in the distance. He stretched out on the sofa and pulled off his boots. He knew Pike's event was tonight. Something about his mother's job. They were giving her a dinner and a plaque. It was later over there—he might be done with it by now. He sent Pike a text:

How did it go?

A minute later his phone buzzed.

"How's the mama's boy?" Slater said as he picked up.

"Hey, I'm in good company," Pike said. "Remember when Aeneas was in the Trojan War? His mama jumped into the middle of the battle to help the guy. No fucks given."

"To be fair, it wasn't that risky for her. She was a goddess."

"I was talking to my mom today. You know she basically picked my career for me, and she doesn't even remember doing it."

"She wanted you to be in law enforcement?"

"Not specifically," Pike said, "but she knew what I'd be good at in college. She actually chose all my courses my freshman year."

"You and Aeneas both, then. Mama's boys."

"I've seen you with Doris. You're not ashamed that you love your mama either."

"Come to think of it," Slater said, "she's the one who got me into community college to do horticulture. It definitely wasn't my idea."

"She knows you better than anyone. She knew you'd be good at it."

"Damn it," he snapped. "So it's the same story. Our mothers mapped out our careers for us."

"They nailed it, didn't they?" Pike said. "I like what I'm doing, and you're passionate about greenery."

"Isn't that a little unsettling? I feel like I just figured out that I've been had."

"I don't think it's just about you. We think we're autonomous, but our mothers kind of hold up the sky."

They talked some more, and after he ended the call, Slater gazed out at the darkness. Guys or booze or both. It was that time of day. Even though the rules said he could hook up with other people when Pike was away, it felt like he shouldn't. He'd just talked to the guy, professed his love to him. But he hadn't stretched that muscle in days. He needed to do something about it.

Opening the hookup app on his phone, he started to scroll through the body parts and torsos and dick picks. There were lots of options on Saturday night. Almost instantly a message popped up:

u hawt. your place?

Slater checked the guy's profile. A little older than him, with a decent head shot, a nice smile. A little scruffy, maybe, but basically fuckable, and just 0.2 miles away. He texted back:

No drugs.

In a second message he sent his address, then heaved himself up, and trotted down to his bedroom to change his shirt. A tight white T-shirt got the best reaction from guys. He was just pulling it over his head when the doorbell rang. That was fast.

He hustled down to the front door and pulled it open. The guy beamed at him.

"You look like your profile photo."

"You don't," Slater said. He was years older and had a thick beard now, wearing a heavy dark-green field jacket.

The guy waved a hand. "I haven't had time to update it. Are you going to let me in?"

"Are you sober?"

"Totally."

Slater moved aside, and as the guy stepped past, he picked up the unmistakable tang of homelessness. Vinegar and ammonia and ancient cheese. Now was the moment to eighty-six him, he knew, and considered doing that, watching him start to climb the stairs. Finally he heaved a sigh and closed the door. A bad smell didn't mean the sex would be bad. People lost their housing before their cell phones, and he couldn't fault the guy for wanting to hook up despite his circumstances. But it changed things. He followed him up the stairs.

The guy paused on the landing. "Where's the bed?"

"Why don't we have a shower?"

"I guess I'm a little ripe, huh."

"I don't mind."

Slater pointed him to the bathroom and followed him inside. Turning to face him, the guy massaged Slater's biceps, then put his palms on his pecs. Leaning in to meet his mouth, it tasted like stale beer and cigarettes.

Slater pulled back. "Why don't I throw your clothes in the washer? You jump in the shower, and when I get back, I'll fuck your brains out."

He grinned. "Deal."

Quickly ditching his jacket and stripping his clothes off, he emptied his pants pockets, and piled his phone and his wallet and some tattered paper next to the sink. As he stepped into the shower stall, Slater scooped up his clothes. He heard the water go on as he started down the stairs.

The clothes really stank, and he had to breathe through his mouth. The machines were at the back of the garage, and he threw the guy's jacket and everything else into the washer and started it. In the laundry sink he washed his hands and forearms with soap and hot water, just in case he'd come in contact with any contagious crawlies.

Back upstairs, the guy was luxuriating in the steamy hot water, humming to himself. When he spotted Slater, he jutted his chin.

"You should come in."

Slater stripped and stepped in with him. He had the water set hot. Grabbing a loofah and the soap, he ran it over the guy's body, both to clean off the grime and because exploring his skin was a turn-on. He washed the guy's hair, and his beard, and his junk, then squeezed his chubby cock. He quickly got hard, and stood close. Slater drew his cock between his legs, and with his hands on his waist, pulled him in, working him by thrusting against him.

The water streaming over them, he locked their mouths together. The guy wrapped his arms around Slater's back, his chin digging into his shoulder, and thrust between his legs, building up speed. A minute later he yelped and came, straining into him.

When the guy pulled back, he was red-faced. He took hold of Slater's woody. "You should fuck me."

"Give me a second."

Slater stepped out of the shower, and walked over to the bedroom, dripping water all the way. He grabbed a condom and lube and went back, rolling it on outside the shower and then stepping in.

The guy stood with his forearms braced against the wall, and from behind Slater ran his hands over his chest, and his belly, and gently penetrated him. The guy whimpered but pressed back against him. Mouthing his ear, Slater shifted deeper, wrapping an arm around his waist, and around his chest. He worked up to pounding him, then came with a roar, straining hard into him.

Pulling back, he ditched the condom, and caught his breath, and stepped out of the shower. He'd mostly dried off by the time the guy turned off the water and came out. Slater handed him a towel, and threw his own on the floor to mop up the puddles and his wet footprints.

"Do you have anything to eat?"

"I'll order you something," Slater said. "You can eat while you wait for your clothes."

He beamed. "Thanks."

"What do you want me to get?"

"Does that Italian place on Sunset deliver?"

Slater grabbed his phone from his jeans, and stepped into the bedroom, and made the order. Once he'd pulled on a pair of boxers and a T-shirt, he trotted down to the garage and loaded the guy's clothes into the dryer. Back upstairs, he found the guy in his bedroom, naked, with all the closet doors open.

"You have nice stuff."

"No, I don't. Do you want a robe?"

He pulled out Pike's bathrobe, and waited while he pulled it on, and led him upstairs.

"Do you have anything to drink?" the guy said.

"Tap water."

"I mean booze."

"No. I've got stuff to do. Why don't you park it here." Slater pointed to the dining table.

The guy pulled out a chair and sat, and folded his arms, and knotted his brow. "I'm not a junkie."

"Nobody said you were."

Slater walked over to the sofa, out of view of the table. He wanted the guy out. He never should have let him in. But that ship had sailed. Picking up his twelve-step book, he got into it. Before long he heard the guy opening kitchen cabinets. He could let it go, he decided. He could eat whatever he found, and there was nothing to steal.

When the doorbell rang, he got up and walked through the kitchen. The guy was standing there eating a granola bar. Every cupboard door in the room was open, the way Rosa had done for the big clean before he'd moved in.

Slater frowned at him. "Did you find what you needed?"

"You've got plenty of booze," the guy called after him.

Trotting down to the front door, he retrieved the food, and hustled back up, and set it on the dining table.

"Sweet calzone goodness," the guy said as he dropped into a chair and pulled open the bag. He looked up at Slater. "There's only one."

"I'm not eating."

He hustled down the stairs again to the garage. The dryer was still running, but he pulled the clothes out anyway. They felt mostly dry. He carried them upstairs, and piled them on the other end of the dining table, and sat to watch the guy wolfing his food.

Finally he sat back. "I'm so happy right now."

"Your clothes are dry," Slater said.

"Nice. So do you have a TV? What do you do in the evening?"

"You have to go."

He frowned. "I thought we could hang out. Maybe I could sleep over. If you don't want me in your bed, I could sleep in that other bedroom. If your roommate isn't around."

"You have to go," Slater said, "and you have to go now."

He scowled and got up. "You don't have to be a dick about it." Tossing the bathrobe on a chair, he pulled on his shirt. "I could call the cops, you know. Tell them you shot me up with dope and sexually assaulted me."

"How do you think that would play out for you?" Slater rose and put his hands on his hips. "If you need a night in the hoosegow, go kick a prowl car. They'll help you out. Leave me out of it."

He scoffed, and tightened his belt, and walked to the stairs. Slater followed him and watched as he grabbed his possessions from the side of the sink and stuffed them into his pockets.

"Can I at least charge up my phone?" he said, stepping out to the landing.

"No." Slater extended an arm toward the stairs. "Out."

"You're kind of an ass." As he trudged down, he spoke over his shoulder. "The sex was totally underwhelming, by the way. I've had better orgasms from rubbing up against a utility pole."

"Lucky you," Slater said, and once he was out the front door, flipped the bolt.

Up in the kitchen he threw the food containers in the garbage bin, and despite the evening chill opened a couple of windows to dispel the stench of greasy tomato sauce. From the fifth he poured two fingers into a tumbler, and stood at the French doors, looking out at the city. The first slurp was always the best, and he savored it, relished the burn in his nose, and coughed involuntarily from the fumes.

"Underwhelming" was the word for it. Maybe that stupid twelve-step book had a point. It talked about feeling empty versus feeling fulfilled. He'd scratched that itch but it still felt like it was a total waste of time.

SEVENTEEN

▧▧▧▧▧▧▧▧▧

IN THE MORNING, WHEN he woke, Slater's head hurt, that familiar dull ache over his eyes. He could smell the nauseating by-products of the booze clinging to his skin. When he sat up, the room didn't spin. Maybe it wouldn't be too bad.

"Idiot," he muttered, and took a deep breath.

In the bathroom he shook a couple of tablets into his mouth from the ibuprofen bottle, then spent some time upstairs lounging with a mug of coffee. He made toast with lots of vegan butter slathered on it. The grease would counteract the hangover.

He needed to leave soon, he realized, if he was going to get to Kim's place before Etta. In his bedroom he pulled on his jeans and a dark work shirt, then went down to the garage, and grabbed a pair of work gloves from the bench.

Most of tony Hancock Park was prewar, with mansions on ordinary lots, before the überwealthy started building sprawling estates in the hills. He cruised through the neighborhood to Kim's address. It was an impressive structure, set back beyond a verdant green lawn. That really ought to be illegal, putting that much water on it, considering the ongoing drought.

Slater street-parked past the pull-through driveway, and grabbed his gloves, and climbed out, tucking them in the back of his belt. When he walked up the drive, in front of the house he found the familiar Benz, and in front of it a car with a Bimmer badge. It was a model he'd never seen before. Whatever it was, it looked new. The third car was gray with sports-car lines. He didn't recognize the logo. Pulling out his phone, he took a photo of the badge and did an image search.

It was a luxury brand called Preliator. This vehicle cost over three hundred grand. He scoffed and walked toward the entrance, but paused to check out the hedge along the front of the house. It was tightly trimmed and blooming in showy pink flowers. A *syriacus* hibiscus. Those were unusual here. It was too warm for them—they grew in places where it was colder and more humid, like the Bay area. And why in hell were they blooming in April?

At the door he rang the bell, and Kim soon appeared, wearing a dark skirt and a tweed jacket.

"There's a workers entrance in the back, next to the garage," Kim said, frowning at him. "Have you never done this before?"

"How did you get the *syriacus* to bloom out of season?" Slater said.

"You mean the hedge?" She looked at it. "It blooms a lot. You'd have to ask my gardener." Beckoning him to follow, she stepped inside.

They were in a grand foyer with an ornate chandelier. With all the intricate plasterwork around the stairs, it had to be prewar.

"You look rough," Kim said over her shoulder. "Are you hung over?"

"I'm not used to working on Sunday."

"Or was it too many *cervezas* last night?"

She led him past the stairway into a hall, and then stepped through a double doorway. The room was dramatic—it was round, with a shallow dome high overhead, and bookshelves lining the walls. The only windows were high up, above the shelves. There were a couple of spindly desks, the kind they had in the public library, with no drawers, and in the center of the room a squat round dark-wood table, directly under the plasterwork in the center of the domed ceiling. A stylized rose, maybe, Slater thought, gazing up at it. Some artisan had crafted that a lifetime ago.

"This is the library," Kim said.

"It's impressive."

"I know. That's my son, Steve." She gestured across the space to one of the desks, where a guy sat gazing at a laptop. In his early twenties, maybe, he glanced up at them, and Slater jutted his chin in greeting. Steve quickly looked down.

"Don't worry about Steve," Kim said. "He's neurodivergent. He won't get in your way."

She stepped over to the desk that sat across the room from Steve's. A stack of cardboard bound with plastic bands sat on the carpet next to it, and on the desk was a utility knife and two rolls of packing tape shrink-wrapped together.

"There should be plenty of boxes," Kim said, and

waved at the room. "All the books have to go. Just box them up."

Slater surveyed the space. Less than half the shelves were filled with books, but there were a lot of shelves. Others sat empty or bore tchotchkes or framed photos.

"Steve," Kim called, raising her voice. "This is John. He's here to work. Leave him alone." With that, she walked out.

Digging out his phone, Slater checked the time. He was running early—Etta wasn't due here for half an hour. Grabbing the utility knife, he cut the bands on the top bundle of cardboard. He folded open a box, and taped the bottom, and set it on the desk. Once he'd pulled on his gloves, he started loading books into it, then taped it closed and heaved it to the floor. By the time he started the fourth box, his arms ached. He hadn't realized books were so freaking heavy.

Steve rose from the desk. His pecs were pleasing under his silky green shirt, and he was wearing a print skirt hemmed just above the knee. Slater mopped his brow with the back of his glove and called to him.

"It's not every day I walk into a round room."

Steve stepped over to him and held his gaze as he spoke. "I live here, so I walk into it every day. But you mean round rooms are unusual."

"In my experience, they are."

Steve looked him over. "You're hot. I like the way your jeans fit. The work gloves make you look strong."

"Are you hitting on me," Slater said, "or is that a neurodivergent thing? Like not having filters?"

"Maybe both."

"How old are you?"

"I'm twenty-two," Steve said.

Studying his face, Slater decided he believed him, even though he could be younger.

"Have you ever slept with a man before?"

"I'm different, John. I'm not disabled. I've had sex with lots of people. Men and women and nonbinary types. Do you do that?"

"I guess I'm more narrow-minded," Slater said. "I only sleep with guys."

"Well, I've probably had sex with just as many men as you have."

Slater seriously doubted that, but he said, "OK."

"The best part about men is kissing them. I really like that."

"Kissing is pretty great," Slater said. "You should let me show you my technique sometime."

"Is that a neurotypical thing, like overpromising events that never happen? Or is it that you don't actually want to do that because I'm a boy in a dress?"

"That's a skirt, not a dress. And I'm not the gender police. I don't care what you're wearing. You've definitely got the gams to pull off a miniskirt." He took his gloves off, and tucked them into his belt, and stepped closer. "You're wearing guyliner."

"Is that a turnoff?"

"It looks great. It makes your eyes pop. I used to wear it when I was in high school. I wasn't nearly as precise about it as you are."

Slater put his hand on the back of his neck.

"Don't touch me," Steve said evenly, holding his gaze.

He dropped his hand and frowned. "I'm getting mixed signals here."

"Only the lips. Your hand is too much sensory input. It conflicts with the oral experience."

"So Steve doesn't want to get pawed. I get it."

"There's an odor too. On your skin. It's not just sweat."

"Dude," he said intently.

"It's not bad," Steve said. "Just noticeable."

"You're probably picking up on my hangover."

"I've never smelled that before. I don't drink."

Slater showed his palms, then leaned in to kiss him. The guy was intent and methodical, and it was more intense because there were no other physical sensations. Maybe there was something to it, the thing about conflicting input. He could feel his dick tightening in his jeans.

Pulling back, Slater massaged his own crotch. "Do you want to take this farther? I can fuck you, or I can smoke you. Where's your room?"

"I don't really want to do that."

"It's your call," Slater said. "But when a man is tired of blowjobs, he's tired of life."

"Aren't you supposed to be working?"

"I don't really want to do that. Where's your mom's office?"

"She doesn't have one. Not in the house. Why?"

"No reason," Slater said. "Does she have a laptop or a safe?"

"You sound like a thief."

"You sound like you want a punch in the face."

"It's just a statement of fact. There's no reason to get angry."

Slater took a breath. He knew he wasn't deliberately trying to provoke him. "Have you met her business partner, Zane?"

"My father isn't happy that she's in business with a man. Zane isn't allowed to come here."

"Is your father home today?"

"He's working. In Seoul. That's him in the photo." Steve gestured to a bookshelf.

Slater stepped over to look. It was a framed portrait of the three of them, dressed formally and posed with a mottled-blue photo studio backdrop. His father had a solid jaw, and great hair, and a keen look in his eye.

"He's a knockout," Slater said. "How did your mother get mixed up with a slab of cream cheese like him?"

"You're being weird."

Slater turned to him. "Because I think he's hot? It's just a statement of fact."

"I'm attracted to you, and you're attracted to my father. It's weird."

He shrugged. "The dick wants what the dick wants."

"Do you want to watch something? A piece I've been working on."

"A video?"

"It's a performance piece."

Slater raised his eyebrows. "Of course I want to watch that."

"You have to sit in one of the chairs." He pointed to the desk where he'd been sitting. "You can't stand up until it's over, no matter what."

"I can handle that." Slater walked over to the desk, and felt his phone buzz in his pants. When he pulled it out to check, he found a text from Etta:

Here. We're set up in the dining room. Left off the foyer, then through the kitchen. Kim's desk and files are in here too.

The dining room seemed like an odd place for a desk in a house this big. He wouldn't be able to poke around in it if they were hanging out in the same room. Even this room would be a better place to do business, but there were no file cabinets, no office equipment. Tucking his phone away, he pulled out a chair and positioned it to face the room.

Steve was over at the shelves, where he picked up a coil of yellow nylon rope. An oblong red object was attached to it. Walking over to the table in the middle of the room, he piled the rope on it, then went to the double doors, and pulled them closed, and flipped off the room lights. It got darker, but the space was still dimly illuminated from the high windows.

Steve walked over to where he was sitting, and stooped to peer at his laptop, and tapped at it. An audio track started playing. It sounded like a synthesizer, with deep bass, and it had a slow tempo. It was almost not even music, just lazily drifting sound.

Stepping back to the table in the center of the space, Steve deftly climbed up on it, his skirt flaring to reveal a glimpse of his underpants. He scooped up the nylon rope, and looked at the red attachment. Suddenly it flared with blue-white light. It was some kind of battery-powered lamp, Slater realized, like the work lights that hung under the hood when you were working on an engine. It was a bright point in the darkened room.

Steve started to spin the lamp around his body, rotating with it, fast enough to get it airborne. As he slowly let the rope out, the lamp gradually made a larger circle, with Steve at the center of it, turning with it, always facing the lamp. His movements were small compared to the growing arc of the lamp, and eventually the point of light was almost out at the bookshelves.

That table had to be in the exact center of the room, as the lamp was within a few feet of touching the shelves as it made the circuit, over Slater's head and around again, never closer to any of them than the others. He saw now why he wasn't supposed to stand up. That nylon rope would wrap itself around his neck.

Slater focused on the orbiting point of light sailing around the room, and the slow flat music. It was kind of mesmerizing. Eventually Steve started to reel it in again, and in a minute the lamp was in his hands, and he turned it off. He hopped down off the table, and went to flip on the room lights, then stepped over to kill the audio.

"What did you think?" Steve said, holding his gaze.

Slater sat up in his chair. "It's a great piece for a round room. I felt immersed in it. Like I wasn't just watching. I was inside it. What does it mean?"

"I'm not really sure."

"How can you not be sure? You created it. You must have some insight."

Standing there, Steve blinked, staring absently at him. "Maybe it's something about knowing that things are happening, but not being directly involved. Like the light at the end of the rope. I know it's there, and it's moving fast, but I can't touch it."

"I can see that."

"In English lit there's a saying: Trust the tale, not the teller. Postmodernists think that's hogwash. They say the quality of something is meaningless, and all that matters is the artist's intention. But personally I think that idea is hogwash. I like the older framework. Where you just have to experience art for what it is."

"You studied literature?"

"English lit is my major. At UCLA. I'm graduating this spring."

"What's the plan once you graduate?"

"I have no plan," Steve said. "I'll have my degree."

"You're not going to work?"

"I don't need to. My parents have money."

"Don't you feel kind of sheltered living here?" Slater said. "If you were out in the world, you could create more stuff like this. In bigger places. You could show it to people."

"Where would I live? It's safe here. My mother is protecting me."

"Maybe you don't need protecting. Sometimes plants do better when you don't coddle them. If you water them all the time and groom their leaves, they don't do very well. But if you ignore them, and let them face the harsh environment, they thrive."

"I'm not a plant."

"Hmm," Slater said, and pursed his lips, watching him. "Where's the bathroom?"

"There's one in the hall."

EIGHTEEN

H E ROSE AND WALKED to the double doors, and stepped out, pulling them closed behind him. Standing there for a moment, he could hear faint voices somewhere deep in the house.

He tried the first door in the hallway. That was the bathroom. The next one opened onto a big room with lounge furniture and windows onto the front lawn. The door on the opposite side of the hall was locked. Stepping back into the foyer, he looked up the staircase. It was risky, but he could always say he'd been looking for the head.

Hustling up the stairs, Slater tried to tread quietly. At the top was a long hallway, and he turned left, and pulled open the first door. A bedroom. Maybe Steve's. It looked like a student lived here, with a big TV, and a crowded bookshelf, and more books stacked on the desk under the window.

Next was a sprawling bathroom. What was the point of taking up all this space? There was enough room for somebody to live in here. Next to that was a bedroom, maybe the main one, with a king bed and a dressing table. Slater stood for a moment and looked around. Was he really going to dig through Kim's underpants? This didn't look like a place with significant secrets.

His phone buzzed in his jeans, and he pulled it out to check. A text from Andy:

I got some juicy details. Call or come by.

Treading down the stairs again, he walked past the library and into the kitchen. It had nice appliances, and a big island. The voices sounded closer. Two of them in conversation. He walked through the kitchen and found Etta sitting at the far end of a long dining table. She was wearing a vest over a white blouse, and an array of paper was strewn in front of her. He could see why Kim put her desk in this room—it sat in a nook under big windows with a great view of the backyard. Etta looked up as he walked in.

"Hi there," she said. "Are you the gardener?"

He shot her a withering look. "Where's Kim?"

Kim stepped in from the next room, a sheaf of paper in hand. She frowned at the sight of him.

"You can't be finished packing the books already."

"Not yet."

Behind him, Steve walked in, and stood facing the table.

"Etta, this is my son, Steve," Kim said. And to Steve, "Are you able to work in the library with John in there?"

"John's not really working. I kissed him."

"Dude," Slater said. "Why would you say that?"

Kim's face contorted, and she raised her voice. "What the hell, John? I let you into my house and you molest my son?"

"He's a grown man," Slater said. "He doesn't need your permission to kiss people."

"He's disabled."

"Steve is more functional than most of the people I have to deal with every day."

"John thinks I should move out," Steve said.

Slater shot him a look. "Filters, man."

"This is what happens when I let the trash blow in," Kim shouted, and waved an arm. "Sexual assault and homewrecking advice."

"You shouldn't be coddling him," Slater said. "Let him live his own life."

"He didn't assault me," Steve said. "It was just a kiss. John wanted to do more, but I said no."

Kim glared at Slater. "I can't believe you did that to him. You really are trash."

Slater flashed his palms. "That's it. I'm out."

"Hold on," Kim said. "You're not finished in the library. Can you come back tomorrow? After your shift at the factory. Maybe I'll get Rogelio to loan you to me for the afternoon."

"So I'm trash," Slater said, "but I'm not too trashy to pack your books?"

Kim raised her eyebrows. "You're a purpose guy, John, and I think you're forgetting your purpose."

Slater eyed Steve. "Can I have a word before I go?"

As he walked out, Kim called after him. "Keep your grubby paws off that boy." Slater heard her speak to Etta in a lower tone. "I have to apologize for all that. It's impossible to find competent staff ..."

Walking back into the foyer, Slater found Steve close behind him. He stopped walking when Slater stopped, and held his gaze, with that open guileless expression.

"Can I give you my number?" Slater said. "In case you ever decide to cut the apron strings and go outside. We could have some fun, you and me."

"I like the way your jeans fit, John, but I don't want to sleep with you. So there's no point."

Slater had to chuckle. "I understand. Thanks for sharing your performance with me."

Walking out the front door, he glanced at the improbably blooming *syriacus*. Did the gardener have some kind of heating for it, or artificial light? When he climbed into the Thunderbird, he tossed his gloves on the floor of the passenger side, and pulled into the street, and headed downtown.

Even on Sunday the surface lot behind Andy's building was crowded. He paid the attendant and walked around to the entrance. When he got upstairs, Andy let him in, and he followed him inside.

A suit jacket hung on the closet door. It was a rich dark-red silky fabric with black accents at the lapels and the pockets. Stepping over and fingering the sleeve, Slater could feel a lump in his throat. That made no freaking sense. It was just a suit.

Andy dropped into his desk chair. "You like it?"

"This is a great color," he said, and turned to face him.

"We're both wearing the same suit. I'm still not ... convinced that's a good idea."

"Why not? You're surrendering your freedom.

You might as well dress like you're in jail."

"The problem is everyone is going to … compare the groom and the other groom, and they'll say … he's hotter than me."

"His mama is the only one who'll think that," Slater said. "Objectively you're way hotter. You know you're completely out of his league, right?" He threw up his hands. "But if you want to marry down, that's on you."

"Even though you're trash-talking my … fiancé," Andy said, "I appreciate you stroking my ego."

"I'm not messing around. It's objectively true."

"So I dug deeper into Kim's cloud drive. I'm pretty … confident she's not running anything on blockchain."

"How can you tell?"

"There's no mention of it anywhere," Andy said. "But I know absence of evidence isn't … proof of anything."

"It does imply that her crypto product is bullshit."

"I'm thinking it's not really a crypto product. At best it … might be an ordinary investment that … Kim is lying about by calling it crypto, because that's a … trendy financial field. More likely it's … just a scam."

"Is it possible the blockchain stuff is somewhere else?" Slater said, "and just not in those records?"

"I found copious documentation of … payments from her investors. It's scary how much money … this woman has acquired from other people."

"Bank records?"

"Right," Andy said. "The money goes directly into a bank account. You can … cross-reference that with the investment dates and amounts in the client list. They line up … exactly. Some of the money moves out, but it's going to … credit card companies, car dealers, Eastside Lightning, and other personal bank accounts. None of it is … moving into the crypto space."

"So Kim is another damn gonif," Slater said. "What kind of bank records?"

"Lots of statements. To me it looks like … the accounts for the whole scheme, dating back to … the first investor."

"Send me all that stuff." He watched him for a moment. "I appreciate you taking time to work on this while you've got your wedding looming."

Andy frowned. "That almost sounded like a thank-you. Are you … feeling OK?"

"My thank-yous come in the form of cold hard cash."

"I'm not busy because Kyle and I aren't … doing the planning. We have the luxury of expressing general preferences and then … just showing up. It's kind of freeing not to be … attached to it."

"That sounds like a twelve-step thing."

Andy chuckled. "I guess it is, in a way. Healthy boundaries. We've … set them up with all the parents involved."

"You're happy, right?" Slater put his hands on his hips. "Is twelve-stepping part of it?"

"That's a big question. I don't know if I'm … happy. Maybe content is a better word. Twelve-step definitely … makes it better. The more I work the program, and the more I … keep it real, the better my life is." He held Slater's gaze, his head undulating slightly with his rhythmic random movements. "If you ever want to come to a … meeting, just let me know."

Slater scoffed. "What good would that do?" His phone buzzed in his pants, and he pulled it out to check. Etta. Before he picked up, he eyed Andy. "I have to go."

"Are we done with Kim?" Andy said. "You have to pay me."

"Not right now. You know I'm good for it."

He walked out, and once he was in the hall, picked up the call.

"I'm out of there," Etta said. "Do you want to debrief?"

"I'm on my way to the office."

Slater climbed in the Thunderbird and drove the few blocks to the Fashion District. The parking lot was almost empty, and no one was in the lobby. Normally the building hummed with the continual on-and-off cycling of sewing machines, but Sunday was the one day the clothing factories took a break. The place was quiet on the ride up, making the clanking of the ancient elevator machinery seem loud. Etta appeared soon after he got upstairs. As she stepped into his office, she set the wire on his desk.

"I can't believe you molested Kim's son."

"Bullshit," Slater said. "It was his idea."

"That's what molesters always say."

He scoffed. "Kim said he's disabled, but he's not. He's just a little different."

Etta chuckled as she sat across from him. "Somewhere on the autism spectrum, if I had to guess. I thought Kim was going to put you on the sex-offender registry."

"The guy is twenty-two and in college. He told me he gets more sex than I do."

"In Kim's mind, he's still a little boy."

Slater waved a hand. "All that paperwork on the dining table. It looked like she was giving you the hard sell."

"There were soft spots. She makes a wicked green tea, and those yummy rice cakes with bean jam in them."

"What's the dope on her crypto product?"

"There was lots of paper," Etta said, "but from what I could tell, it's all marketing. She yakked about it but didn't get specific, even when I asked questions. I didn't want to sound too well informed, but I wanted to press her a little on the details. It felt like she dodged my questions. You can listen to the audio."

"Did she say it runs on blockchain?"

"There was no mention of that, but then I didn't ask. She hit hard on the twenty percent return."

Slater frowned. "Nobody can guarantee that kind of gravy."

"Unless it's illegal. Like a pyramid scheme, where the returns depend on getting more and more people in at the bottom."

"Do you think that's what she's doing?"

"I'm not sure. There was no talk of a schedule for dividend payments. She said they'd come down the road, once the product really took off." Etta shrugged. "That kind of return is a fantasy, right, so it comes down to believing her. That's basically the definition of a con job."

"Everything I've seen says that's what's going on,"

Slater said. "Any other insights?"

Her brow furrowed as she thought about it. "The sales job is subtle, and it's personal. It doesn't feel like the interpersonal warmth is natural, though. More like it's contrived to suit the purpose. Other than that, she's no dummy. And I think she's got dough. That big house, and the cars."

"That might partly be the husband. Steve said he's overseas."

"I didn't stay much longer," Etta said. "I actually used the excuse of her treating you badly to break it off and leave."

Slater frowned. "Was she treating me badly?"

"She was totally condescending. She also called you trash to your face."

"I guess I'm used to it. It's probably wise to make a clean break. Kim is a bearcat, but she won't bug you anymore. She'll shift her focus to the next person on her sucker list."

"She's definitely breaking the seventh commandment."

"Is that some kind of Jesus thing?"

"It's just a turn of phrase," Etta said. "It means she's stealing."

"You know what a con job looks like without a priest 'splaining it for you," he said. "I know you treat people well because you're a decent person, not because you're afraid Jesus is going to punish you in the next world."

"That's not how it works."

"Free your mind, Etta."

She stood up and gestured to the wire on the desk. "Just listen to the recording."

Etta walked out, and he heard the front door close, then the muffled rattle of her keys and the *thunk* of the deadbolt shifting. He found the little memory card in the hardware box on the wire, coaxing it out of its slot with a fingernail, and slid it into his computer. Clicking on the audio file, he listened to Etta and Kim's voices. The mike had been under her clothes, but the sound was clear.

As the conversation unfolded, he heaved his boots up on his desk and stared absently at the statue of Pollux with his horse. He wasn't big on tchotchkes, but the little guy had great hair, and it had been a gift from Pike.

On the recording Etta ran a good game—she sounded engaged and interested but not too bright. Kim was definitely doing a sales job. She'd never spoken to Slater in that upbeat tone or with that level of enthusiasm. As she talked about her crypto product, she didn't really provide any details. When Etta got close to anything substantial, asking pointed questions, Kim redirected her. He listened up to the point that he and Steve walked in, then killed the playback.

Once he'd copied the conversation onto his computer, he wiped the card, and slid it back into the wire, and put the device in the safe.

It was already dark outside, and he hustled across the street to the surface lot, and drove to his house. Trudging up the stairs, he went to the sofa, not bothering to turn on the lights, and pulled his boots off. He stretched out, and sank into it, relishing the comfort.

They were both crooks, Zane and Kim. Stealing landscaping to make their phony booze, stiffing their suppliers, conning low-information investors with a nonexistent crypto product. What Slater was lacking was an obvious way to take them down.

Conrad might have ideas. His idiot ex-boyfriend was a dick-smack but he was also a cop, a detective nowadays, so he knew how the legal system worked, and what it was capable of, and where it fell short. Pulling out his phone, he sent Conrad a text:

Can you do breakfast tomorrow?

It was weird not knowing where he was. For a long time after they split up he'd been able to monitor his whereabouts, keep tabs on him, with tracking software he'd hidden on the guy's phone. But he'd given that up when Conrad got a new one. Now he had no idea where he was. It was liberating, in a way, not to be tuned in to what that idiot was up to.

Conrad's reply came a minute later:

Sure! I'm busy early. It'll be closer to lunchtime.

Slater scoffed. Such a dick. He thumb-typed a response:

Pick me up.

His stomach hurt, he realized. He hadn't really eaten today. On his phone he ordered Thai, and when the doorbell rang, he started awake and hustled down the stairs. Digging in his pants for his wad of cash, he tipped the driver a fin, then ate at the dining table, and stowed the leftovers in the Frigidaire.

Back on the sofa, stretching out again, he was sated, but things felt off. Like he was supposed to be doing something but he'd forgotten what. He wasn't even craving his quotidian ration of applejack, with yesterday's overindulgence still weighing him down. He'd drink it, of course, but later on. No way was he going to arrange a hookup either. The last one had been a big waste of time. He'd had to do the idiot's laundry for him and scrub him down just to tolerate him.

Pike was busy with his people, off in another time zone. He knew he'd call later if he could. Slater gazed out the French doors at the glow of the city in the dark sky. A full belly but no booze, no man. What else was there? And why were the nights so damn long?

NINETEEN

⌗⌗⌗⌗⌗⌗⌗⌗⌗⌗⌗

IT TOOK SLATER A minute to remember why he was alone. He was in his own bed, he knew, and daylight lit the room. His head was clear. That meant he'd actually stuck to his ration last night.

Upstairs he made coffee, then got dressed, in yesterday's jeans and a black dress shirt. Before long Conrad texted:

I'm out front.

Trotting down to the street, he stepped outside and locked the front door. Conrad's SUV was idling in front of his garage, and he stepped over and climbed in the passenger side.

Barrel-chested, Conrad had thick dark hair, and greeted him with that smile. Such a beautiful man. Even after so much time, so long since he'd thrown Slater out on his ass, just the sight of him made his heart beat faster. Today he was dressed in a basic gray suit without a necktie, and a blue shirt, his sidearm clipped to his belt.

"What are you wearing?" Slater said, frowning as he pulled on his seatbelt.

"What are you talking about?"

"Your look is so cop."

Conrad glanced at his side mirror and pulled into the street. "So what? We're not going on an undercover op."

"It's embarrassing. People are going to think I'm an informant."

"I'm sure the servers at the diner won't be judging you. Do you want to go to that place on Sunset?"

"As long as we can get a table in a dark corner. I wish I'd brought sunglasses."

"Innocent people don't need to be afraid of the police," Conrad said.

"That's what they say right before they snap the cuffs on."

"In your case, we'd have to chase you over the back fence first."

Slater eyed him sidelong and spoke through his teeth. "Spread out."

Conrad laughed. "What are you working on these days?"

"It's a whole thing. Let's order first."

The eatery wasn't far, and Conrad slowed as they came up on it, and turned into the driveway. The parking lot in back was tiny, but there was room for his vehicle, and they walked into the place through the back door.

It was a narrow space, with a glass-fronted deli counter facing the booths, and the clerk at the register waved them to one near the front window. The server stepped over. A twenty-something guy with thick dark hair, his T-shirt showed off his wiry musculature.

"What'll it be, boys?"

"How's the BLT?" Conrad said, meeting his gaze.

"Fabulous," he said flatly. "The critics rave."

Conrad chuckled. "It sounds like I have to order that. And a coffee."

Looking to Slater, he raised his eyebrows.

"The jackfruit quesadilla," Slater said. "Is the cheese vegan?"

"Everything's vegan." He gestured impatiently. "It's a vegan diner."

"Bring me that, and hit me with the joe too."

"Thanks, Ernesto," Conrad said, and smiled at him.

"You don't have to be so sappy with people," Slater said as the guy walked away. "I know you don't know him. You just read his name tag. If you want to fuck him, just ask."

"Being friendly isn't sappy. And when I'm dressed for work, I kind of have to be in PR mode."

"Having lunch is just a transaction."

He raised his eyebrows. "Kind of like you and me. I only ever hear from you when you need something."

"That's because you stabbed me in the heart and dumped my lifeless body in the gutter. Why would I come around for more of that?"

Conrad groaned and sat back as the server set down their java.

"In the case I'm working I've uncovered a con job," Slater said. "I wonder if there's anything officialdom can do about it."

"Who's the fraudster?" Conrad said, and slurped at his cup.

He told him about Kim's grift, in broad strokes, and the documents he'd seen. He left out the part about getting her bank records, and explained about Etta's recording, and interviewing some of Kim's clients. He paused as their meals arrived, and they started in on the food.

Once he'd eaten half his sandwich, Conrad wiped his hands on a napkin. "Recordings and photos aren't enough evidence. Unless the other person consented to be recorded, it's not admissible in any legal proceeding. Whatever paperwork you found snooping around isn't admissible either, no matter how damning it is. It doesn't sound like a big enough deal to put detectives on it to get clean evidence, especially if none of the investors claim to be victims."

"Right now they don't. Not yet. But it's obvious what's going on."

"Those white-collar things have to be pretty egregious for an investigation to make any headway."

"The son of one of the investors I talked to was a beat cop," Slater said. "A guy named Lee. He works K-town. Do you know him?"

Conrad frowned. "You know there's like ten thousand of us, right?"

"You'd remember this guy. Buff, great hair, kind of hot." He looked him up and down. "The total opposite of you. Do you think he could push for an investigation?"

"Unless he knows more than you do, he wouldn't be able to sway the detectives to do anything. You have to get people to identify as victims, then make a complaint." He furrowed his brow. "Maybe if you inform her clients that it's not really crypto, they'd change their tune, and be smart enough to file a civil suit. That might be the way to shut it down. Even starting a lawsuit like that would dissuade new investors."

"I hate that that's the best option," Slater said. "It'll take years."

"Sometimes you do what you can do but there's no tidy result. No satisfying conclusion. I see it every day." Conrad picked up his cup. "How's your G-man?"

"A smoking-hot pillar of grade-A man flesh. He transferred his post, so he's working here now."

He nodded. "Doris told me."

"Such a gossip," Slater said, and folded his arms.

"It's news, not gossip."

"He's on the road a lot. B-field, the Central Valley, the Inland Empire."

"There's crooks everywhere."

"He says it feels different here," Slater said. "Like everyone is trying to kill them. He didn't feel so besieged in New Mexico."

"That's probably about LA being an urban setting. Small towns are a lot more chill." He waved a hand. "Lots of people I work with have that mindset. We actually do training to deal with it, to remind us that the public isn't the enemy."

"It makes me think I've dragged him into a bad environment. Into worse circumstances."

"He's given up a lot for you."

Slater watched him for a moment. "Fuck me. What the hell have I done?"

"He's a big boy. He chose to come here. Besides,

Albuquerque isn't exactly arcadia."

"Have I ruined his life?" Slater demanded.

"Maybe that's a good thing to remember about him. Part of your narrative complex is that he made sacrifices to be with you."

"I have no perspective on Pike, and the choices he's made. It's impossible to be objective about him when I'm so wrapped up in it." He threw up a hand. "Impossible."

"I think he's good for you," Conrad said, absently rubbing his thumb on his cup. "Like you've mellowed out a little. He's definitely an upgrade from me."

That look in his eye, Slater thought. It wasn't like he was jealous. It wasn't wistful. There was something else. He couldn't quite parse it.

"Not better," Slater said quietly. "Not worse. Just different."

"You're deep into it, though. I can tell. All that raw emotional stuff. It makes everything else seem less important."

"That's exactly what's happening. You can see right through me."

"It's not that you're transparent," Conrad said. "I know you. I know that side of you. I've seen it."

Slater jutted his chin. "Yeah, well, loose lips sink ships."

He laughed. "Who am I going to blab to about your private life?"

"Doris," he said, and waved an arm.

"That doesn't count."

The server stepped up, holding a black tray with a slip of paper on it. "Your check."

"I'll take it," Slater said.

The guy handed it to him but kept his eyes on Conrad. "How was that sandwich?"

"Transcendent, Ernesto. You were right."

"You'll be in a good mood the rest of the day, then."

"I'd be in a better mood if I could get your phone number," Conrad said.

Ernesto gestured impatiently. "Are you going to write it down, or do you have a photographic memory? I don't have all day."

Conrad chuckled, and fished his phone out of his jacket, and tapped at it. "Hit me."

He rattled off the number, and Conrad thumb-typed it.

"When do you finish your shift?" Conrad said, looking up at him.

"Seven, but I need to decompress for a while," Ernesto said. "After that, however, I'll be ready to rock your world." With that, he walked away.

Slater scoffed. "PR mode, he says."

"I didn't expect to get a date out of it."

"Hey, smoke 'em if you've got 'em. I get the feeling Ernesto is a firecracker."

"I can't help it if I'm a dick magnet." Conrad shrugged. "I can't really switch it off."

"It's probably that suit. Some guys have a fetish for the hopelessly square and unfashionable."

After he'd paid, they walked out the back to Conrad's car, and he dropped Slater at his house. Pike's rig was parked on the street. Just the sight of it, with that turquoise plate, made his heart pound. He trotted up the stairs and found Pike in the bedroom, wearing an olive-drab tank top and his high-cut bright-red underwear, propped up on the pillows with his phone.

"I see you got the Thunderbird back."

Slater stood near the doorway, hands on his hips. "It's as good as new."

"Where were you just now without it?"

"I had lunch with Conrad. He drove. I needed some cop advice."

Pike's brow furrowed. "Are you going to come closer? Maybe kiss me hello?"

"Red means stop. You can't just lie there in those underpants and expect me to act like everything is all normal." He squeezed the burgeoning woody in his jeans. "If I get any closer, I'm going to have to fuck you."

He laughed. "I'm supposed to be working, but I needed to chill out after the flight. We can do something if it's quick."

Slater pulled off his boots, and stepped over, and straddled Pike on the bed. Pike grasped his biceps and massaged them as Slater put his hands on his chest.

"You drive me crazy," Slater said softly, holding his gaze, shifting his weight on Pike's pelvis. He raised his voice. "Crazy."

Pike pulled him down by the neck to meet his mouth. Pressing his woody into his crotch, he could feel him getting hard too. He pulled back and unbuckled his belt, and popped his fly, and pulled out his cock. Pike sat up and grabbed it, and mouthed his neck and his ear, then pushed Slater onto his side, and shifted down, and took him into his mouth.

He gasped at the intense sensation, then shifted to face Pike's lurid red underpants. He was already hard, distorting the stretchy fabric, and Slater pulled his cock out, and went down on him, and worked him intently.

It had been too long, and they both got close quickly. When Pike came, thrusting into him, it was enough to set Slater off too. Pulling away, he rolled onto his back. Pike sat up and pushed his arm under his neck.

"I missed you."

Once his breathing had slowed, Slater studied his face. "Have I ruined your life?"

Pike chuckled. "Why would you say that?"

"You moved here for me, and your job is more dangerous now. I pulled you away from your family."

"I just saw them. My mother dropped me at the airport this morning."

"Still, it's like you sacrificed a lot for me."

"Not for you," Pike said. "For this. For us. For our narrative complex."

"I don't want you to hate me because I upended your life."

"I'm a better person when I'm with you. And I love that you're aware of it. That you know I gave things up to be here."

Conrad had been aware of it, at least, and pointed it out this morning. It had been news to Slater. But he didn't need to tell him that. He leaned in to nuzzle his neck.

Eventually Pike got up and started to get dressed. "I'm going to work out on the deck. I think it's warm enough today."

Slater got up and tucked in his shirt. "I'll see you tonight."

Down in the garage, he backed the Thunderbird into the street and waited for the door to roll down. Once he was downtown, he parked behind Andy's place.

When Andy opened the door, he frowned. "You should have called."

"You want to get paid, don't you?"

Slater followed him inside, and found Kyle standing beside the bed. The guy was lean, his trendy jeans revealing his buff physique, and as usual he had a sharp money haircut.

As Andy dropped into his desk chair, Kyle scowled at Slater. "What are you doing here?"

"If it isn't the blushing groom," Slater said, and put his hands on his hips. "You're as pretty as a picture, Kyle, but it's like that fondant icing they put on cakes. It looks all polished and sweet, but it tastes like paste, and it sticks to your teeth, and nobody's quite sure what the hell the point of it is."

"Wisdom from the booze hag," Kyle said. "Or is it your herpes medication talking? You remind me of those people who get into car chases with the police on the freeway." He waved a hand. "Breaking news. Sooner or later you're going to be spread-eagled on the asphalt and on your way to jail."

"Where did you learn all those multisyllable words, sweetheart? Your teacher will have to give you a gold star."

"You are an emotional wreck," Kyle said, raising his voice.

"I think that's common knowledge, son. I guess I shouldn't be surprised you're a bit slow on the uptake."

"This is probably good," Andy said. "Both of you

can … get it all out now. You can't be doing this at the ceremony."

"What are you two doing loafing around here anyway," Slater said. "You're getting married tomorrow. Or did that slip your mind?"

"The preparations are all done," Andy said. "I just need to shave and get dressed."

"Still, most people would be stressed out."

"We wanted a low-key event," Kyle said. "There's no need for stress."

"How many people did you invite?"

"Less than three hundred."

"That sounds extremely low-key." Slater waved at the room. "You could have just done it here in the loft."

Andy spoke louder. "Slater. Focus. You owe me money."

"I know. What's the damage?"

"It was a lot of work."

"Just rip the bandage off, man."

"Eleven hundred."

Slater groaned and pulled out his wad. As he stepped toward the desk, he eyed Kyle. "You're marrying a chiseler."

"I'm kind of amazed that you make that kind of money, sweet pea," Kyle said. "And it's all under the table. Just seeing the cash change hands like that, it feels like you're a crook."

Slater furrowed his brow. "And yet you're marrying him."

"Don't be trash-talking my work," Andy said. "I earn … an honest living."

"I need you to prepare something for Kim's

investors," Slater said. "I want to show them that Kim's crypto product isn't really crypto because it's not on a blockchain. Show them what she's doing with the money—buying cars and paying her credit cards. Explain it for laypeople."

"It'll take some work to simplify it."

"Do what you can," Slater said. "Just a few pages. It shouldn't be traceable. Once you've spelled it out, I want to email it to everyone on Kim's client list. Is that something you can do anonymously?"

"Anonymous is easy," Andy said, "but Kim will likely … get wind of it. She'll be able to figure out someone … hacked her."

"One thing about dealing with crooks is that they have little recourse. If she figures out it was me, she's not going to sue me." He waved a hand. "Those people on the client list work hard. I've met some of them. They should know what's really going on. That they're being scammed."

"I'll set it up," Andy said, "but it'll be … later in the week."

"I get it. The big nuptials."

"Listen, Ibáñez," Kyle said. "I'm only going to say this once. About tomorrow." He raised his eyebrows and spoke intently. "No drama."

Slater narrowed his eyes. "Did you ever notice that the people who say 'no drama' are the ones who generate all the drama? Nobody's going to be focused on me, toots. It's your day."

"Still—I'm concerned that you'll make it about you. Somehow, some way." Kyle's lip curled in a sneer. "With drunks it's always the ego."

Slater took a breath, forcing himself not to react.

"I drink to make you people tolerable," he said evenly. "And I respect Andy too much to punch you in the face. But you know I want to. You know I'm picturing it. You in your monkey suit tomorrow with a fat lip and a grade-A shiner."

"Slater," Andy said, raising his voice. "Enough. Shut the fuck up and … get out of here."

He eyed him for a moment. "Bye, beautiful."

TWENTY

⌦⌦⌦⌦⌦⌦⌦⌦⌦⌦

ON THE WAY DOWN to his car, Slater saw there was a text message from Claudine:

Another blue agave got stolen last night. Is it the same people?

"Damn it," Slater muttered, and opened Svetlana's app. Sure enough, the tracker labeled труб-3 had moved last night—its current location was at the Eastside Lightning factory.

He couldn't shut Eastside Lightning down, just like he couldn't shut down Kim's grift. But there were steps he could take. Climbing in behind the wheel of the Thunderbird, he called Claudine.

"It was the same people," Slater said when she picked up. "Do you know the total value of what's been stolen?"

"I can tell you exactly," she said. "Hester asked me to figure it out for an insurance claim. Thirty-five hundred and fifty."

He ended the call, and drove to the Eastside Lightning factory, and parked nearby on a side street. When he walked through the gate, he saw the blue Town Car sitting next to Zane's Bimmer and Rogelio's pickup. Striding back to the factory door, he went inside. Sitting on the worktable was a big blue agave, on its side, roots exposed. He could see the plug in the piña where he'd buried the tracker.

"Do you even work here anymore?" Rogelio said, stepping out of the back room and frowning at him.

"Where's the *jimadore*?"

"He was here a minute ago. He brought that blue agave."

"His car is still out front."

"So he's probably meeting with Zane. To get paid."

Slater went into the office, and saw that Zane's door was open. Walking in, he found Zane behind his desk, still wearing that stupid red sports jersey, and Mauricio sitting across from him. They both looked surprised as he approached the desk. Maybe sensing Slater's determination, Mauricio stood up.

"You," he said, his brow furrowing. "What are you doing here? I thought my boys already taught you a lesson."

"You know this grunt?" Zane demanded.

"Let me tell you what I know." Slater gestured to Mauricio. "I know you're stealing those blue agaves." He looked to Zane. "And I know you're in on it."

"They come from rich people's houses," Mauricio said. "It doesn't matter. They'll just buy another one."

"So you're enriching this asshole instead?" He waved at Zane. "Stealing from the rich and selling it to a lowlife?"

"I don't need to explain myself to you, *vato.*" Mauricio reached behind his back, and drew a handgun, and leveled it at him.

"Don't point your gun at me," Slater snapped. It was an unusual weapon, a nine mil, tan in color but with a traditional black slide.

Mauricio didn't waver. "Why do you care about rich people's landscaping?"

They were standing close enough that Slater could easily grab the weapon. It was a risky move, and he might wind up gut-shot, but the way Mauricio was holding it, like it was a sandwich—he didn't have a firm grip.

"I got hired to care. I'm also sick of the bullshit," Slater said, and held Mauricio's gaze, and waved toward Zane. "This nebbishy moron is selling industrial ethanol as if it were high-end booze. He acts like he invented something new, but it's a grift as old as civilization. He's the worst kind of lowlife skid mark."

Zane sat up. "Fuck you," he spat.

Slater was watching Mauricio closely. He needed to get the timing just right. As the guy glanced toward Zane's outburst, he made a grab for the pistol from his other side. Slater yanked it from his grip with almost no resistance, and took a step back, next to the little conference table, and quickly flipped the weapon around to aim it at Mauricio.

At first his eyes grew wide, then his face went red with anger. "Motherfucker."

"Here's what's going to happen," Slater said, and eyed Zane. "You're going to wire seventy-one hundred bucks for the blue agaves you stole."

"No, I'm not."

"The other option is I ventilate you." He eyed Mauricio. "This is loaded, isn't it?"

"I don't walk around with an empty rod."

He waggled the weapon at Zane. "Pull out your phone. Go on, do it. I know you have the dough."

Zane scowled but dug it out of his pants pocket. Taking another step backward, Slater used his free hand to pull out his own. He looked at the screen, and tapped with his thumb to pull up the number for the bank account he and Max had set up for their business, and read it aloud.

"Once you've sent it, you're going to show me the confirmation."

"You know I can just phone the bank later and have this reversed."

"If you do that," Slater said, "I'll take all my evidence to the cops. Maybe you won't get charged with anything, or maybe you will. Do you really want them poking around your factory, looking into your business?" He eyed Mauricio. "I'm sure you'd prefer that this idiot doesn't attract the attention of the *placa*."

"You don't speak much Spanish, I'm thinking." He heaved a sigh. "No, let's not bring the cops."

"What's the status, Zane?" Slater said, glancing over at him. The guy sat staring at the little screen.

Mauricio jutted his chin. "Would you really use my own rod on me?"

"You want to find out?" Slater said.

"I don't think you would." Mauricio took a step toward him, extending a hand, a wry grin on his face.

Aiming slightly above his head, Slater squeezed the trigger, then pulled it again. The sharp *bang-bang* was deafening, and the recoil jolted his wrist.

Mauricio instantly ducked into a crouch, raising one hand to shield his face and flattening the other on top of his head.

"Back where you were," Slater growled.

Mauricio took the step back, dropping his hands to his sides and keeping his palms exposed. Slater could see the rush of stress heaving his chest, reddening his face. High on the wall behind him were a pair of dark little bullet holes in the white expanse of wallboard. With any luck those rounds hadn't traveled any farther.

Slater eyed Zane. "Have you made the transfer?" he said sharply, raising his voice over the ringing in his ears.

Zane's eyes were wide, his face ashen. He hadn't expected gunfire. He tapped rapidly at his phone, then held it up. "There it goes. I sent it."

Stepping over, Slater leaned in to glance at the screen. It looked like he'd actually done it. As he took a step back to the conference table, a soft high-pitched tone filled the air, a sustained *beep-beep-beep*. It came from Zane's direction.

Mauricio raised his eyebrows. "That's a lame-ass ringtone." The guy had managed to recover his composure. He sounded almost bored now.

"It's my watch," Zane said, and held up his wrist to peer at it. "It's an alarm. It says my heart rate is too high. Not surprising, with somebody shooting holes in my walls." He frowned at Slater. "I'll have to get a drywall guy out here to patch it."

"You've really got him upset," Mauricio said. "His watch thinks he's having a heart attack."

"It's not just about bullet holes," Slater said. "I know

why his emotions are running high. He's hopped up on meth, for one. Tweakers always think nobody can tell. Plus we have a preexisting sexual relationship."

Mauricio cackled and looked to Zane. "Oh, *jefe*, sleeping with the help. That'll mess you up every time."

"I didn't sleep with him," Zane snapped.

The seventy-one hundred would cover the landscaping and what he'd charged Hester, Slater thought, plus a little extra as damages. But this idiot should pay for his labor too.

"How much have you got in petty cash?" Slater said.

Zane frowned. "Like business cash? We don't have that."

"Then what have you got in your pocket?"

"You're seriously going to rob me at gunpoint? Think about what you're doing."

"It's money you owe me, you idiot. My wages and the cost of tracking down the stolen agaves. You can get into it with the cops after. Go ahead and call them. I doubt you'll want to explain the full story, with all the details that'll be in my version when they come to talk to me."

His mouth a tight line, Zane pulled a bundle of cash from his pants pocket, and pulled off the bill clip, and riffled through it.

"I've got twenty-eight hundred." He set the bills on his desk.

"That sounds about right," Slater said, and stepped over to scoop it up. "We'll call it even."

Mauricio had a grin on his face, like he was enjoying the show.

"I know you're not playing," Slater said to him,

"so I'm not going to mess with you. My beef is with this cheap dipshit."

"I am not cheap," Zane snapped.

"Did he pay you yet?" Slater said.

Mauricio spread his palms. "We didn't get to that."

"What does he owe you?"

"Eight dollars."

"But he doesn't pay you fairly, does he?" Slater riffled half the C-notes off the wad he'd just picked up. "Here's fourteen."

The weapon still aimed at him, Slater stepped toward him and handed over the cash, then moved back a few paces to the table. Popping the mag out of the handgun, he quickly unloaded it, and deftly pulled back the slide to empty the chamber. Once he'd pocketed the bullets, he peeled another C-note off his wad.

"That's for the ammo I'm taking," Slater said, and set the weapon and the empty mag on top of the bill on the conference table. "Are we square?"

Mauricio shrugged. "Close enough. I can see you're not disrespecting me."

"You're not going to let him get away with this," Zane said.

"He's your problem, gringo," Mauricio said. "I got paid, and I got my piece."

Looking to Zane, Slater jutted his chin. "Next time just buy the agaves from a farmer. It'll be a lot cheaper."

Meeting Mauricio's eye and flashing his palms, he walked out, then went out the front door. Glancing over his shoulder as he headed to the street, he saw that no one was following him.

Zane was just a frat boy, but he had to be careful

with Mauricio. Dude was a gangster, and he'd be embarrassed at getting disarmed. But Slater had let him save face by returning his heater, and making sure he got paid—that should be the end of it.

As he walked up on the gate to the street, Kim's stupid Benz turned in, and stopped next to him. She rolled down the window.

"Where have you been?" Kim demanded. "Rogelio said you didn't show up. He said we should look for somebody else."

Slater paused on the sidewalk, his heart still pounding.

"I know what you're doing with crypto is a scam," he said. "There is no crypto product. You're just ripping off people in your social network. Taking their money. How long do you think you can keep that up?"

Kim's face hardened. "What the fuck would a fungible blue-collar grunt know about my business?"

"Not enough to get you arrested, but I know you're a crook." He pointed a finger at her. "You're going over for it, sister."

"Are you the one who's been spooking my clients?" She scoffed. "You know nothing. I run a legitimate business."

"Like a crypto product built on blockchain? It doesn't wash."

"My investors are perfectly comfortable with what's happening to their funds."

"And there it is," Slater said. "You know, when Agamemnon was gathering his troops to attack Troy, he had no idea how demoralized they were. They bailed on him at the first opportunity. Ran for the hills."

"The fuck are you talking about?" she demanded.

"You have no idea what your investors are thinking, or what they're going to do. I'd bet money you can say good-bye to all your bougie cars." He waved at the hood of the Benz. "The sheriff will seize them to pay restitution."

As he walked away, Kim shouted after him: "You don't know me." A moment later she added, "Fuck you."

Not looking back, Slater rounded the corner and climbed into the Thunderbird. He took a deep breath to slow his pounding heart. That had been really stupid. He should have held his tongue, but instead he'd told Kim exactly what was coming for her. That gave her an advantage. He really was an emotional wreck, the adrenaline from the gunplay still thrumming in his veins. Mouthing off was always a mistake. He knew that.

"Idiot," he muttered, glancing at himself in the rearview, then started the engine.

TWENTY-ONE

WHEN SLATER GOT DOWNTOWN, he parked across from his office. There were still some day laborers in the lobby, waiting for gigs in the sewing factories. Upstairs the office was dark. He flipped on the lights, and stuck his head into Max's office to make sure he really was alone, then sat at his desk.

On his phone he checked their business bank account. The money from Zane had landed with no hold on it. He swiveled to the safe, and dialed in the combination, and pulled open the heavy door. There was way too much folding money in here, even though they were gradually trying to smurf it into their bank accounts, and he pulled out a rack, and broke the dark-yellow currency band. Once he'd counted out seventy-one C-notes, he tossed the rest back inside. Digging a pen out of his desk drawer, he made a note on the list they used to keep track of the cash, with the date and the details:

Slater -7100, for deposit to business acct.

Mauricio's ammo, he remembered. He dug all the bullets out of the pockets of his jeans and piled them in the safe, between the stacks of cash and the pile of paperwork. Max would pop them off at the gun range or leave them there for someone else to use.

Once he'd locked the safe again, he heaved his boots onto his desk, and pulled the keyboard into his lap. He needed to write his report for Hester. In terse language he laid out what he'd found with the trackers, and how Eastside Lightning had used the blue agaves, and how the owners knew they were stolen. He included everyone's names, although for Mauricio he only used his first name—he needed to stay as distant from that guy as possible. At the end he added a separate line:

Restitution: $7,100 was obtained.

Once he'd read through it again, he added "confidential—not for distribution" at the top of each page. Max said that made them less vulnerable to a lawsuit, even if it got into the hands of a journalist or the people he'd fingered as crooks. If it wasn't a public statement, it didn't qualify as libel.

Next he printed out all the details Andy had scraped from Kim's files—the list of investors, and dozens of pages of bank statements. Gathering up the printouts, he shuffled them into a file folder, then pulled out his phone and called Ellen Jung, from the handbag store.

"My name is Ibáñez," Slater said when she picked up. "We met on the weekend."

"I remember."

"Are you around today? I have some documentation for you."

"Seriously?" she said. "That's great. I'm at the shop."

Slater stuffed the cash in the pocket of his jeans, and locked up the office, and rode down to the street with the file folder in hand. Cruising around the corner, just a few blocks and still in the Fashion District, he parked in front of a narrow storefront with ENVIOS DE DINERO filling the window in big red letters. A print shop and shipping store, it was convenient to the office, but even more significant, the owner hadn't put up any security cameras.

Stepping inside, he greeted the clerk. She was short, and thick, and wore her hair tied back, with a stretchy red top covering her ample breasts.

"I need a copy of these," Slater said, and set the file folder on the countertop. "Just one."

"Give me a minute," she said, and took the folder, then stepped into the back.

The repetitive mechanical sound of the photocopier came as it started to spit out pages. Slater stood at the window, looking out at the street between the big red letters. Svetlana had told him that printers and copiers had built-in software to mark every printout with microdots. They weren't noticeable to anyone looking at the printout, but they contained the device's serial number. It gave law enforcement a powerful forensic tool, but it meant everything that got printed was traceable. If anyone decided to go after whoever had hacked Kim's files, they wouldn't get any farther than this print shop.

The woman stepped out of the back, and set both

stacks of paper on the counter, and rang up the sale.

Once he'd paid her, he scooped up the paper, sliding the new copies into the file folder, and went out to the Thunderbird. Traffic wasn't bad yet, and soon he was in Koreatown, in front of Ellen's shop, and pulled in at a meter.

Like on Saturday, there were no customers inside. Behind the counter was a woman in her sixties, her short hair run through with gray. She called out a perfunctory greeting as he stepped in.

"You must be Jung Ji-young," Slater said.

Her brow furrowed. "How do you know me?" Her accent was thick.

"I'm here for Ellen."

Before she could respond, Ellen came out of the back. She said something to her mother in Korean, and after a brief exchange, Ji-young stared at Slater, curiosity burning in her eyes.

Behind him a customer walked in, and Ji-young called out a greeting, then stepped out from behind the counter.

"Does she know why I'm here?" Slater said.

"She asked me if we're dating." Ellen sighed. "It'll take me half the evening to undo that."

He set the file folder of photocopies on the counter. "What do you know about crypto?"

"I've done some reading. It's so complicated."

"I hear you, sister. My understanding is that crypto products run on blockchain. To me it looks like Kim's product doesn't."

Her brow furrowed. "What does that mean?"

"It's not really a crypto product, even though she says it is. One of my operatives did some digging.

He's going to write up an explanation in plain language, then send that to your mother and all the other people on Kim's client list." Slater tapped the folder. "This is the raw data. Documentation about what Kim does with the money."

Ellen folded open the file on the countertop and leafed through it. "These are bank records," she said, and met his gaze. "Who gave you these?"

"Don't ask. There's also a list of Kim's clients in there, and some communications with them. I don't even know what half of it says because it's in Korean."

As she dug through the pile, Ellen inhaled sharply and muttered, "Oh …"

"My operative said you can compare the buy-in listed for each client with the deposits to one of the bank accounts. They line up exactly. But the money in that account doesn't turn into anything crypto—it goes to Kim's car dealer and her credit card company and her tequila venture."

"I can see it in the investor list," Ellen said, pulling aside a sheaf of paper. "This column is the buy-in, and next to it is the date. Did you hack her computer?"

"That's the problem. None of this was obtained legally, so you can't show this to the DA. It can't be used as evidence in a criminal probe."

"But what she's doing is a crime," Ellen said intently. "Can't I give this to the DA anyway? They might be able to use it."

Slater shook his head. "Don't do that. They'd charge you with data theft, and then you'd have to rat me out, and they'd come after me."

"I could say someone gave it to me anonymously."

"I talked to a guy who knows the system. He

said the DA won't investigate unless there's clear and egregious fraud." Slater tapped the sheaf of paper. "This doesn't qualify. None of the investors I talked to have tried to cash out yet. They're still in the believing-it phase, like Ji-young. So technically there's no evidence that Kim is doing anything illegal. Not yet. Kim could easily tell an investigator, 'Oh, the big crypto purchase is happening next Tuesday. The money is in escrow until then.'"

"So what can I do?" she demanded.

"Show this to your own lawyer, and team up with this list of patsies, and sue her in civil court. The email from my operative will be coming later this week."

"I wonder if that will be enough to convince any of them. Wrong beliefs are next to impossible to change, and these people believe in Kim."

Slater shrugged. "At least you know the score. If you can band together with some of them, at least, with a civil suit you might be able to get some of your money back."

"That's basically what the cop said."

"Lee? You talked to him?"

"He came by here earlier today."

"So he's motivated too," Slater said. "Get him to help you."

"I guess I have to think about this with the American side of my brain."

He frowned. "What does that mean?"

"There's no government authority to sort it out for us. Even the police can't do anything. We have to do it ourselves."

"Taking things into your own hands can be satisfying. It's why I'm here—there's not much I can do to stop this crook except share this information."

Ellen nodded. She looked tired now. "OK, Slater, I get it."

"Have you been to Kim's house? It's a mansion. There are three luxury vehicles parked out front. One of them is so expensive I'd never even heard of it. I had to look it up. If you check these financial records, you'll see that your mother and Lee's parents paid for those cars."

"That's infuriating."

"So stay pissed. Go after her and nail her to the wall. Get your money back."

"I guess I've got some work to do."

"And leave my name out of it. When the provenance of this stuff comes up, call me anonymous."

"You said that already."

He threw up his hands. "You're welcome."

Walking out, he climbed into the Thunderbird, and pulled out his phone, and called Hester.

"I wondered when you were going to check in," she said when she picked up.

"Can I see you today?"

"Why not? I'm at home."

He plugged her address into his navigation app, and it sent him to the 101 and onto the 5. Traffic was starting to slow down, and eventually he was pulling up at Hester's house, with its absurd faux Greek columns. Claudine hadn't replaced the missing agave yet, he saw as he cruised up the driveway, but she'd smoothed out the sandy earth so it didn't look like something had been uprooted.

Hester opened the door when he rang the bell. She was wearing a billowy top and plaid capri pants even though it wasn't really warm out, and her blond mane looked freshly styled. Just the fact that she could make it look that way said money. She beckoned him in, and he followed her through to the kitchen.

"Is it too late for coffee?" she said.

"I don't need anything."

Hester waved him to a breakfast table, at bar height with a set of stools around it, positioned next to a tall window that looked onto the backyard.

"What exactly have you been doing?" She climbed onto a stool. "Another plant got stolen last night."

Pulling out his phone, he took the seat across from her.

"What's your email?" he said, and thumb-typed it as she recited it. "I just sent you my report."

"Can you summarize it?"

"I know who took the plants, and I know where they wound up. But knowing that isn't enough to get anyone arrested. I did get you some money to replace the blue agaves, plus a little extra."

She frowned. "What kind of money?"

"Right." He briefly stood up, and pulled the thick wad from his pocket, and set it on the table.

Hester stared at the pile. "Cash?" she said, her tone rising.

"That's seventy-one hundred. Claudine said replacing the blue agaves will cost half that. The rest is for your trouble."

"You got the thief to pay this?" She laughed and picked up the stack of bills, fanning through them. "How did you manage that?"

"I threatened to make trouble for them. It's a bluff, though. I can't really do anything."

"Who was this?"

"It's all in the report."

"Why can't you do anything? They stole from me. It was pretty blatant."

"It's about physical evidence," Slater said. "No one saw them take the plants. I know where they wound up, but they could easily claim ignorance, that they bought them from a nameless middleman, not knowing they were stolen. A prosecutor wouldn't touch it."

"So they're free to keep doing what they're doing, and rip off somebody else."

"Unfortunately, yes," he said. "I don't think it'll be you again. They know it'll cost them."

"Well, if that's as good as it gets, I guess I should be satisfied." Hester tapped the pile of C-notes. "Claudine said you were good at this. What do I owe you?"

"I got the thieves to cover the rest of my time. You and I are square."

They both looked over as Big Mike strode in from the foyer, wearing his jodhpurs and riding boots.

"You're back," Hester said, pulling the wad of cash into her lap, out of Big Mike's line of sight.

"Temporarily. I'm headed out again." Big Mike eyed Slater, his brow furrowing. "If it isn't the slappy gardener."

"You two have met?" Hester said.

"When I was here last week to plant the trackers." Slater slid off the stool. "Let me know if anything in the report is unclear."

"I'll walk you out," Big Mike said quickly.

Once they were through the foyer, and in the

driveway, Slater went to the driver's side of the Thunderbird.

"Sweet ride," Big Mike said.

"I know."

"I'm on my way back to the stables. There's only
horses there at this hour. Do you want to come with
me? We could do some equestrian stuff."

Slater looked him up and down. "Those boots are
totally giving me a stiffy, big guy, but I can't. I've got
a man who expects some loyalty."

"I have that expectation on me too." He gestured
toward the house with his thumb. "It doesn't really
slow me down."

"That's because you're a *gantse macher*, with the big
house and the horses and those fuck-me boots. You
can do whatever you want. I can't." Slater shrugged.
"I'm not sleazy."

Big Mike scowled. "Are you sure about that?"

"I'm not cheating on anybody."

"But you are a dick."

"I know," Slater said. "Enjoy the horses."

He got behind the wheel and fired up the engine.
The sun was sinking low as he drove to his house in
the stop-and-go freeway traffic. When he finally got
there, he headed up the stairs, and heard Pike call a
greeting from the back bedroom.

Parked at the desk under the window, Pike was
working on his laptop. Outside the daylight was fading. There was a decent view from this side, as the
next street was quite a bit lower down the hill. Pike
could contemplate the greenery and the rooftops of
the neighborhood while he worked.

"Did it get too cold out?" Slater said, walking over

and leaning down to kiss him.

"I was OK up there until about four." He grabbed his phone from his desktop. "Listen to this. It's a text from Andy: 'Big day tomorrow. Can't wait to see you there.'"

"That's nice of him. The personal touch."

Pike furrowed his brow. "Did he think I'd forget?"

"It's an LA thing. You have to remind people the day before. Otherwise they flake."

"Even for a wedding?"

"He's just covering his bases," Slater said.

"Do you flake on people if they don't remind you?"

"I try not to. But you can only change what you're willing to change, not what you think you should change."

Pike's eyes narrowed. "Are you quoting your addiction book at me?"

He chuckled. "Is it that obvious?"

"I'm so glad that it's sinking in."

"You're glad about the twelve-step," Slater said. "It makes me think you want my twelve inches."

He folded his laptop closed and rose to embrace him, nuzzling his neck. "You wish that's what you were packing." Pike sniffed audibly, and pulled back. Drawing Slater's hand to his nose, he sniffed again, then checked the other hand. He looked Slater in the eye. "What were you up to today?"

"What are you talking about?"

"I smell gunshot residue," Pike said. "It's unmistakable."

He groaned. "I feel like no matter what I say, it's not going to end well for me."

"Try the truth."

"How about this," Slater said. "Max took me to the shooting range today, and we plinked some targets. It's a great way to relieve stress."

"You know I have Max's phone number, right? I can run down that story in a hot minute."

Slater frowned. "Why are you acting like you have to investigate me?"

"Because you're lying to me," Pike said, raising his voice.

"It wasn't a lie. I offered it as one possible explanation."

"Honesty, remember? The foundation of trust in a relationship."

Slater took a breath. "A gangbanger pulled a gun on me. I disarmed him, and I had to fire a couple warning shots when he came at me."

"How did you disarm him?" His brow furrowed. "That sounds really risky. And where did the rounds go? Bullets do strange things in enclosed spaces. They ricochet off concrete floors and steel beams, and then wind up right back in your torso or your brain."

"See, this is why I don't tell you the whole truth. You're judging me."

Pike flashed his palms. "Fair enough. I want to be able to listen without doing that. Let me try. But I really want to hear the story." He raised his eyebrows. "All of it."

Slater huffed. "You're not going to like it."

TWENTY-TWO

IN THE MORNING SLATER woke when Pike wrapped his arm around his chest and drew him close. He luxuriated in it, the warm heady feeling of his skin, as he gradually came up to consciousness.

"I hear wedding bells," Pike murmured.

"Fuck."

"You should probably blow me," Pike said. "That way I won't get too distracted by all the guys. It is a boy-boy wedding after all."

Slater shifted onto his back. "Knowing Kyle and Andy, all their friends are going to be affluent zombie twinks."

"I don't mind a twink now and then."

Climbing up on him, Slater straddled his hips. He could feel Pike's morning wood beneath him. "If that's what you want, I'll smoke you, punk, and you'll stay smoked."

"I love it when you're on top of me like this," Pike said. "Get a condom."

Reaching for one in the bedside drawer, he rolled it on for him, and grabbed the lube. As he slid down onto him, grimacing with the intensity of it, Pike was breathing hard, and kneaded his chest. He rocked back and forth, and Pike stroked his cock as he thrust into him. It was such a turn-on to see the expression on his face. Slater came in Pike's fist, and a moment later Pike climaxed, straining deeper.

He climbed off and stretched out beside him, relishing the magnetic feeling of Pike's skin. Once he'd caught his breath, he spoke.

"We need to eat."

"Maybe just a snack," Pike said. "There'll be food at the event."

"Doris texted last night to remind me of a salient point: it's a Protestant wedding."

"Oh, yeah. We need to eat."

After they'd had coffee and bread and fruit upstairs, Pike spent some time at his desk in the back bedroom. Eventually Slater summoned him to get ready.

"Who gets married on a Tuesday?" Pike said, pulling his suit out of its garment bag.

"Andy said it was the only day the ballroom they wanted was available."

"What did you come up with for your best-man speech?"

"I thought I'd wing it."

Pike paused and stared at him. "I wish they all could be California boys."

Buttoning his shirt, Slater frowned. "What does that mean?"

"You can't do that. You have to have a plan."

"I sort of know what I'm going to say."

He pulled on the trousers of his tux, in a deep midnight blue, and watched Pike step over to the floor mirror to adjust his jacket. It was traditional black, and it fit him well.

"Great threads," Slater said. "You look good in a tux."

"Everybody looks good in a tux." He turned to look Slater over as he pulled on his jacket. "I like the way yours is cut. It shows off your assets."

"Hey," he said sharply. "My eyes are up here."

Pike chuckled. "In that suit, no one is going to be looking at your eyes." He pulled his bow tie around his neck, and turned to the mirror, and deftly knotted it.

"Can you do mine?" Slater said, and draped it around his collar, and stood facing him.

"Come over here."

Pike positioned him facing the mirror, then stood behind him. Slater watched their reflection as Pike reached around his neck and pulled it together into a knot, his brow furrowed in concentration. How lucky was he to have this guy in his life, this beautiful man? Once he'd finished the bow, Slater turned to him, and put his hands on his neck.

"You're the best thing that ever happened to me."

Pike beamed. "Because I can tie a bow tie?"

"You know what I mean. Because you're you."

Pike kissed him, and they got lost in it for a minute.

"Snap out of it," Slater said finally, pulling back. "We'll be late."

They climbed in the Thunderbird and drove downtown. It was still mid-afternoon but the traffic was already getting sluggish. He nosed the car onto the ramp that led down under Pershing Square.

"Is the hotel nearby?" Pike said.

"Right across the street. The city lot costs a fraction of what they'll be charging over there. It's valet only."

Once they'd ascended the stairs to the square, they crossed to the Baltimore and went inside. In the wide hallway Pike pointed to the coffered ceiling and the paneled walls.

"All this mahogany, and all the detail work," he said. "They don't build stuff like this anymore."

There were several ballrooms, but only one had its doors open. A cluster of people stood in the hall-way outside it, in suits and dresses, and the din of the crowd inside grew as they got closer.

There were a lot of people here, he saw as they stepped in. Round banquet tables were set up at one side, and a low stage was at the other. The guests were standing around in small groups talking or lined up for the bar.

"Look at that chandelier," Pike said. "This is a great place to get married. And the music stands. There must be a live band."

"A big one, I'd say." There were eight chairs, and some of the instruments were already set out.

"There's the gift table," Pike said. "You should drop your envelope."

Slater pulled it out of his jacket and set it on the table with the array of others. It wasn't very secure, but at least it wasn't near the doors. That made it harder to steal from.

"We should get drinks," Slater said, and they joined the end of the bar line.

Pike looked around the room. "There's Andy."

He was standing with his walking sticks, Slater saw, the cuffs around his forearms, in the open space between the stage and the banquet tables. That patch of bare floor was tiled in wood parquet—it must be for dancing.

"So that's Kyle," Pike said.

"Oh, yeah," Slater said, following his gaze. "That little toothache."

"The grooms are wearing matching red suits. That's so adorable. You never told me Kyle was so hot. He could be a model."

"That seems far-fetched. Unless you mean a spokesmodel for a weasel ranch. When he opens his mouth, he instantly loses eight points of hotness. You just want to punch him in the face."

Over by the doorway Slater noticed a guy step in from the hall. In his fifties, maybe, he had a slick haircut and wore dress pants and a necktie but no jacket. No one was checking invitations, and the guy glanced around as he entered. He knew that look—furtive, shady, trying to fit in. The guy stepped over to the bar, and cut the line to talk to one of the bartenders. That was a total dick move, a shortcut to get a drink without waiting for it like everybody else. But maybe the bartender refused to serve him—he stepped back again with nothing in hand.

Slater strode toward him, hustling the few paces to the front of the bar line. Stepping up behind the guy, he grabbed his bicep, and then the other one. He tried to turn around, but Slater had firm hold of him.

"What the hell?" he demanded.

Shoving him forward, Slater frog-marched him

out into the hallway, and growled in his ear.

"You can't crash other people's weddings. Hit the bricks."

"Get your hands off me."

"I've had enough of your guff," Slater said. Once they were out in the hall, he spun him around and delivered a rapid kovac, left and then right, slapping hard. "Why do you make me do this to you?" he demanded.

"Stop it," the guy shouted, batting at his arms.

"You'll take it and you'll like it." He landed one more slap as the guy shoved him off.

Glaring at him, he was red-faced. "What is wrong with you?"

"I get asked that a lot." Slater put his hands on his hips. "You've almost got the look to fit in, but not quite. Although if I had your pecs I'd probably wear a shirt that showed my nipples too." He gestured toward him. "And those fuck-me trousers. They look like you painted them on. At least everybody can see that you're stacked."

"Who the hell are you to be judging my clothes?"

"I said beat it, you damn stumblebum." Slater moved toward him, but at that moment Kyle stepped between them.

"Leave him alone," he shouted. "Dad—what's going on?"

"Who is this thug?"

Kyle scowled at Slater. "Believe it or not, he's supposed to be the best man." He took hold of his arm and steered him into the ballroom.

Taking a breath, Slater adjusted his jacket, then walked back inside, and joined Pike in the bar line.

It didn't seem like giving a crasher the bum's rush would draw a lot of attention, but he could feel a lot of eyes on him right now.

"You're doing double duty as security?" Pike said.

"I thought he was trying to crash. It turns out he's Kyle's father."

Pike winced. "Ouch. He did look pissed."

"It's the way he was dressed. I thought he was an interloper."

"We're definitely dressed better than him. And better than the grooms."

"You make it sound like that's OK," Slater said. "I totally blew it on the dress code. Kyle is so bougie I just assumed everyone would be in black tie."

He surveyed the crowd. "There's some other tuxes. Lots of the women look just as formal."

"You're so damn upbeat. Not concerned about it at all." Slater scoffed. "I made you look stupid and you're not even upset with me. It kind of drives me crazy, but I love that about you."

He chuckled, and wrapped an arm around Slater's shoulder, and squeezed. "We don't look stupid."

As they slowly inched toward the front of the line, he saw that Doris was here now. She was wearing a great dress, not overly formal, shiny and gold and hemmed just below the knee. Stupid Albert was on her arm, in a suit without a tie, his stupid gray hair thin on top and clumped around his ears. Slater scowled at the sight of him.

"There's your mom," Pike said. "And that must be her boyfriend."

"Is that old croaker still alive? His name is stupid Albert. Accent on the stupid."

"He needs a haircut."

"Like I said, stupid." Slater looked around at the crowd. "Lots of their friends are gay guys. A few of them are junkies from Andy's NA group, but the rest look like somebody put out an open casting call that just said 'twink.'"

"At least there's some diversity. It's not all white folks."

"I'm glad you notice things like that."

"New Mexico is pretty diverse, even though it's rural. And it's way more integrated than this town."

"That's because there's next to nobody there," Slater said. "You have to integrate or you'd be alone."

"When I worked in Native American communities, you quickly figure out who the elders are."

"Because they call the shots?"

"More like they know everybody, and they know what everybody's up to." Pike nodded to the cluster of people where Andy and Kyle were standing, near the long head table. "Who are their elders?"

"The bottle blond in the blue dress is Andy's mom. The crasher with the pecs is Kyle's dad, so the other woman must be Kyle's mom."

"I bet the older couple are somebody's grandparents. She looks Asian."

"Not on Andy's side. I would have heard about it."

"So Kyle's grandmother is Asian," Pike said.

"You're such a cop. I'm surprised you're not writing it down in a little notebook."

He chuckled. "It's interesting, isn't it?"

"It's actually depressing," Slater said. "It means there's one interesting thing about Kyle. Until now I thought it was zero."

Finally they were at the front of the line, and Pike leaned in to talk to the bartender. "Can you do a screwdriver?"

The woman shook her head. "I've got beer or wine."

"Red, then," he said, and Slater asked for the same.

She handed the glasses over. "Eight dollars."

Pike handed her a sawbuck, and they stepped away.

"It's not every day you see a cash bar at a wedding," Pike said, surveying the crowd.

"It's the most *goyishe* thing I've ever seen."

"And no snacks. I hope nobody passes out from low blood sugar."

"Doris called it: Protestant wedding. I'm surprised they weren't charging admission."

A woman stepped up to them, her dirty-blond hair styled expensively to tumble on her shoulders. It was meant to look casual and wind-blown but it probably took three hours of intensive work to get it to look that way. Her makeup was subtle, considering the occasion, and she wore a flowy white minidress.

"Slater, right?" She smiled at them both. "I'm Juniper. The groom's woman."

"You're Kyle's sister," Pike said, and introduced himself, and squeezed her hand.

"Do you really think it's wise to wear white to someone else's wedding?" Slater said.

Juniper laughed. "I knew the boys would be in red. I'm working my own look here. Because it's April, I call it 'the first breath of spring.'" She pulled out the side of her skirt and waved it with a flourish.

"That's exactly what I thought when I saw you," Pike said. "Optimism returning as the world warms up again."

"See? You get it." She touched his arm. "Thank you for that. Andy said you were a honey-dripper." She eyed Slater. "I'm sure we'll talk later. I just wanted to say hello."

As she walked away, Pike was beaming. "Am I really a honey-dripper? What does that imply, exactly?"

"That you're a positive person. People interpret whatever you say as positive. With that smile on your face you could have told her that her hair was on fire and she would have been happy to hear it."

"I guess we balance each other out."

Slater gestured with his wineglass. "You're saying I'm a downer?"

"Not at all. But the first thing you said when you met her was to question the wisdom of her outfit."

"Why is she wearing white? It's weird. And who would name a kid Juniper? There's lots of juniper species, but the leaves are either sharp needles or oily and scaly. There's no flowers. One little spark and they go up like a Roman candle. Wilderness firefighters call them gasoline bush."

"Maybe they picked it because they use juniper to make gin."

Slater eyed him sidelong. "That's like naming your kid Malt Barley, or Sour Mash."

He laughed. "I bet there are kids running around with those names too."

Slater groaned as he caught sight of Kyle making a beeline for them. "Here we go," he muttered.

When he stepped up, Kyle introduced himself to Pike, and Pike grasped his hand.

"I know who you are," Pike said. "You're hard to miss with your matching suits."

"It's not too much?"

"They're brilliant. You both look like a million bucks."

He made it look so effortless, connecting with people, Slater thought, watching him talk. Effortlessly charming, effortlessly making a good first impression. Why was all that so irritating?

They chatted some more, and finally Pike gestured with his glass. "Congratulations on all this."

"Thank you." Kyle briefly touched his bicep, and held his gaze. "Could I have a minute to talk to Slater?"

"I need to check in with Doris anyway." Pike clapped Kyle on the shoulder as he walked away.

"I get it now," Kyle said, watching him go. "He's hot, and he's got social skills. What's a catch like that doing with a wastoid like you?"

"We're embroiled in a multidimensional narrative complex, cupcake. It's extremely complicated. In broad strokes it's similar to what you've got with Andy, only much, much more meaningful."

"I can't believe you tried to eject my father. Were you drunk already?"

"Nobody's going to get drunk when it's a cash bar." Slater jutted his chin toward the head table. "He's not bad looking, your pop. I never would have guessed you were related."

"Thanks," he said flatly.

"So how many of these guys are you sleeping with? I heard you weren't actually exclusive, except when it comes to me."

"You know damn well why we're not sleeping with you."

"Because of your sex hang-ups?" Slater said. "Because you're a selfish little control freak who despises humanity?"

Kyle raised his eyebrows. "That's actually the man you see in the mirror every morning." He poked Slater's shoulder with his index finger. "You can't be sleeping with Andy because Andy has feelings for you. It was his idea to ixnay the hookups. So that we'd have the space to bond."

Closing his eyes for a second, Slater inhaled deeply. It took all his strength not to grab his finger and dislocate it. He pushed the impulse out of his mind. Finally he met his gaze.

"What is it you're supposed to say at weddings? I wish you every happiness, Kyle."

"Why is it that coming from you it sounds like an insult?"

Slater narrowed his eyes. "Do you seriously want me to give you a tune-up at your own wedding? Don't think I won't do it, son."

Looking him in the eye, Kyle squeezed his bicep. "Have fun, Slater."

As Kyle walked away, Slater saw that Pike was standing with Doris and Albert, engrossed in conversation. Pike was grinning like a loon. His optimism wasn't the part that was irritating. Slater was actually in awe of that, because it wasn't bundled with naïveté or stupidity the way it was with some people. Maybe they did balance each other out. But why did he have to lay it on so damn thick?

When he stepped up to them, Pike was talking to Albert.

"Doris tells me you're a medical doctor."

"An orthopedic surgeon," Albert said.

"Can I ask you about this mole on my back? Just let me get my shirt off."

"You're funny," Albert said. "I like that."

Listening to them, Slater gritted his teeth. Doris stepped closer, and leaned in, and kissed his cheek.

"You look beautiful," Slater said. "That dress is stunning. The woman in gold."

"Thank you, sweetie. What was all the tsuris with Kyle's father?"

"I thought he was trying to crash."

"There's no point in crashing when there's a cash bar," Albert said.

"You're not the bouncer." Doris held his gaze. "You need to behave."

"I know." He huffed. "You're the only person on the planet who can get away with talking to me like that."

She raised her eyebrows. "I bet Pike knows how to keep you in line."

A woman stepped up to them, wearing a pale-blue dress with a gold belt, her Afro in delicate little twists. In one hand was a thick dark-covered book.

"I'm told you're the best man," she said to Slater. "Could I have a word?"

He followed her a few steps away.

"My name is Lisette," she said. "I'm officiating today."

Slater frowned. "Are you a priest or something?"

"You're not a fan of priests?"

He raised his voice. "I'm Jewish."

Lisette's eyes grew wide. "I'm not a priest," she said quickly. "Kyle is a nontheist. How do you not know that? I'm a biologist. They wanted to get married by a scientist instead of clergy."

"Then why are you packing a bible?"

"That's not what it is."

She handed him the book, and he looked it over. It was old, and a little ratty, bound in timeworn dark-green cloth. The cover was embossed in faded gold: THE ORIGIN OF SPECIES BY MEANS OF NATURAL SELECTION.

"Darwin," Slater said, and handed it back. "Clever. I get it—with the first wedding, you put a lot of thought into it."

Lisette chuckled. "You make it sound like you think there'll be more than one."

He raised his eyebrows. "No one can predict the future."

Tucking the book under her arm, she dug in the pocket of her belt.

"These are the rings," she said, and held them in her palm. "I'll ask you for them at the ceremony."

Slater scooped them up. Two simple gold bands. He'd seen them before, many times, as Andy and Kyle were already wearing them.

"Wouldn't it be easier if you just kept them?"

"It's symbolic. You holding them shows that you're supporting the happy couple."

"Fine," he said flatly, and tucked them into his jacket pocket.

"For the ceremony I'll stand in the middle," she said, "and you'll stand with Andy on my left. Kyle will be on my right, and his sister will be with him."

"Got it."

"After dinner is when you'll make your toast to

Kyle. I'll introduce you, and you can stand up, and take the mike. There's no lectern. You can stand next to the head table."

"It's supposed to be for Kyle?" he demanded. "Nobody told me that."

"The groom's woman will make the toast to Andy, and you toast Kyle."

"Did you just come up with that?"

Lisette frowned. "You talk like I'm a flake. I'm taking this very seriously. I've given up speed for the whole rest of the month. I did that so that I can be fully present today. I want this to be a cherished memory for those boys."

"What an admirable sacrifice."

Her face softened, and she cracked a smile, and squeezed his forearm. "Thank you, Slater. You'll do just fine."

He watched her walk away. Clearly she wasn't quite fully present enough to detect sarcasm.

TWENTY-THREE

OT LONG AFTER, LISETTE'S voice came through the sound system, and she summoned everyone for the ceremony. Andy and Kyle walked onto the stage, just a little higher than the ballroom floor. Andy was using his walking sticks but he managed to step up without assistance.

Only a few chairs had been set out, with Kyle's grandparents parked in a couple of them. Everyone else stood facing the stage. Juniper stepped up next to Kyle, and Slater took his position next to Andy, and stood with his feet apart, his hands folded over his belt buckle. Andy greeted him, and flashed a smile, then gazed out at the crowd. He looked a little nervous, his random muscle movements more pronounced than usual.

Slater leaned close and spoke quietly. "There's still time to call it off."

Andy laughed. "You would say that."

"Did you at least get a prenup?"

He lifted one of his sticks and whacked Slater's butt with it.

Lisette stepped between him and Kyle, holding a mike, her voice loud through the speakers. She asked everyone for quiet, and spoke her preamble. Mercifully it was just a few thoughts. Brandishing the book, she mentioned Darwin, and Einstein, and Newton, and Galen, linking them all to the arc of human enlightenment and progress that in her mind somehow culminated in everyone standing here today.

"Andy and Kyle have written their own vows," she said finally, "and I'd like them to express those now."

Slater stifled a groan and watched as Andy turned to face Kyle. Lisette held the mike in front of him so that he could focus on maintaining his balance.

"Kyle, I love you," Andy said. "I love the way we are together. Up here in front of … our friends and family, I want to say that I'm committed to you, and I'm … committed to our future together." He looked out at the crowd. "That is all."

Some of the guests tittered, and Kyle took the mike.

"Andy, when I met you, you told me you were sober. I assumed you meant California sober, but I soon found out that you're sober-sober. So I know you have this incredible strength within you. It made me love you even more. You make me happy, and you treat me so well. I want to spend the rest of my life with you."

There was a smattering of applause, and Lisette spoke.

"May I have the rings?"

Slater dug them out of his jacket and handed

them over. After she'd spoken a little more about what they symbolized, Andy and Kyle slipped the rings on each other's fingers, Kyle gently guiding Andy's hand.

"By the power vested in me by the people of California," Lisette said, "I pronounce you legally wed."

The pair of them leaned in for a lingering kiss, and the crowd hooted and whooped and clapped. Watching them, Slater had to frown. He wanted to say *Break it up,* but their guests were still clapping for this. Eventually they stepped down among their friends and were quickly surrounded. Slater walked around the side of the crowd, back toward the bar.

He spotted Doris then, dabbing at her eyes with a tissue. Stepping up, he put a hand on her arm, and studied her face. Her eyes were red. Slater glared at Albert and spoke through his teeth.

"What did you do?"

"It's not about him," Doris said. "Lots of people cry at weddings. It's emotional."

He took a breath and nodded. "I get it. Andy's giving up so much."

Doris chuckled. "And gaining so much."

"Good thing you wear waterproof mascara."

"I should go fix it up," she said, and squeezed his arm, then walked toward the hallway.

"You get a pass today," Slater said, eyeing Albert. "But if I ever see her in that condition because of something you did, I'm coming for you."

"I'm not afraid of you," Albert said firmly, holding his gaze. "And I'm not afraid of your vague threats."

"It's not a threat, Albert. It's a promise. And if it's too vague for you, picture your little doll car with your corpse in it, two hundred feet down a cliff off the Angeles Crest Highway, wedged between the pine trees. They might not find the twisted wreck for months. Think coyote chow."

Walking away, Slater went out into the hall, and headed toward the men's room. When he stepped inside he found a guy leaning over the counter next to one of the sinks. He was in the same demographic as Kyle: Anglo and buff, with an expensive haircut and a trendy suit. It was odd that he looked surprised to see him, considering this was a public restroom. As he straightened up he palmed the rolled-up bill.

Slater paused and tapped his own face. "There's still some on your upper lip."

"Thanks," he said, and wiped at it. "Do you want a bump?"

"Are you a duster?"

He frowned. "What does that mean?"

"PCP," Slater said. "Angel dust."

"Why would I be doing that? It's just coke. I can sell you some for later if you want."

"I'm not a junkie."

Walking past him, Slater went over to the row of urinals. As he was zipping up his pants, he heard a long snort. The twink had his rolled-up bill in hand again, he saw as he walked back toward the door, and he was leaning down, his face next to the counter.

The door swung open, and Kyle's dad stepped in. His face clouded at the sight of him, and his eyes flicked to the other guy.

"What's going on?"

"I came in to use the head," Slater said. "If you're shopping for dope, talk to the nickel rat."

Walking out, he headed back to the ballroom. People were starting to sit at the banquet tables, and he spotted Pike standing near the front. Pike caught sight of him and pointed to the table he was at. Doris was at a different table, farther back, and he walked over to her.

"We're sitting way the hell over there," he said. "Why aren't we with you?"

Doris waved a hand. "You're in the wedding party. You have to sit close to the head table."

Slater scoffed. "It's always something."

The table Pike had pointed out was like the others, with eight chairs around it. He was sitting next to Juniper now, chatting with her. Slater sat on his other side and whipped his napkin into his lap. When Pike turned toward him, he spoke in a low voice.

"I'm almost afraid to ask, but what's California sober? Kyle mentioned it in his vows."

"It's when you've given up your main substance," Slater said, "but you still drink and smoke weed."

"So it means you're not sober at all."

"I suppose that's subjective."

Pike's eyes narrowed. "By that definition, you're completely sober."

He chuckled. "Don't put that on me. I never claimed sobriety."

The servers, dressed in black and white, started circulating, and as he'd expected, the meal was minimalist, the portions paltry. After the plates were cleared, Pike folded his napkin on the tabletop.

"Would it be rude to order in from that Oaxacan *tlayuda* joint?"

"As long as you charge it to Kyle's parents," Slater

said. "They're responsible for this. All style, no substance."

Pike turned to Juniper and chatted with her. Over at the head table, with the newlyweds and the parents and the grandparents, Andy and Kyle looked animated as they talked, happy with each other. He knew that shouldn't piss him off, but it did, and he had to force himself to look away.

He didn't know the guy sitting on his other side. Older than the grooms, his blond hair was slicked back, and he had big ears, and wore a tweed jacket. Basically fuckable, Slater decided. When he finished eating the guy spoke to him.

"Does Kyle work in the entertainment industry?"

"I'm not sure he works at all," Slater said. "I thought he was a trust-fund baby."

"The family has money, I heard, but not that kind of money. So many of their friends seem to be artsy types."

Slater looked out at the room, at the guests sitting around the other tables. "You mean actual artists?"

"You know—actors and musicians. Entertainers. There's enough of them in here they could put on a spontaneous floor show."

"And I thought this event couldn't possibly get any worse."

He laughed. "I was comparing notes with your mother. She said the same thing: she's met a lot of show people tonight."

Slater frowned. "How do you know my mother? And who the hell are you, exactly?"

"The name is Ray. I'm Andy's uncle. Doris introduced herself as the mother of the best man. That's you. She's thoroughly charming, by the way."

"She used to be a teacher. Doris can interrogate you without you even realizing she's doing it."

"Teachers are people-oriented," Ray said. "They know how to bring out the best in others. They can see that people are basically good."

"It's funny that I grew up with her, then, considering I think people are basically fucking crazy."

He chuckled. "So you're Andy's best man. Did you go to school together?"

"Something like that."

"His mother told me this wedding is something of a relief," he said, leaning toward him and lowering his voice. "Apparently Andy got mixed up with some Mexican thug who was stringing him along."

"Interesting," Slater said. "I wonder if I know the guy."

"You haven't heard this story?" Ray furrowed his brow. "I doubt that he's here. She said the guy was emotionally unavailable but he'd hang around anyway, just to get free sex. He basically broke Andy's heart." He waved a hand. "An underworld type, supposedly. Maybe he disappeared back to Mexico, or got incarcerated."

"It sounds like Kyle rescued him, then." Slater double-clicked his tongue and grabbed his wineglass. He really wanted to tune the guy out, and he sat back as the servers stepped around the table, depositing champagne flutes in front of each chair. But Ray kept talking.

"I work for Metro," he said.

"The homeless distribution system. I know it well."

"That's not really fair."

"I haven't been on a bus or a train lately that wasn't full of homeless people."

"The key word there is people," Ray said. "People who need to get around, just like we do. People like you and Doris."

"Well, I've never pissed on a bus seat, and Doris has never pulled a knife on a train car full of strangers." Slater gestured with his glass. "Not that I know of, anyway. At least they're not all Mexican thugs."

Ray huffed, and got up, and walked away. Other people were doing that now too, milling around, talking to people at other tables. Juniper got up and went to talk to Andy and Kyle.

Reaching around his shoulders, Pike gave him a squeeze. "Juniper is on a TV show that's filming right now. Can you believe that? It's so LA."

He looked at Juniper, over at the head table, leaning in to talk to the grooms. "I believe it. She's good-looking."

"You know, you're showing remarkable restraint."

Slater frowned. "What does that mean?"

"I know you," Pike said. "I know what you're feeling."

"You've gone psychic now?"

He pulled out his phone and tapped at it, then held it out. On the screen was a photo of Andy and Kyle on the stage, during their extended kiss, with Juniper and Lisette next to them, both grinning like idiots. Slater stood to the side, his brow knotted, his mouth a tight line.

"You look like you want to murder somebody," Pike said.

"Busted."

"And yet you didn't do anything. That's restraint. There's probably a dozen people here that you want to punch in the face, and you haven't."

"A dozen minimum," Slater said. "But Andy's my friend. I'm not going to turn his wedding into a brawl."

Lisette's voice came through the sound system, asking people to quiet down and take their seats. As people started to drift back to their tables, she walked over beside the head table, holding the mike just below her chin, and gestured widely.

"Look at these two. Are they beautiful together or what?"

There was a round of clapping and hooting, and Kyle leaned in to kiss Andy yet again.

"To make the first toast," Lisette said, "I'm going to summon the best man, or as Andy explained it to me, the second-best man."

A ripple of laughter went through the room as Slater rose.

Pike tapped his arm. "You'll need your glass."

Grabbing his champagne flute, Slater walked over and took the mike from Lisette, and held it at throat level.

"It's not funny," he said. "She's not wrong." He cleared his throat and looked over the crowd. Lots of people were smiling at him. Were they expecting a stand-up routine, or were they just nervous?

"When I met Andy, we quickly became friends. If you know him well, you know there's no bullshit with this guy." Slater glanced over at Andy and Kyle. "He's not on anybody's sucker list, even though I'm sure many of you have tried to sign him up." He waved at the room with his glass. "Nobody could fool him into doing something like this."

Someone in the room called out, "Yeah."

"When Kyle came along, I wondered ..." Slater gestured helplessly with his flute. "Where is this going, you know? I thought his limo had dropped him in the wrong neighborhood, or he was on some kind of frat-house dare." He paused as some of the guests laughed. "Kyle and I have had a couple of serious conversations since then, and I can say that for all his flaws, and his entitlement, and his privilege, I'm convinced that when it comes to Andy, it's not a grift. He really does care about him. Kyle wants Andy to be happy, and that's enough for me."

The guests applauded, and Juniper stood up, stepping toward him.

"Slow down, Seabiscuit," Slater said, holding the mike to his lips to get more volume. "I'm not finished here."

Juniper hesitated, and cocked her head.

"Move it, toots." Slater jutted his chin. "Back on your perch."

She frowned but sat down again.

"So I've been reading the classics," Slater said. "Most recently the *Iliad*."

From the table he'd been sitting at he heard a skeptical laugh. Slater gestured in that direction with his glass.

"This guy laughs. I get it, Uncle Ray. I'm not really a high-tone person. Kyle once called me the drunken gardener. Anyway, during the ceremony Lisette talked about the arc of human enlightenment. Before all that, in mythology, there's these different ideas about the nature of reality. One of them is that the earth is held up by a tortoise. The logical question then is, what's holding up the tortoise? Well, there's another tortoise. So what's under that? The answer is that it's tortoises all the way down." Slater waved his glass. "That's just stupid. We know it's not fricking tortoises. Lisette here is a scientist. She can tell you there's no planet-size tortoises."

"He speaks the truth," Lisette called out. "There's no tortoises."

People laughed, and Slater looked around the room before he continued.

"I certainly don't see any tortoises. But I do see lots of chaos. It makes me think everything is chaos. This city, this world we live in. It's all chaos, all the way down. So if you can find someone to love, someone who loves you back, amid this perpetual grinding chaos, that seems like a huge victory. Like you've beaten the odds when everybody else is rolling snake eyes. You're in a well-watered garden in a world that's on fire. Lo, for reasons that escape me, these two appear to have pulled it off. This toast is to Kyle, and to Andy, and to love." Slater raised his flute and looked at the grooms. "Mazel tov, and confusion to our enemies."

Once he'd taken a sip, Juniper approached, and he handed her the mike as he walked away. The guests clapped for a while, and as it faded Juniper beamed at the room, standing in the confident pose of a practiced actor.

"Thank you, Slater, for those heartfelt words," she said. "When Kyle told me about the best man, I said, what's he like? Kyle said, think of Jack from *Lord of the Flies*. I understand that now. He seems civilized at first blush, but then you see the face paint, and you notice that the forest is burning."

People laughed at that, and as Slater took his seat, he scowled at her.

"But I'm here to talk about Andy," Juniper said. "The man who won my brother's heart."

Slater looked sidelong at Pike. He had a grin on his face, in rapt attention to her words. The guy was so good at this, the social skills, the civility.

After Juniper's toast, Lisette took the mike again. "Everybody have fun. The bar is open. I want to see you on that dance floor."

Pike turned to him, his expression deadpan. "I'm really glad you clarified that their relationship isn't a grift."

"Hey—in my world you're either the grifter or the mark," Slater said. "It's exceptional when that's not what's happening. I thought it was worth pointing out."

He chuckled, and leaned in to kiss his neck. They watched the band taking their seats across the room, and soon a woman stepped out in front of them in a sequined navy-blue dress, her hair intricately styled up. With no introduction, the band started up, and she launched into a song:

> Stars bright in the sky above
> Their light sends you my love.
> Poorwill singing for us up in the tree
> Their night song just for you and me.

"She's got great pipes," Slater said.

"Come on." Pike rose and held out his hand. "Dance with me."

Slater took his hand and followed him onto the

expanse of wooden floor. Several couples were already up dancing. Pike put his arm on his waist, and folded his other hand around Slater's.

"We're doing this old school," Slater said.

"It's that kind of song."

He had to focus to follow his movements, but it wasn't overly complex: two side steps, then back. He soon picked up the rhythm.

"This is the first time we've done this," Pike said.

"You're pretty good at it. You realize that increases your hotness by several degrees."

He chuckled. "We should take a class, and both get good at it."

"You're so freaking beautiful," Slater said. "And you're into me, and you're here with me. I'm trying to convince myself that I deserve this. That I deserve you. I love you so hard."

Pike drew him closer, and met his mouth, and lingered in it.

After the song he found Doris, and took her onto the floor, and put his hand on her waist. Looking up at him as they moved to the slow song, she had a smile on her face.

"Tortoises."

"You know what I meant," Slater said.

"I got the gist of it."

Gazing past his arm, she maneuvered Slater so that he could see what she was looking at. Pike was dancing with Juniper, and they were both good at it, their steps synced, making it look effortless.

"I love that he knows how to dance," Slater said.

She gestured at the room. "Maybe this will be you and Pike before long."

"Good god, woman, slow your roll."

"I've seen you together. The way you look at him."

"I love the guy," Slater said, "but love stories tend to end badly. It's a thing."

Doris raised her eyebrows. "I thought it was a narrative complex, not a mere story."

"At least I'm the one with the house. He can't very well pile all my stuff in the driveway when he decides to dump me."

"Don't get ahead of yourself." She nodded toward the head table. "You should dance with Andy."

"He can't dance. His legs don't work well enough. No way am I dancing with Kyle. I'm surprised they even wanted this."

"I was talking to Kyle's mother," Doris said. "She said people expect to dance at a wedding, and the room had a big dance floor, so it was a waste not to. Same with the stage. She said she couldn't very well leave all the music stands empty, so she hired a band."

"That sounds insensitive, when one of the grooms can't dance. Andy told me it was supposed to be low-key. Just a few guests."

She chuckled. "Just a few hundred. Maybe this is low-key for Newport."

TWENTY-FOUR

FTER THE SONG ENDED, Slater saw Albert at the side of the dance floor, a goofy grin on his face. Doris waved him over. Slater shot him a look as he approached, then walked away.

At the head table he saw Andy was still in his seat, talking to a guy squatting next to him. The guy rose, leaving Andy on his own for a minute. Slater walked over and dropped to one knee next to his chair.

"That was quite the toast," Andy said.

"I nailed it, huh."

He laughed. "Let's say it was memorable. So what's … a nickel rat?"

"A small-time crook. Somebody who does penny-ante jobs. Why do you ask?"

"Kyle's friend Tyler said you … called him that in the men's room."

"Tyler's your friend now too," Slater said. "You just married it. Did Tyler mention he was shilling coke in there, and also sampling his own product?

He looked pretty crunk."

"I've told him you have to stick to … one drug at a time. Otherwise you'll wind up … on a slab in the morgue."

"Getting caught selling it is also suboptimal. It's a one-way ticket to the hoosegow." Slater waved to dismiss it. "You look amazing in that suit. I don't think I've ever seen you clean-shaven."

"It's not too trashy that we wore matching outfits?"

"It's beautiful. Pike said you look like a million bucks. Even Kyle looks decent. I'd say he looks like a hundred bucks."

"I'll take the compliment."

Slater tried to swallow the lump in his throat, and held his gaze. "I'm really happy for you, and for him. I want the best for you. I want you to be happy. I want you to have someone who can give you what you need, I just …" His voice broke. "That wasn't me. I want your life to be good."

Andy put an unsteady hand on his cheek, and wiped his thumb under Slater's eye. "That means a lot."

There was nothing else he could say, and they shared the silence for a moment, the tacit understanding of their history, their connection, until someone sat on his other side, and Andy turned away. Rising, Slater squeezed his shoulder before he walked away, and wiped his eyes with the back of his hand. What was that about? He was getting weepy, like Doris. It made no freaking sense. It wasn't like the guy was being sent up or leaving town. He could go see him anytime.

Back at their table, he sat next to Pike.

"What happened? You're all verklempt."

"Lots of people cry at weddings," Slater said, and put his arm around his back. "It's emotional."

"Did Lisette tell you that?"

"Actually it was Doris."

His phone buzzed in his jacket, and he pulled it out to check. Etta. She knew he was busy tonight. Why was she phoning him? He picked up.

"Turn on channel 6," she said.

"I'm not near a television. What's going on?"

"The Eastside Lightning factory is on fire."

"You're serious?"

"As a heart attack, brother. I wasn't sure it was the same place, but the TV news showed the sign on the fence. Eastside Lightning."

He ended the call and leaned in to Pike. "I have to go. It's work."

"Seriously? Should I come with you?"

"No—I don't have time to explain. Tell Doris what happened. That I didn't leave because I'm a hoodlum. It was an unexpected work thing."

"I'll talk to her," Pike said. "Just go. Be careful."

Slater hustled out to the lobby, and into the street. It was already dark outside. Trotting down the stairs in the parking garage, he found the Thunderbird, and headed toward Soto Junction, driving fast and hard.

Well before he got close to the factory he could see a plume of smoke on the horizon and a warm glow illuminating the night sky. He parked on the boulevard, a block before the street where the factory was, and ran the rest of the way.

As he came up on the place, he could see the

white ladder of a firetruck, extended high into the air and towering over the building, spraying a thin stream of water down on it. The air was lit by the flickering orange glow of flames. Parked just beyond the gate, at the street corner, was a TV news van, its microwave mast high in the air.

On the fence the Eastside Lightning sign had broken in half, each side clinging to the steel pickets at a drooping angle. How had that happened? It was too far from the building to be heat damage.

A thick hose snaked out the gate, connected to the hydrant across the street, where a guy in a yellow jacket stood with a big wrench in hand. As he stepped in the gate he could see there was a second fire truck, parked past the one with the ladder, near the loading dock, or where the loading dock used to be.

A TV news camera operator was standing here, just inside the gate, filming the scene. A big 6 was emblazoned on his camera. The reporter stood nearby. He knew this woman—what was her name? Her platinum-blond mane was carefully styled around her ears, and she was showing a lot of cleavage. Right now she was gazing at her phone screen, her face illuminated in its eerie blue light. Mary Louise, he remembered.

Hustling over to her, Slater hailed her by name. Briefly glancing at him, she held up a palm.

"I'm not doing any interviews right now."

"You interviewed me a while back," Slater said, still panting from the run. "Downtown LA. I'd been assaulted."

Mary Louise flashed a thin smile and looked him up and down. "I do a lot of those. Are you a maître d'?"

"I remember thinking then that your work is such a gift," he said. "It's remarkable how much you uplift our community."

She preened a little. "You're very sweet."

It wasn't about pointless platitudes. Telling her what she wanted to hear was a way to get her talking.

"Listen, I know people who work in this building," Slater said. "Were there any injuries?"

"Do you know Rogelio?"

"Is he OK?"

"I interviewed him already for my eleven o'clock package. He's over with the paramedics."

He looked where she was pointing, and saw there was an ambulance parked close to the gate. Striding over, Slater found Rogelio sitting on the bumper of the vehicle, hands on his knees, a clear plastic mask on his face.

"Dude—are you injured?" Slater said.

Rogelio sat up and pulled his mask down. "The oxygen is just in case I breathed in the smoke." His brow furrowed, and he gave Slater the once-over. "Were you working a *quinceañera?*"

"I had a wedding."

"What are you doing here? I thought you abandoned your job."

He waved impatiently. "What happened?"

"I was the only one inside." Rogelio gestured helplessly. "I was cutting up the new piña. I made one cut with the machete and it started smoking. Why would it do that? It never happened before. I ran to get the extinguisher, and when I got back, flames were shooting out of it. I had a barrel of ethanol open. It was too close. The vapor must have caught a spark. It flashed and went out of control."

"But you got out OK."

"I ran through the offices, and called the fire department, and moved my truck to the street." He took a breath. "Zane is going to kill me."

"Listen to me," Slater said intently. "Do not let them blame this on you. It wasn't your fault."

"I hope he sees it that way."

"It doesn't matter what he sees, or what he says," Slater said. "He's a crook. You know that, right? Don't apologize to him, or to Kim. And don't talk to anybody without a lawyer."

Rogelio frowned. "You really think I need one?"

"Somebody is going to try to pin this on you. Zane or Kim or some insurance company. A lawyer will help you avoid taking the fall for them."

"Well, that sucks."

"You know it's true, brother. You've been through the meat grinder before. You're a valued employee until something goes wrong—then you're the fall guy and you're up in front of a judge. Don't let them do that to you."

The uniformed paramedic stepped out of the back of the vehicle and scowled at him.

"Sir, please step back."

Slater threw up his hands and jutted his chin at the guy, then walked away and stood near the gate. The flames were less dramatic now, lower to the ground, not leaping into the sky. But there was still a lot of smoke, white clouds of it billowing into the air.

Standing with his hands on his hips, he looked over the smoldering wreck. The building looked totaled—at this end the office door and the windows were blackened empty holes. His heart was pounding, and there was a nauseating lump in the pit of his stomach. It wasn't Rogelio's fault, but was it Slater's? The smoke and the sparks from the piña had to be the tracker, the one that showed in the software as number 3. That's the one that had been stolen Sunday night—and it was the one that had a dent in one end.

In his periphery he noticed a figure striding up from the direction of the boulevard, and he turned to look. It was Etta, he realized, dressed in jeans and a plaid shirt.

"What are you doing here?" he said as she stepped up.

"I wondered if you needed backup." Knotting her brow, she looked at the factory. "What happened?"

"There were no injuries."

"The structure looks like a total loss."

She was right. The long side wall had collapsed inward, and the steel of the loading dock door was piled in an unrecognizable twisted mess.

"They were storing a fuck-ton of ethanol in there," Slater said. "Hundreds of gallons. That stuff burns hot."

"I know how fires work. I mean what do you know about it? Was it an accident?"

Slater huffed. "This is business talk. Not for public distribution."

"You know I can keep my mouth shut."

"I think one of my trackers started the fire."

"Oh, Slater, no."

"Whoops."

"I guess when you say 'I will burn you to the ground,' you mean it literally."

"I have an airtight alibi. I was at a wedding until you called. When the fire started, I was making a toast in front of three hundred people."

"Slater, you weirdo—that's not the point." Etta waved at the smoldering ruins. "That factory was somebody's livelihood."

"It was based on stolen inputs and copyright infringement."

"That's no excuse to burn it down."

"I didn't burn anything," Slater snapped. "It was an accident. Malfunctioning Russian technology."

She sighed. "At least you didn't kill anybody."

A guy in a yellow jacket and a rimmed helmet stepped up to them.

"You can't stand here," he said, waving them out the gate. "You have to go across the street."

"I've seen enough," Slater said, and they stepped out to the sidewalk. "Where did you park?"

"On the boulevard. Right behind the Thunderbird."

As they walked, Slater told her about the dent in the tracker, and what Rogelio had just told him.

Etta paused at the driver's door of her little red car. "So what are you going to do?"

"I don't think there's anything to do. The damage is done."

Climbing into the Thunderbird, he took a deep breath. He felt nauseous, and he could still smell smoke. It had permeated his suit. He started the engine and headed toward his house. How culpable was he? Was he the villain here, the lowlife who burned down a building? Pike had told him not to booby-trap the agaves, and he'd effectively done it anyway.

Turning onto his block, in the glare of the street-lights he could see the first jacaranda blooms. It was that time of the year, the start of a month of purple haze high overhead, slowly raining down onto the asphalt bloom by bloom. The lights were on upstairs, and when he got up to the kitchen, he saw Pike's suit jacket draped on a dining chair. Pike was on the sofa, still wearing his tuxedo pants, the ends of his bow tie hanging loose at his collar.

Rising, Pike embraced him, concern in his eyes. "Are you OK?" He pulled back. "You smell like smoke. Were you setting off your M-80s?"

"I need a drink."

"Get me one too."

That meant he could use the good stuff. Slater went to the kitchen, and pulled out the fifth of scotch, and poured a couple of fingers into two tumblers. Back at the sofa, he handed one to Pike, and clinked his glass against it before he dropped into the adjacent lounge chair. Slurping at the scotch, he closed his eyes a moment to savor the nutty heady burn. Was this the last time he'd be able to? His last drink on the outside before his only option was prison moonshine?

He told Pike about the fire at Eastside Lightning. "There was so much ethanol inside. I counted fifteen barrels. It would have gone up fast."

"Why did you have to go down there?"

"I was worried about the guy who works in the factory. Rogelio. I was with him all last week. He's OK, but he's lucky he got out." Slater took a breath, absently swirling the contents of his tumbler. "We're working on honesty, right?"

Pike raised his eyebrows. "What about it?"

"I need to be honest with you."

"Did you hook up with someone tonight?"

Slater scowled. "No—it's about the fire. I think it started because of me."

"You booby-trapped the agave plant," Pike said, "even though I told you not to."

"I didn't do that," he said, raising his voice. "You really do think I'm crazy."

Pike spoke in the same even tone. "You know I can handle that. I can handle you."

He watched him for a moment. That wasn't the same as saying *You're not crazy.*

"I put radio trackers inside my client's blue agave plants," Slater said. "There were three of them. They all worked fine. It's how I found the tequila facto-ry—I followed the first blue agave that got stolen. But one of the trackers had a dent in it." He threw up a hand. "Maybe I dropped it. I don't know. It was still broadcasting, so I used it anyway. I think the battery might have been damaged. The trackers have these great big batteries so they can work for days. Maybe the agave's fluids seeped in through the gap that the dent made. The heart of the plant is moist. The bat-tery heated up and caught fire."

"Those lithium ion batteries do that all the time," Pike said. "It's why you can't put them in checked baggage on an airplane. Do you know for sure it was the tracker?"

"It's the only explanation. Rogelio said the plant started smoking and burst into flames before he could do anything. Maybe hacking into it started it. He was cutting it apart with a machete."

"Is there any way it can be traced to you?"

"No one at the factory knew about the trackers," Slater said. "Nobody knew I was following the blue agaves. Even if they figured it out, I used an alias with them. And if the fire department finds the tracker, my supplier is extremely careful. The gear is untraceable."

"You told me you got those from your Russian friend," Pike said.

"I'm leveling with you about me. I'm not going to rat out anyone else." Slater took a slug of scotch. "So is this it? The end of the road?"

"What are you talking about?"

"I'm putting my fate in your hands here. Telling you the whole truth. That means you get first dibs on arresting me."

Pike was watching him, his expression thoughtful. "Was the tequila company renting the building?"

"One of the morons who runs the company owns it, I was told."

"So there's no landlord who got screwed out of an asset. Even if the fire department identifies the tracker as the origin of the blaze, I'm thinking the tequila people aren't going to be very helpful about where the plant came from, since it was stolen and they hired the thief. The blue agave won't be traced back to your client."

"Zane and Kim will both have amnesia, undoubtedly," Slater said. "I made Zane pay for the plants and the damage to my client's yard, but he wired the dough to my business account, so there's no direct connection to her. If that transaction ever gets scrutinized, I suppose an investigator could finger me, but Zane isn't going to cop to paying for stolen goods.

He'll tell them it was some legitimate business expense."

"So Zane knows you knew the blue agaves were stolen, but not how you knew. What about the guy with the machete?"

"Rogelio. The lone employee. He did all the factory work but he had no idea where the agaves came from. From a farm, they told him. As far as he knows, I'm just a flaky worker." Slater sighed. "I guess he's out of a job now. At least he managed to save his truck."

"So nobody knew the tracker might malfunction," Pike said. "It was unintentional."

"I should have considered the possibility when I saw that it was dented."

Sipping at his tumbler, he gazed out the French doors for a moment before he spoke. "The truth is so elegant, isn't it? It stands out because it's so rare."

Slater gestured with his glass. "It's the golden thread that knits the world together."

"So these knuckleheads stole someone's landscaping as a business input, and it caused a fire. That sounds like karma more than a crime."

He furrowed his brow. "You're not going to cuff me and haul me down to the hoosegow? If that's the thing to do, I won't squawk. I'll take the rap. In the morning, though. So I can hold you in my arms one last time."

Pike sat up, leaning toward him. "Does your twelve-step book talk about catastrophizing?"

Slater frowned. "I haven't got to that chapter yet."

"This isn't doomsday. And I wouldn't pop you no matter what you did. I'd just let it eat me up inside knowing what you'd done."

"I don't want to be the cause of your ulcers. I'll take my lumps. You already know I'm no damn good."

Pike slowly shook his head. "This isn't one of those. You didn't do anything wrong. One minuscule misjudgment. And I can tell you're remorseful for it." He cracked a smile. "That means you have a conscience. It actually makes me happy."

<hr />